Publisher's Note:

Thank you for purchasing this book. It began as an idea, was shaped by the creativity of its talented author, and was subsequently molded into the book you have before you by a team of editors and designers.

Like all EDGE books, this book is the result of the creative talents of a dedicated team of individuals who all believe that books (whether in print or pixels) have the magical ability to take you on an adventure to new and wondrous places powered by the author's imagination.

As EDGE's publisher, I hope that you enjoy this book. It is a part of our ongoing quest to discover talented authors and to make their creative writing available to you.

We also hope that you will share your discovery and enjoyment of this novel on social media through Facebook, Twitter, Goodreads, Pinterest, etc., and by posting your opinions and/or reviews on Amazon and other review sites and blogs. By doing so, others will be able to share your discovery and passion for this book.

Brian Hades, publisher

VOLUME ONE OF THE
BOOK OF WEST MARQUE

THE CALL

RICHARD PARKINSON

EDGE SCIENCE FICTION AND FANTASY PUBLISHING
An Imprint of HADES PUBLICATIONS, INC.
CALGARY

The Call
Volume One of the Book of West Marque

Copyright © 2019 by Richard Parkinson

EDGE SCIENCE FICTION AND FANTASY PUBLISHING
An Imprint of HADES PUBLICATIONS, INC.
P.O. Box 1714, Calgary, Alberta, T2P 2L7, Canada

The EDGE Team:
Producer: Brian Hades
Acquisitions Editor: Ella Beaumont
Edited by: Michelle Heumann
Cover Design: Brian Hades
Cover Art Elements: rvika, Svetlana Alyuk
Book Design: Mark Steele
Publicist: Janice Shoults

ISBN: 978-1-77053-188-8

EDGE Science Fiction and Fantasy Publishing and Hades Publications, Inc. acknowledges the ongoing support of the Alberta Foundation for the Arts and the Canada Council for the Arts for our publishing programme.

Library and Archives Canada Cataloguing in Publication
CIP Data on file with the National Library of Canada
ISBN: 978-1-77053-188-8
(e-Book ISBN: 978-1-77053-101-7)

FIRST EDITION
(20190320)
Printed in USA
www.edgewebsite.com

Dedication

Dedicated to all those who helped keep the story alive, my wife, Shelley, my family and friends; and to my mom and dad, who shared with me their love of reading.

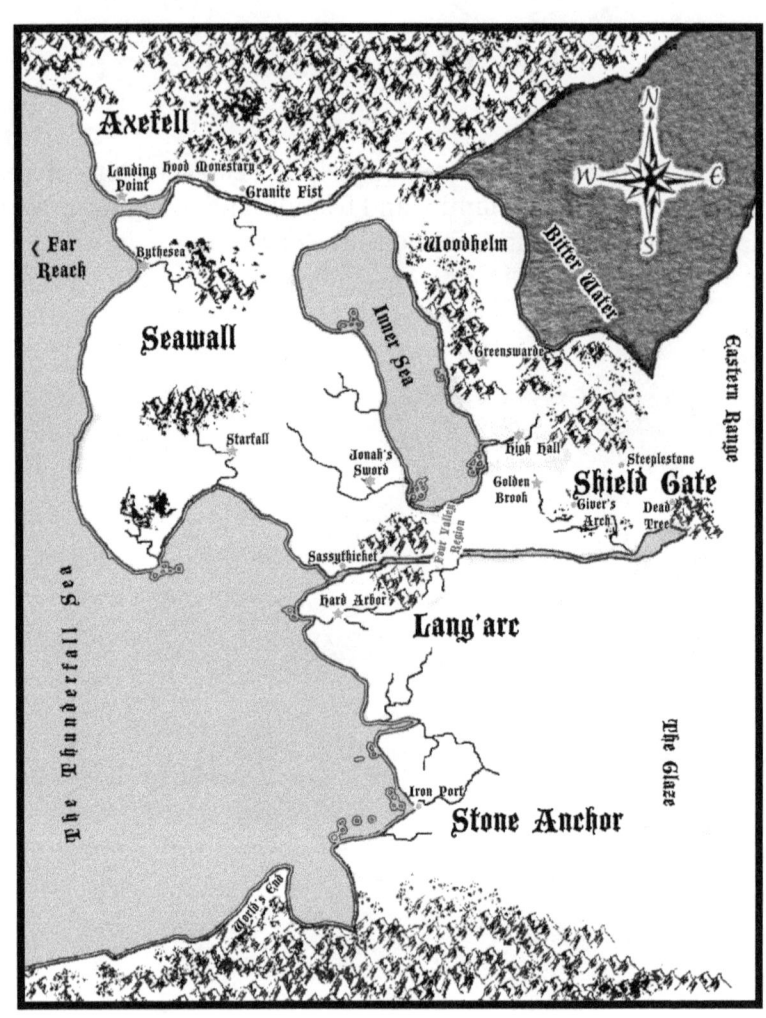

Prologue

She ran across the field, the long grass tugging at the hem of her skirt. Her shoes had fallen off and she had torn a heel on a jagged rock, but she couldn't afford to stop. She had to keep running.

Tears were on her cheeks and sobs escaped her with nearly every breath. She took a chance and glanced over her shoulder. Was *he* coming? No. Back there, washed out by the orange of the setting sun, there was only meadow grass and weeds, and beyond that low, treed hills. Still, she would not stop. She would not stop until she was certain she was safe. She wasn't sure, however, when that would be. *Maybe never.*

Her shadow stretched out in front of her, looking like a deformed giant. There was a chill in the air. It was early spring and the night would be cold.

How much distance had she put between herself and her pursuer? Was it enough? She was just a child on foot, but *he* was mounted. No matter how fast Tabitha Pillar thought she was — and she *knew* she was fast — she couldn't outrun a horse. The man would soon be on her.

The man...

They had given him dinner, offered him a bed, and he had *betrayed* them. He had repaid their hospitality with death, something worse than death, Tabitha knew. Father, Mother, Gran, Rufus, Dan, all of them.

She was sobbing loudly now, snot running down her nose and over her lips, making them slick. Her dark brown hair stuck in her eyes and she swiped it away. She stumbled, but quickly regained her footing, a terrified moan escaping her. If she fell hard, she might be doomed. The trees were just ahead — maybe a quarter of a mile away — skirting the hills that blocked out the horizon. They were thick and green, the gloom they promised inviting. *I can make it to those trees and if I do my chances will be better.* She could hide in the undergrowth like a wild hare.

Your kindness will get us killed.

Those were Mother's words. She would say them to Father whenever he offered a traveler some food and a bed. Grandma agreed with Mother, but she never said so to Father. "His house, his rule," she would say to Mother. "It's not my place to interfere."

"We live too close to the Range to trust strangers, Joe," Mother would say. Father would shake his head and respond, "We're the Giver's folk and it's our lot to give a little when we can."

"Pious fool," Mother would snap back, sometimes with Grandma nodding in agreement behind her.

Your kindness will get us killed.

There was truth in those words. Tabitha knew that now. She moaned again as she thought of the man, the horrible things he had done.

It seemed almost a nightmare, and not quite real. But it was, it was too real. Terrible images rolled through her mind. Mother naked in the barn, father and Rufus groping at her. Danny — her older brother Danny, not quite thirteen — leering and laughing at the act as Grandma's eyes rolled in her head and she babbled loudly in words Tabby didn't understand. And in the middle of it all there was the man, in his coal black duster and hat. He was smiling, and his smile was the worst thing Tabby had seen in her life. Somehow she knew he was controlling the grotesque acts that went on about him and when his cold dead eyes turned on her, those white eyes, those empty eyes with no color and no pupils...

She had screamed as she felt the man's mind slithering into her own, filling her head with indecent and terrible thoughts. She made to scream again, but it came out as a choke as she recalled that moment. She was nearly at the trees now, their darkness and the cover promising comfort. She looked behind her and saw only empty field. *I am safe,* she thought. She plunged through some bushes, the branches scratching at her arms and legs, face and neck. She stumbled into the woods, tripped over a root, regained her feet, and kept her legs going.

She didn't see where the forest floor disappeared and the gully opened up. She cried out as she went over the edge, her hands grabbing for any purchase, her nails breaking on roots and rocks. She skidded all the way down the gully's steep side and was on her hands and knees when she came to a halt at the bottom. She was next to a shallow stream, staring at a pair of boots and above those boots a pair of dark pants and above that… Tabatha let out a scream.

Your kindness will get us killed.

One

The Fifth Wheel — John Gray

The spring storm had harried John Gray for two days. It was a great ugly thing, a bank of boiling black clouds that rose high into the sky, scratching the belly of the heavens. The winds came with it, whipping the rain and hail into his face as forks of lightning stabbed the countryside and crashes of thunder rang in his ears.

It had only broken the day before, the heavy clouds scattering and disappearing, giving way to a clear blue sky. There was no sign that the weather had ever been anything other than perfect.

It was a hellish ride that matched his mood — dark and sour.

The storm had seemed to push him onward, toward his duty, to here.

Dead Tree.

The town was aptly named. In place of the vibrant forest that once surrounded it, centuries ago, were fields filled with petrified white trunks.

John Gray was not happy to be riding into this backwater. He had left Barres Beacon three days ago. Forty-nine people called *that place* home, the town consisting of a dusty saloon, a shed that served as both railway station and telegraph office, and a handful of shacks. All the same, it held vital clues as to the whereabouts of the Gambler and his wife.

Gray had pursued them up and down the frontier all winter. He had chased them into the burning desert of the

Glaze and followed their tracks deep into the wilds of the Eastern Range. Every time Gray thought he was about to run down his quarry, they would elude him. The Gambler's wife had nearly laid Gray low once, but the bullet meant for his head had only put a hole in his hat. The Gambler, Gray conceded, was an exceptionally clever man and his wife a cunning and nasty she-devil.

Their crimes were many, but only one of their crimes really concerned Gray. Treason.

In Beacon he had obtained some vital intelligence from a nearly toothless farmer who had sold the Gambler a pair of solid horses. The Gambler and his wife, the farmer said, were heading south to book passage on a river runner. They were tucking up their tails and running home, which meant their work was done.

They only had a two-day head start and Gray *knew* he could ride them down.

But an urgent telegram came to Barres Beacon that roadblocked Gray's pursuit. It wasn't addressed to him directly, but rather to any Fifth Wheel in the region. And as there were no other Fifth Wheel operating in the region that meant Gray.

As a Fifth Wheel, Gray was bound to the realm. His Order was an ancient one that had existed for nine centuries or more. *The Knights of the Realm,* they were called, and there were many in his Order who took great pride in that. But when Gray thought of knights, he thought of fools riding around in shining armor, with flowers on their helmets, out saving damsels. They carried swords and shields in the days of yore. Now they carried guns.

The telegram had contained orders directing him to this place, to Dead Tree.

THREE MURDERED IN DEAD TREE. SHERIFF REPORTS ALL FIFTH WHEELS. FRESHLY GUNNED. INVESTIGATE AND BRING THOSE RESPONSIBLE TO JUSTICE.

Gray cursed aloud when he read the words and he nearly struck the old, scrawny telegraph operator who was trembling, wide-eyed in his chair. The murder of three of his

Order was no small thing. It was certainly not something he could ignore. *Freshly gunned.* The three were wet-behind-the-ears, mere boys, not necessarily new to the saddle, but certainly new to the trail. As much as Gray wanted to catch the Gambler and his wife, he would have to leave that work to others. It was more than likely the pair would pass unmolested and slip safely into Seawall, beyond the hands of justice. Gray cursed one more time, crushing the telegram in his hand as he did so, and left.

— ‹› —

Dead Tree was not much to look at. Still, with a population of two hundred or more, it was a metropolis compared to Barres Beacon.

He put his heels into Horse's sides, and the chestnut mare responded at once. He had given up naming his mounts years ago. It was tough to get attached to the animals only to have them die under him. Horse was the fifth mount of that name.

Gray was tall and broad of shoulder. His features were ordinary, but his blue eyes were bright. His face was weathered from years of hard riding, his wide jaw covered in stubble from lack of a sharp razor. His hair, which was still brown despite his forty years, hung long and limp about his shoulders. His riding clothes were well-made but worn, any color they once had faded to a dull grays and browns.

He wanted to make an entrance into town, so he urged Horse into a healthy trot. The stark white trunks of the trees disturbed him and the sour yellow grass that surrounded the trunks disturbed him even more. There was something queer about the countryside, which wasn't unusual being so close to the Range.

White dust puffed off his shoulders with each step of his horse. He had ridden through a storm to get here, but it had refused to rain in these parts for weeks. On the horizon, though, storm clouds were gathering again. Dead Tree would have rain soon enough, and lots of it.

It was a two-day gallop from Barres Beacon to Dead Tree. Gray had made the journey in three. Foul weather be damned. He was bitter about being thrown off the Gambler's trail, and he saw no reason to blow Horse. Horse had been with him for a while. She was a stubborn mount, but loyal. Tough to get going, but good on the trail when she finally did. Whether Gray made the journey in two days or three, it made little difference. The bodies of the young men he was sent to examine would still be there. *Men?* In truth, they were only boys. They had yet to earn their spurs. Nonetheless, they were of Gray's kind, Fifth Wheels. It took some nerve to kill one Fifth Wheel, let alone three, even if they were *just* boys.

The first house he came to on the edge of town was a leaning structure with a sagging roof. There was an old man sitting on the porch and a large brown dog was curled around his feet. The man had the same hard look that most landed folk wore this close to the Range. Gray tipped his hat to him and he nodded in return. The dog didn't even lift its head. The old codger's expression was sour, as sour as the yellow grass on his doorstep. *At least he had the good grace to nod,* Gray thought. It was a better welcome than he received in many a frontier town.

Gray would make no detours. Now that he was here, he would get right down to business. His first stop would be the sheriff's office. It was the sheriff's appeal that had ultimately summoned him here, so Gray was determined to rattle his cage first.

The town was crowded in on itself, the buildings square boxes made of wood. It was mostly bland and brown with a rare splash of faded red or blue paint on some of the windowsills and walls. There were a few dogs lolling around and some people going about their business. An old woman gave Gray a quick glance, but the rest kept their eyes to the ground. The only living thing that seemed to have any spirit in it was a ginger cat. The tom was sitting on a fencepost and seemed to wink at Gray until he realized the critter was missing an eye. The cat had a leg cocked high, lazily licking its genitals, pausing only briefly to watch horse and rider pass with an arrogant look before getting back to its grooming.

The sheriff's office was small and dusty, built up against the wall of the livery, looking almost like an afterthought.

The smell of horse and manure was thick in the air and so were the flies. Gray waved the flies aside as he hitched Horse to the post in front of the building. He stepped up and rattled on the door. No answer. He knocked again, louder. *Never hurts to knock with your guts, rather than your knuckles*, he thought. Still, his second knock met with the same silence as the first. He turned and looked around. A few townsfolk were eyeing him from a safe distance, old men, loitering on the steps of the saloon.

"Where's the sheriff?" he shouted, more forcefully than he intended, angry about the summons that had turned him from the Gambler's trail.

One of the men proved braver than the rest. He gestured with a thumb toward the saloon door behind him. Gray left Horse hitched to the post in front of the sheriff's office and strode across the square, kicking up dust as he went, until he stepped in a pile of dung. Angrily, he shook it off his boot and then went up the saloon steps, the old men quickly getting out of his way. A scrawny cat hissed at him before scurrying away on black paws.

The saloonkeeper had yet to close the outer doors against the approaching storm, so Gray banged open the flimsy batwings. The taproom was almost empty. Four men were playing cards at a table in the corner next to a window and a long, lean man tended the bar. The card players didn't look up when Gray entered and the barkeep barely gave him a glance.

Gray walked to the bar, spurs rattling, and threw back his coat to reveal his badge of office and guns. *That* got the barkeep's attention. He straightened up and moved to greet Gray with the worried look all common folk had when there was real authority about. "W—wanna d—d—drink...?" he stammered.

"No," Gray replied. "I want the sheriff. Where is he?" The barkeep's beady brown eyes flashed over to the table in the corner and he pointed at the card players. Gray tipped his hat and surveyed the quartet. The sheriff sat closest to the window like a dope. *Anyone outside could shoot him*, Gray thought. He had a soft, fleshy face and was thick around the middle. He was licking his lips, staring hard at the cards in his hand. They must have been good. His three friends were middle-aged, well-dressed, and probably well-to-do. They were, however, still commoners. Gray knew there were no true gentry in Dead Tree. Only pretenders. He walked up to their table with purpose. It was covered with stained and faded green cloth to indicate it was the gaming table.

The sheriff did not even glance up from his cards. He had a bent cigar stuffed in the corner of his mouth, which he removed to say, "No room for another. Table's full," before shoving it back into his maw.

"I'm not here to play any games, *sheriff.*" The sheriff's head snapped up, angrily. His hand dropped to his gun, a gun that looked too oiled and new to be used. Gray pushed back his coat, so all could see his badge. The color drained from the sheriff's face and his hands went to the table.

"I'm s—s—sorry, sir," he stammered.

"We've got business, I think," Gray replied, nodding toward to the door.

The man on the sheriff's right, an old gent with a long bent nose, droopy eyes, and skin like old brown paper, had the audacity to whine, "But we're in the middle of a game."

Gray quickly looked at each man's hand in turn, shoved the money — a tidy pile of the smallest of copper coins — toward the sheriff, and declared, "You all lose." To the sheriff, he said, "Let's go." The lawman gathered the coins from the table with a shrug and followed Gray out of the saloon.

"I didn't think you'd be here so soon," he said, as soon as they were outside. He tossed away the stub of his cigar and quickened his pace to keep up with Gray. "I just sent the telegram a few days ago. I never realized. If I knew you were coming this quickly, I would have been waiting for you on the edge of town."

"I didn't need a welcoming party," Gray snapped, looking hard at the man trotting beside him. He was a damn prattler, a talking sheriff. The Fifth Wheel was well acquainted with his type. Every backwater had a lazy lawman in it. They were good at breaking up fistfights, coaxing drunks into jail cells so they could sleep it off, and scolding boys for flinging night soil onto doorsteps, but they were good for little else. Gray had no time for wasted words and headed straight to the sheriff's office. "Inside."

The man pulled a heavy key from his pocket and fumbled it around the lock. Gray was close to snatching the key from the sheriff's hand when it slid in.

The sheriff's office, such as it was, smelled of sweat, manure, and something rotten. A pot-bellied stove, older than the sheriff, was against the back wall. Dust was everywhere. The only desk looked unused. A wall was covered in wanted posters, most of them yellow with age. "Any of these men still alive or have they all died of old age?" Gray asked, waving a hand at the posters as the sheriff waddled to his desk.

"A few," the sheriff said. It was hard to tell whether he meant they were alive or had died old geezers. The sheriff opened the desk drawer and produced a bottle of whiskey and two greasy glasses. "Drink?"

Gray *was* thirsty. "Sure."

The sheriff uncorked the bottle and poured with a shaky hand. Gray watched as a few drops hit the desktop. A shame. He took the closest glass, raised it in salute, and gulped the contents down in a single swig. The sheriff sipped at his.

"So, where are they?" Gray asked. The man looked puzzled for a moment and then there was a flash of realization. "Oh, the bodies." He let out a nervous chuckle. "In one of the cells." That was a fair enough place for them. Gray doubted the jail cells got much use.

"Let's see."

The sheriff took another sip of his drink and then wandered over to a small iron door. Gray followed. The door clanked loudly when he turned the handle, but before opening it, he said, "I want to warn you about the smell."

"I have smelled dead men before," Gray replied impatiently, "Many more ripe than these three." The sheriff shrugged, opened the door, and gestured for Gray to take the lead.

Gray stepped in and the smell hit hard. *The sheriff wasn't kidding; these boys stank.* The sheriff's face blanched and his nostrils flared. He hauled forth a snot-encrusted handkerchief and held it to his nose. "Why do they stink so bad?" Gray asked, as they headed down a narrow hall. He glanced over his shoulder at the sheriff.

The sheriff shrugged to indicate his ignorance. "They were only dead a day or so when we got them." That was enough. The area had not seen rain in a long time and it was uncomfortably warm in the back of the building.

They passed a strong room and came to two jail cells. The boys were tucked in the one closest to the back. Gray looked through the bars and saw that they were packed in tarred canvas. "To keep the flies off," the sheriff said.

Gray nodded. "Obviously." He gestured at the door. "Open it up."

The sheriff unlocked the cell door and swung it open, the iron hinges screaming when he did so. That sound was music to Gray's ears. It was a song he lived by. He stepped in and crouched next to the nearest canvas bundle. He pulled out his skinning knife and slit the canvas open. The stench slammed into him and he almost gagged. The sheriff did gag. He scurried off, the sounds of retching resounding in the hall. Gray pushed back the canvas with his blade.

The boy's face was chalky white, with touches of green and grey. Gray noted that he might have been handsome in life, but death is the great equalizer. *Everybody is ugly in death.* As he gazed down on the face, all the dead faces of his past paraded through his mind.

Gray's first acquaintance with the great equalizer came when he was a young boy. He was five or six, and — his cousin, Lily, who was only a few months older than he was, had died of the Black Kiss. Her face was a rigid white mask, her lips black as midnight. His mother would not let him near the corpse in fear he would also catch the Kiss.

"But, Mother," he whined. "I never kissed Lily." Gray's father had boxed his ears for what he perceived as insolence. So Gray stared at his dead cousin from the far side of his uncle's parlor. She was on display as was the custom. Gray cried and his father scolded, "Buck up and be a man. Tears are for women and small babes. If you are *ever* to take the gun, then you must do so with dry eyes."

Gray flipped the canvas back over the boy's face and sheathed his knife. "Why the hell am I here?" he muttered. "I was *so* damn close to the gambler."

He got up and went to the office. The sheriff was there, pale-faced, chewing his lip and nursing a drink. There was a bit of vomit on the man's collar. Gray went and poured himself another. "Well?" the sheriff asked.

Gray took a deep swallow of whiskey. "They're dead alright. Let's head to the saloon. I'm hungry and my horse needs a stable. You can tell me the particulars over dinner."

"Yes, sir," was all the sheriff had to say as Gray drained his glass. Gray looked at the man, scowled at his softness, and left.

— «» —

The Greenberry Saloon & Hotel served decent fare. Over a meal of roasted hare, swimming in gravy, with fresh veggies and a small loaf of warm bread, Gray found out the sheriff's name was Dan Croft. While Croft picked half-heartedly at his meal, Gray wolfed his down. He had been eating jerky, dried peas, and hard bread for several months, washing it down with lime beer. Before that he had eaten roasted lizard and snake on the Glaze, and fiery dishes in Far Reach so laden with spices that they were almost inedible for anyone with a civilized palate. One of Croft's card player friends joined them as they finished their meal. He was introduced as the mayor. "Ron Brook," he said, extending a hand. Gray stood and shook. The mayor's hand was as soft as a maiden's and as moist as a steamed clam. "John Gray."

The Mayor was short and thin. His pinched, lined face carried the blemishes of an older man and his trimmed moustache and beard were so black they had to be dyed. *This one is vain*, Gray thought. His vanity extended to his attire. He wore a burgundy coat, which Gray noted was worn in places, gray breeches, poorly polished riding boots, and a black felt top hat that the fool didn't even have the grace to take off indoors. The sheriff quickly moved to pull out a chair for Brook. *This one is a* somebody *here*, Gray thought, *but he'd be a nobody anywhere else.*

After they were seated, Gray ordered a flagon of beer. He would reserve whiskey for later in the evening. He took a sip and the mayor cleared his throat. Gray cocked his eyebrow. "Yes?"

"There is — uh — the matter of your credentials," Brook said. "I mean, that is not to say that you aren't who you say you are ... it's that this is a delicate matter and ... and living this close to the Range, we..." He trailed off.

Gray ignored the mayor for a moment. He'd need something stronger than beer to wash down Brook's words. "Whiskey," he shouted to one of the saloon's doxies, a pretty wench for such an ugly town. The sheriff had been winking and smiling at her since they had entered. She nodded and scurried off to the bar. A few moments later she brought a whiskey bottle and three glasses balanced on a wooden serving tray. She set down the tray and Gray paid her.

Gray noticed the place was filling up and that the customers were thirsty. Many of the patrons were watching Gray and his companions out of the corners of their eyes. *Is the killer, or killers, of those boys in this room?* He reached into an inner pocket of his coat, pulled out an oilskin pouch, and thrust it at Brook.

The mayor opened the envelope and pulled out Gray's letter of marque. As he read it, Gray ignored the beer and poured some whiskey for himself and his companions. Croft nodded his thanks. When Brook finished reading, he returned the paper to its pouch and handed the packet to Gray. "My apologies and my thanks. I hope you understand." He lifted his glass in salute to Gray and the sheriff hesitantly followed suit. Gray lifted his glass in return. "So now the formalities are over," he said, "is someone going to tell me what the hell is going on here?"

Croft's face reddened. Words had abandoned him. Brook took a sip of his drink, cleared his throat, and said, "We don't get much crime here in Dead Tree."

Gray looked at the bumpkins who crowded the Greenberry's common room. "No, I reckon you don't. Still, you have three dead Fivers in one of your jail cells and I assume they didn't drop dead through natural circumstances."

Croft found his tongue. "No, no. They were *murdered*."

"And there's the other one, as well," Brook chipped in.

"The *other* one? What *other* one?" Gray said loudly. There was a lull in the conversation around him. Someone coughed. Gray fixed the two men with a withering stare. "What — other — one?"

"The dead man the Fivers found," Brook replied, as a cool as a cucumber. "He was murdered, too."

Gray shook his head and took a swallow of whiskey. "Hold on. Let's start from the beginning." Brook and Croft looked at one another. There was some silent debate as to which would do the talking. Gray made the decision for them. "Sheriff, start talking." He reckoned the sheriff would give a more honest account than the mayor.

Croft licked his lips, took a fortifying sip of whiskey, and began. "Two of the boys rode into town ahead of the other boy eight days ago. They rode in from Jersey's Spit, a small town about twenty miles from here. They came in at an easy canter and made their way straight for this saloon.

"I didn't see them come in myself," the Sheriff noted. His plump cheeks reddened and his eyes flashed to the pretty doxy. He gave a little cough. "But it was early, about eight o'clock or so. From what I hear they were full of themselves, talking a lot about this being their first time out and all the great things they were gonna do. Ed, the barkeep, would be able to give you an account of what they said." Croft turned and pointed at a squat fellow with a bushy beard and bald head who was tending the bar.

"It doesn't surprise me they were full of themselves," Gray remarked. "I was the same when I first got my guns, a real swaggerer. I thought the world was my oyster and I had dreams of glory in my head."

Gray reflected on when he rode with company rather than alone. His partners those many years ago were Luke, Dan, and a boy they called Fatty. Luke and Dan were big youths and the chips on their shoulders were bigger than his own. Fatty was big, too, but in a different way. Like all newly gunned Fifth Wheels, the quartet was sent to patrol the Range. "Baptism by fire" they called it. Gray was unsure whether he agreed.

Luke, Dan, and Gray had fared well in those first weeks of Range riding, but Fatty suffered. When the elements weren't plaguing the beefy boy, Gray, Dan, and especially Luke, hammered him with insults. It was, Gray decided, the way of mean youths. There was many a night when Gray heard Fatty crying himself to sleep. Pangs of guilt had stung Gray at times, but his desire to be accepted by Luke and Dan proved greater.

That was years ago, Gray reflected. Luke was killed in a place called Turkey Run, shot through the hip and side by a two-bit dirt rider named Stan McAusley who was hanged for his crime and was long deceased. Dan was thrown from his horse while jousting in a tournament. He shattered both his legs and became a cripple and a drunk. As for Fatty, Gray couldn't say. Fatty was recalled to Posting House only a few months in and he never saw him again. *I can't even remember his real name.*

"Sir?" Brook shook Gray's arm gently. Gray gave the mayor a sad smile and turned his attention to Croft. "Sorry. Go on. The two boys were in town, but the third had yet to arrive."

"That's right," Croft nodded. "The third boy came into town a few hours later. However, unlike the first two, he rode in hard by way of Short Cut Pass. I suspect he was straggling behind the others and took the pass to make up for lost time. Still, his horse was just about blown by the time he got into town."

There was a clatter by the doors as a man stumbled into the saloon. He was dressed in farmer's clothes, and manure was thick on his boots and the bottom of his canvas pants. It was clear the man was well into his cups. He swayed a bit and then steadied himself on the back of a chair. His eyes darted about the room and settled on Croft, Brook, and Gray. He took a step back and then several quick steps forward, working his way over to the table. When he arrived, he gave Croft a mock salute, "Sheriff." He bowed to the mayor and grinned at Gray.

"Irwin," Croft sniffed. "Pickled as usual, I see."

"Just a bit," Irwin drawled. A dribble of spit ran down his chin. He lurched, bobbed, and turned to face Gray. "Hah! I see you brought a *real* lawman in. I reckon you're here 'cause of the murders."

"That I am," Gray gave him a steady stare.

"*Irwin*," Brook snapped. "Don't you have some other business? Or, at least, some manners?"

The drunk cranked himself around to face the mayor, "My apologies, your Worship. I was –"

Croft had had enough. "The Giver has patience to deal with you, Irwin, but I don't. Public intoxication is a crime. Must I run you in, *again*?"

As drunk as he was Irwin saw the point. "No, sir. My pardons." He stumbled to the bar to argue with the bartender about his sobriety or lack thereof.

"We're sorry for the interruption," Brook said to Gray. He turned to Croft. "Do continue."

The sheriff took a sip of whiskey and continued. "So, the third boy came into town excited. He asked around to find the whereabouts of his friends and was directed here. By all accounts the boy was worked up when he came in and he spoke to his friends quickly. No one heard much of what they said, but a number of people say there was talk of a dead body. The boys paid their bill and came to my office at once."

He paused at this point, cleared his throat, and took another sip of his drink. "The boys discovered I was not at my office quite yet, as I was delayed. But they found me soon enough." His eyes flashed once again to the saloon doxy. It required little intelligence to figure out that the sheriff had been cavorting with her. Gray let it pass. A man's bed business was his business. "The boy who rode in last told me he stumbled upon a body in Short Cut Pass.

"That wasn't particularly peculiar as people do die on the trail, whether they get thrown from a horse or have some other mishap. I inquired into the nature of the person's demise. The boy said that the man was definitely murdered, shot through the head and neck at close range."

Croft stopped at this point as if that was all there was to tell. There was a moment of awkward silence. "That's it?" Gray said. "How did the *boys* die?"

Brook opened his mouth to speak, but Gray stopped him with a sharp gesture. "I'm asking *him*." Gray pointed at the sheriff.

Croft looked about nervously, from Gray to Brook and back again to Gray. "I'd asked the boys if they'd mind collecting the body and bringing it back to town," he admitted.

Gray snorted and took a long look at this supposed sheriff, this supposed *lawman* who sat across from him. "You sent three *boys* out on their *own*, to their demise?"

"No, no," Croft protested. "It wasn't like *that*."

"Then just *how* was it?"

"At first, I said we'd ride out together, but they were all heated and eager and insisted that they would do it themselves. I agreed. That's all."

Gray nodded. Croft was bending the truth, telling a lean tale that could only get thicker in the telling, but he saw no reason to pursue the issue. "Go on."

"They rode out of town to the Pass. A day passed. I got concerned and I approached Mayor Brook." Croft glanced at his friend. "After a bit of deliberation it was decided that I would ride out with some men to see what happened to the boys.

"My thought," he continued, "was they had taken it upon themselves to do some investigating, to have a little adventure."

Gray swirled the contents in his glass. "But it wasn't like that."

"No." Croft slowly shook his head. "It wasn't. We found the boys dead on the trail with the body I presume they went to gather up. They were shot down, robbed of their guns and horses and whatever wealth they might have had."

"Where is the body they went to fetch," Gray asked. "Was it a man, woman, child?"

Brook answered. "It was a man. Someone thought he might have been a farmhand from Jersey's Spit, named Rufus, but they couldn't be sure. Whoever he was, he wasn't a local, and he was too ripe to have lingering around. We buried him promptly." Gray could understand that.

Croft chimed in. "When I got back to the town with the boys' bodies, I immediately sent a telegraph to the marshal's office."

"And he sent a message to my commanding officer who sent a message to me in turn and here I am," Gray concluded. The three men sat and nursed their drinks in silence, each wrestling with his thoughts. Gray looked suddenly at the sheriff. "You said the boys were lying with the man's body?"

"Thereabouts," Croft nodded. "They were all in the same area, I mean."

"What about tracks? Horse hooves? Footprints?"

"There were many about, but none that I could say weren't caused by the boys or the horses."

"Spent cartridges or anything of the like?"

Croft shook his head.

Gray finished his drink. "Peculiar." And it was. "Well, a phantom couldn't have killed those boys."

"It was a *demon*." The words startled Gray. The drunk, Irwin, had been eavesdropping from the bar. He looked hard at Gray and repeated, "It was a *demon*, I tell you."

"*Irwin!* Enough of your poppycock," Brook barked, as he slapped his hand on the table. Croft was about to reinforce Brook's message, but Gray interrupted. "Let him speak." He gestured for Irwin to come over.

Irwin came over and took a seat. "Drink?" Gray offered. "Much obliged," Irwin said, as Gray tipped the bottle, filled his glass, and slid it over to the man. Brook and Croft sat uncomfortably as Irwin gulped down half his drink. He was a worn old coot, with a scraggly gray beard and unwashed hair. As he swallowed the whiskey, his protruding Adam's apple did a little dance.

"So tell me about this demon," Gray said. "And don't mix any manure in with the dirt. Just the truth."

The old man nodded. He took another pull of whiskey, forcing it down with a hard swallow. "I'd bet a whole gold crown, if I had one, that it had something to do with the death of those boys and probably the other one, too. I don't know how long it's been lurking around these parts or how it got here, but it's here now. I know that because I saw it myself."

"Anyone else see it?" Gray asked.

"None that'll admit it." Irwin drained the glass and burped. *Why is it always a drunk who sees the unbelievable*, Gray thought. *Why for once couldn't it be a sane and sober man?* "And what's this demon of yours look like?"

Irwin squinted his eyes and furrowed his brow. "That I couldn't accurately say. I saw it from a distance. It was big."

"How big?" Gray poured more whiskey into Irwin's glass. Irwin ignored the drink for a moment and said, "I reckon about eight feet, nine feet, ten feet tops."

Gray sat back in his chair and folded his hands in his lap. "If you saw it, how is that you avoided ending up like the other four?"

"It had its back to me."

Brook guffawed and Croft smirked. "Honest," Irwin snapped. "Upon my soul and as the Giver is my witness, I *saw* it."

Gray sat for a moment in silence, his face expressionless. He leaned forward. "And where did you see it?"

"In Short Cut Pass. It was just a day or two before those boys showed up, and the weather was foul. No rain, but high winds and ominous skies. I was bringing up a team of horses from the Spit and was running late. With the wind kicking up dust and the color of the sky I couldn't say how close to dusk it was." Irwin seemed to sober up as he told his tale. "The horses started getting skittish and there was a hell of a racket in the hills. I thought it might have been coyotes, but a closer listen assured me it was not. It was something ... *strange*."

A shiver ran through Irwin. He grabbed his glass, but then released it. "With the horses worked up I began to fear that it was a pack of Range wolves, venturing into the interior. I put my spurs in and started riding hard." Irwin gulped. "It was only by chance I glanced up the eastern slope and saw it against the skyline, something big and ugly. Loping along. Like it was a man, but it weren't."

"Maybe it was a man and a trick of the light," Gray suggested.

"If it was, it was the most awful man ever formed by nature," Irwin replied.

Gray rubbed his chin, looking hard at Irwin. He leaned back on his chair and was silent for a long while. Then he said, "Well, I reckon I'll have to head down Short Cut Pass and take a look myself." Irwin nodded in fierce approval.

Croft blanched and Brook piped in, "What's this, sir? You actually believe him, this tale of a ... a ... *demon*," he snorted in disgust.

Irwin gave Brook a dirty look and then turned his attention back to Gray. "Others have heard the cries of this creature at night, too. Not just me. You just go and ask them." He looked around at all the people in the Greenberry's common room. If anyone was eavesdropping, however, and Gray suspected more than a few were, no one acknowledged Irwin's words. Gray said to Croft, "You and I will head out early tomorrow morning."

Brook was incredulous. "You're actually going to chase this man's phantom?"

Gray responded. "Well, Your Worship, I am. Unless, of course, you have a better idea. I have four dead bodies, lots of questions, and no damn answers." He glared at the mayor and his face bore an expression that discouraged any argument. "This talk of a demon is all I have to go on. Maybe it *isn't* a demon and it's only a man or pack of men. No matter. Man or no, this killer, or killers, must be dealt with." He turned his attention to Croft. "Tomorrow we ride out."

"But who'll w—watch the t—town?" Croft stuttered. "Who'll m—mind the law here?"

Gray pointed at Brook. "He will, until we return."

"I'm coming with you," Irwin volunteered. Gray saw a man of courage there, rather than a drunk. Sheriff Croft he realized was so white he made snow look black. Gray nodded his assent to Irwin. "Good."

Over Irwin's shoulder Gray saw some men pitching cards at the gaming table, four bumpkins betting nothing but the smallest bits of copper. It made him think about the Gambler. *How close I was.* He sighed. The Gambler would have to wait.

Two

The Gambler — James Gallant

James Gallant had shaken the Fifth Wheel, *or more likely*, he thought, *something has diverted the Fifth Wheel's attention.* Although the lawman had proved bothersome, he would have preferred the Fifth Wheel's company, or even a jail cell, to the company he kept at the moment.

Gallant was staring at the working end of a .44 long, a fine pistol to be sure. The tip of the barrel quivered a few inches from a spot between Gallant's eyes.

Gallant was hoping that he would get a chance to speak before the trigger was pulled. But he was uncertain. Guns, after all, are temperamental tools, liable to shout out any given moment. Particularly when they were in the hands of men like Gregory Dent.

Unfortunately for Gallant, his wife was not with him. She had *real* business to attend to. She had a way of pulling his fat out of the fire, and right now his fat was dangling over the flames.

The two other men in the room sat rigidly in their chairs. They lacked the courage to breathe, let alone to lift their fingers to help the likes of Gallant. True, Gallant wore the finery of a gentleman, but the soil of his recent travels had embedded themselves into the cloth. His cream-colored coat was stained at the elbows, his soft brown breeches were worn at the knees, and his tall boots of supple leather were looking much worse for wear. Even his face looked trail-worn — his strong jaw covered in stubble, his dark blonde hair unkempt despite his best attempts to keep it groomed. There was even some dirt under his nails. *Quite frankly*, he thought, *you cannot trust a man whose veneer is as blemished as mine.*

"Well, Gregory," Gallant ventured, his deep blue eyes shining with something between amusement and interest, "it would appear I have offended you in some way." He was careful to keep his hands in plain view, dirty nails and all. It was stifling in the confines of the small room set aside for the riverboat's card players. Dent's face, wide and covered in coarse black stubble, was bright pink, the color brought on by anger, liquor, and the heat.

"You, sir, are a *cheat*," Dent snarled. The barrel quivered a bit, and Gallant prepared himself for the blast. What angered Gallant the most was that he had not cheated at cards this evening. Normally, Dent would have been correct in his assumption, but on this night Gallant had played only for the joy of it. It was Lady Luck who sent the cards and coins his way. But Lady Luck was a fickle bird and she had flown the coop.

"Greg, I don't think he—," began one of the other players, a plump fellow with a fine bowler hat.

"Shut it," Dent snapped, his bloodshot eyes not wavering from Gallant for a second. The other man shut it. "I say this bastard has been cheating us," Dent continued.

"That simply isn't the case," Gallant began, playing this game like any other. But in this instance the stakes were damn high for him. They were negotiable for Dent. "I didn't cheat you, sir. But if you feel I did, you are entitled to the portion of the money on the table that is mine. You can take it and leave and I won't say no."

Dent sneered. "You aren't in any position to stop me, or say so much as boo." He had Gallant there, so Gallant tried a different approach. "Right you are, Gregory, but let me make you aware of a little fact."

Dent eyed him suspiciously. "What *fact*?"

Gallant cleared his throat as he prepared to pull a clipped ace from his sleeve. It was a cure-all sale, but it was something a man as dull as Dent might buy. "If we are still in Frontier Edge you *may* be in your rights to shoot me *if*, and only *if*, I was cheating.

"However, if we crossed the border into Arbor ... well then, if you shoot me it'll be murder. In Arbor the law condemns those who shoot other men over a game of cards, regardless of whether cheating was involved or not." Gallant saw something in Dent's eyes. Awareness? He pushed the point home. "They'll hang you for certain and on that I'd stake my—,"

"Life," Dent raised an eyebrow and a cool smile curved his thick lips.

"Mr. Dent," Gallant said with all the calmness he could muster, "it's in your best interest to take the money, call it even, and go. No harm, no foul."

Dent licked his lips. Gallant could see that the wooden gears were turning slowly, ever so slowly, in that big, thick head of his. "Maybe you're right," Dent said.

"Of course, I'm right, Gregory." Gallant adopted the tone of an understanding uncle. "Go ahead, take what's yours." He inclined his head towards the coins on the table. They were mostly copper commons, but there were a few silver quarters and silver marques as well.

Dent's eyes flashed to the money and back to Gallant. There was the glint of greed there. "Go ahead," Gallant coaxed.

A smile broke across Dent's moon face. "Right," he nodded. "Damn right. He's a cheat, boys." His flashed a crooked smile to the two onlookers. "That money is mine coz he tried to swindle me." He giggled and licked his sausage lips. His gaze settled on the copper and silver, winking in the lantern light. And Gallant made his move.

Gallant was quick. His hand flashed out, plucked the .44 long out of Dent's hand, and he turned the pistol on his foe. The coins were forgotten as Dent wet himself. Gallant chuckled. "Uh oh, Mr. Dent. The tables, it would appear, have turned."

Dent's mouth opened and then quickly closed. His hands went up and Gallant noticed great sweat stains on his shirt under each armpit.

"Now, gentlemen," Gallant said to the two spectators, while keeping his eyes on Dent. "I reckon you are decent

enough fellows, but are used to a softer sort of living. Please
let yourselves out. I fear Mr. Dent and I have some matters to
square up, the outcome of which I am uncertain. I would not
want either of you two fine men subject to any unpleasant
business."

Neither needed prodding. They left in a hurry, the man
with the bowler hat toppling his chair in the process. He did,
however, have the discretion to close the door behind him.

"Gregory, you know what bothers me *so much* about
this disagreement?" Dent shook his head. "It is not that you
accused me of cheating. I could live with that. It's the fact
that I *didn't* cheat. And that being unusual for a man such as
myself, it truly hurts me to the core.

"Gregory, here's some advice. Never, *ever*, accuse a
natural cheat of being a cheat." Gallant cocked back the
hammer on the gun.

"Wait," Dent cried. "Please, *please*, don't shoot."

"Now why the hell not?"

"You just said we might have crossed the border into
Arbor, and if you shoot me, you'll hang." The panic was
riding across Dent's face.

Gallant smiled and shook his head. "Gregory, there is
something that you have forgotten about me, even though
it is as plain as that pimple on your nose. I, sir, am a true
gambling man, and as such I am willing to wager that we
haven't cleared the border yet." He pulled the trigger and
planted a bullet in the middle of Dent's forehead.

— «» —

The heat of the riverboat's strong room was stifling. No
breeze came through the open porthole. The room, reserved
for customer valuables, doubled as the office of the riverboat
agent. He was an untidy man, but Gallant didn't hold that
against him. The agent was a bachelor and undomesticated.

The agent sat stiffly behind a desk that was strewn with
papers, inkpots, whiskey bottles, filled ashtrays, and the
like. He managed to find the only clear space on his desktop to rest his folded hands. Gallant sat on the other side of
the desk, calmly smoking a cigar while the agent stared him
down.

A pair of pince-nez was perched on the end of the agent's bulbous nose. He was well past his prime, riding out the end of his days on the river. He had a disapproving look and Gallant felt like he did in school when he was hauled before the headmaster. The entire situation was ridiculous, Gallant decided. He blew a plume of smoke at the wall lamp to make his feelings known.

The agent cleared his throat. He started to say something, thought better of it, pulled a few nuts from his pocket, and popped them in his mouth. He stood up, crunching on the nuts and stared out the porthole. Then he turned, faced Gallant, and said, "I do *not* approve of the likes of you on *my* boat. I've seen your type before." He waved a finger, his jaws working hard as he chewed. "Despite your blue blood you act anything but noble, sir. Shooting a man in cold blood, indeed."

Gallant let the agent's words hang for a minute. He took another puff on his cigar. "Mr. — uh," he picked up the brass nameplate on the agent's desk, "Trumbar, far be it for me to correct you in any way, but I did not shoot Gregory Dent in cold blood, as two witnesses have testified." He returned the nameplate to its place in the clutter. It was true, the other two card players had given their accounts and both said that Dent drew a gun on Gallant first. One of them also pointed out that Gallant was unarmed. "Furthermore, no one actually saw me *shoot* Gregory."

Agent Trumbar sputtered at that. He spit what remained of the peanuts in his mouth out the porthole. "Are you actually going to *deny* that you shot the man?"

Gallant chuckled and stubbed his cigar out in one of the ashtrays. "Oh, no, sir. I will admit that I shot Gregory and a fine shot it was, too. I reckon he did not feel a thing."

Trumbar turned scarlet. "You speak of him as though he was nothing more than a *dog*."

"No, no," Gallant snapped back, his ire rising now. "Gregory Dent is nothing like a dog. A dog has many characteristics I admire and a certain charm that Gregory clearly lacked."

"I ought to see you hang." Trumbar put his hands on his desk, leaned over and glared down at Gallant.

"If only you could," Gallant responded, his usual calm returning. "I'm so sorry to cheat you of your desire, but I shot Gregory Dent before we crossed the border into Arbor. According to the laws of Frontier Edge, a man, and I quote, 'has full right to defend his person, to meet force with force, even if said force ends in the death of the assaulting party'."

Trumbar's face screwed up. "I am well aware of the law." A few flecks of spittle flew from his mouth with his words and landed on Gallant's cheek.

"Then I am free to leave?" It was hot and uncomfortable in the storeroom/agent's office. Gallant sought the comfort of his stateroom, and more than that, the comfort of his wife's embrace.

"Yes, you can go," Trumbar said with a look of disgust, waving his hand toward the door.

Gallant got up and started to leave, but the agent held up a hand. There was a small look of triumph there. "While I am not free to hold you for any crime, I have been instructed by the captain to tell you that you are to disembark from this vessel at the next port of call."

Trumbar fumbled in a coat pocket and produced a watch, a tarnished, pathetic looking thing. He opened it. "By my estimation we should make Exeter shortly."

He grinned at Gallant and Gallant said, "You, sir, are an ass."

"That may be," Trumbar replied, "but you *will* still leave my boat."

Gallant noted that the agent had twice now referred to the *Pike* as his boat, while he knew for a fact that Eugene Masters was the registered owner of the *Pike*. Too many men, he decided, took liberties, declaring this thing and that theirs when they had no more stake in them than he did in the sun. Gallant tried to muster some dignity. "Very well then," he sniffed. "I will be on my way."

Three

The Novice — Marcus Dawn

As Marcus settled into the cot that served as his bed, he thought *today was a wondrous day.* True, it had started like most of the days in the past few months — bleak, boring, and dull — but it had picked up quickly and rose to great heights. *Tonight*, Marcus decided, *I will sleep easy, and maybe with a smile on my face.* He closed his eyes and recalled the day's events.

After he had choked down the usual boring fare they served at the seminary — oatmeal with no honey or raisins to sweeten it, a dry apple, and chunk of dry bread washed down with small beer — Marcus prepared, with no enthusiasm, to shoulder his daily routine.

He looked around and thought what a bleak place the Holy Citadel was. The fathers said it was to prepare the soul for service. Marcus believed it was to break the spirit of anyone who had the misfortune to be sent there. Most *were* sent. Very few came willingly. Like Marcus, most were the third sons of noble families who had nothing better to do with their third sons than parcel them off to the Church. There were a few volunteers, those who believed they were called by the Giver and so opted to dedicate their lives to the cloth.

Although he was only fifteen, a year younger than most of the other novices, Marcus had a low opinion of his fellow priests-in-training. He considered them fools, content to shepherd the landed folk, to preach at — not to — them from creaky, dusty pulpits in backwater parishes. He had no spiritual connection to what he was doing. He knew he'd fare better than most, that he'd be given a rich parish to lord over, but still he hoped his father would rot in hell for exiling him to this place. Marcus had wanted to go into the cavalry (he thought he would look quite dashing in an officer's uniform), but his father had said no. "You're not big enough to fill out a cavalry uniform," his father had said, the disappointment apparent on his face. His father, a block of a man, believed men should be strong and powerfully built. Marcus was not. He was thin, even for his age. His features were delicate, almost feminine, his brown hair soft and shiny, and his brown eyes framed with long lashes. When he was young a girl had once called him pretty, and he made the mistake of mentioning it to his mother in his father's hearing. His father had laughed and said his mother must have taken to some woman's bed to sire Marcus. A year ago, his father had pointed a thick finger at Marcus and said, "You will represent the family as a servant of the Church." There was no opposing his father, *the* Lord Dawn, so here he was.

After breakfast Marcus went to his college's chapel to pray. Twenty others knelt beside him. While the acolytes said their prayers and gave their devotions, Marcus glared at the back of Father Allard, the gouty old man who was his college's head. *Of course he kneels in front of us,* Marcus thought. *His piety, I presume, allows him to be closer to the altar.*

Even from five paces away, Marcus could smell Allard. It was mostly garlic he could smell. Allard tended to the hothouses and gardens. He loved to cook and he loved even more to eat. His favorite ingredient was fresh garlic and he ruined many dishes with large doses of it. Allard claimed it cleared the body of ill humors. Marcus thought it made people stink. He loathed Allard's odor and saw the old priest as nothing more than a tub of flesh, hiding under holy robes.

As usual, the stone floor hurt Marcus' knees. He squirmed. The novice next to him hissed his disapproval. Marcus farted in response.

After their prayers, the novices scurried off to tidy their cells. Marcus was always the last into his cell and the first out. After his inspection, Father Allard showed his disapproval by wagging a finger at Marcus. "I hope you tend your birds better than you tend your cell, *Novice* Marcus Dawn." The father loved to address the novices by their full names.

Marcus put on his most solemn face and stared down at Allard's gross brown toes sticking out from the ends of his sandals. "Yes, Father." When he looked up, Father Allard nodded and moved on to Henry Hume, the novice whose cell was next.

After inspection, Father Allard rang the brass bell at the end of the corridor, announcing the official start of a new day. Hume and Marcus were to mop the latrine before moving on to their regular duties.

Henry Hume was sixteen, a year older than Marcus. He was so near a peasant as to be a clod of soil. He was poorly educated, provincial, and Marcus thought him as thick as two planks nailed together. He was incredibly strong, had a wide, freckled face, and a pair of small, brown eyes that looked like two pissholes in the sand.

Hume was at Marcus' side as the last ring of the bell echoed in his ears. "Go fetch the mops, the soap, and the buckets," Marcus said. "I'll meet you in the latrine." Hume gaped, took a suck of air, and then scurried off. *Obedient, like a peasant.* Marcus approved.

He took his time heading to the latrine. He was careful to avoid the fathers who were strutting around like peacocks, exuding self-importance. He stepped into the kitchen and stole a sticky bun bound for a pen pusher's plate.

Two women were working in the kitchen. They were commoners from the city, employed by the Church. One was old and stooped with a long, jowly face, and a large hairy mole on her pointed chin. The other was young, plump, and ugly, but her breasts were large and firm. Marcus attempted to give one of the breasts a squeeze, but the woman giggled and slapped his hand away. Discouraged, he went to the latrines.

When he arrived he found that Hume had already added lye soap to the water in the buckets and was dutifully mopping what looked like an already clean floor. "Look at this." Marcus gestured to the stones. "You could eat off it."

"Our duty is our duty," Hume replied, moving the mop around. "And besides, if we didn't mop them every day the filth would accumulate and the job would only be harder." He was an obedient mule and would make a magnificent country parson one day. Marcus snorted to show his disgust, hefted a mop, and sloshed water here and there.

"You know, Hume, I have never seen a father move a mop, push a broom, or carry out *any* incidental chore." It was a lie. Marcus knew the fathers worked hard, setting an example. Father Cloitus, a large man with shoulders like a bridge arch, could split a cord of wood quicker than anyone he knew.

"Still," Hume replied, "they were novices once as well. They did what we do now."

Marcus toyed with the idea of smacking the ox in the face with his dirty mop when a bishop, of all things, burst into the latrine. The bishop was out of place here in the novices' ward and Marcus did not recognize this one. His gown was made of rich red cloth trimmed with gold. His face was flushed and he ignored the two novices as he rushed on old spindly legs toward one of the privy stalls. The combustion coming from his anointed behind told both boys he was about to let loose his bowels.

He banged the flimsy privy door open, plunked his arse down on the stone bench, and let loose a torrent of night soil. Hume was mortified. Marcus smiled. Perhaps Hume believed the claptrap about the upper officers of the Church, that they were more than mortal men. A great watery trumpet signaled the end of the first wave, but a few short blasts announced the start of the second. Marcus caught a whiff of the holy stink and curled his nose. With grunts and farts, the bishop rid himself of whatever disagreeable food shook his insides. Marcus stifled a giggle and Hume worked away, face red with embarrassment.

The bishop looked at the two novices when he exited the stall. Hume dutifully bowed his head and Marcus followed suit. The man cleared his throat, straightened his robe and left without saying a word. *Perhaps*, Marcus thought, *he is ashamed*. When the bishop was safely out of earshot, Marcus turned to Hume and said, "You see. Even the Giver's primary servants shit and fart like the rest of us." Hume gawked at Marcus, who laughed in his face.

— «» —

After they had cleaned the latrine, Marcus left Hume the duties of stowing away the mops and buckets and slowly made his way to the aviary. The Holy Citadel, which included the Metropolitan's Palace, was centered in the heart of the large city-state, Jonah's Sword. The Citadel itself was, in truth, a city within a city. Marcus was but one of around ten thousand inhabitants, and a novice to boot. He could easily feign that he lost his way and frequently he did — although the fathers were accepting this excuse less and less.

Marcus walked through the Gallery of Whispers. The Gallery was open on the side facing the Plaza of Prayers. Hundreds of pilgrims crowded the plaza. Many groveled on the ground, whispering prayers to a god that Marcus thought might not exist. An urchin stepped from behind a pillar and held up his grubby hand. "I'm a novice, you fool," Marcus snapped. "I have no alms to give you. Seek out one of the fat fathers." He cuffed the boy in the ear and sent him sprawling to the ground.

A few minutes later a wine vendor approached. He had a great bladder of wine on his back and a large flask bulged from under his coat. "Do you not know it is a crime to sell liquor to one of the cloth?" Marcus sneered. The wine vendor gave a sly grin. Marcus decided he liked the fellow somewhat. He reached into a pocket in his robes and handed the man two copper pinnies. "Give me a squirt." The vendor obliged, deftly aiming the stream of red wine into his mouth. It was Valley Red and quite good. He smacked his lips and patted the man on the arm. "The Giver's blessing." The wine seller cackled and moved on.

Marcus left the Gallery of Whispers. He wandered down lanes and alleys, crossed courtyards and plazas, went through lecture halls and libraries, past studies and meditation rooms. Finally, he opened a small door that led into one of the Citadel's many gardens. A blind father and two novices Marcus didn't know were working there. He ignored them and moved with false solemnity to another door through which lay his destination, the aviary.

The smell of ammonia was thick in the aviary, emanating from bird droppings that coated the walls and speckled the floor. Wooden cages were stacked row upon row, bank upon bank, and birds of many varieties chirped, sang, squawked, quacked, quirked, and made a hellish racket. Father Shirrup was waiting, impatiently, a few steps inside the door. He was the Holy Citadel's Master of Birds, one of the most powerful priests in the realm. Even some of the bishops were cautious around this one. His yellow skin hung in folds from sharp bones. A bent nose gave him the look of a vulture. His grey eyes glittered and his thin mouth quivered in contempt of the lazy novice. "You're *late*," he snapped, the folds under his chin wobbling like a turkey's wattle. "You're *always* late."

"Good morning to you too, Father," Marcus returned, a smug smile on his lips. There was mutual dislike between Marcus and the father. It was no secret. Their hostility was open.

"You're also *insolent.*"

"As you have said countless times before," Marcus drawled, while he absently teased a dove with his finger.

Father Shirrup looked like he was about to say something, but decided to change his tack. "Today is an *important* day and a fortuitous one," he said. "It is a rare day and one wasted on the likes of you."

"Really? I am intrigued." Marcus wasn't. Important, fortuitous, and rare to Father Shirrup was the launching of a carrier pigeon or the discovery of an exceptionally large egg. Marcus loathed the aviary. He had only chosen to work here because he thought his duties would be light. He was wrong. Every day there were over a thousand beak to feed, bedding to change, water to fetch and pump, eggs to collect, hatchlings to move, and many other things besides. Marcus took his frustrations out on his feathered wards. He wrung the necks of troublesome birds when Father Shirrup wasn't looking and *accidentally* dropped fertile eggs when he was.

"If it wasn't for your father's sake and your noble blood, I'd see you tossed out of the Citadel," Shirrup said.

"My father can go to hell," Marcus replied, "but I am grateful to the Giver for my noble blood." Being the son of a Marshal's Man, even a third son, had its privileges. "Anyways, I do not wish to fight with you, Father," and Marcus didn't. He was tired. "Tell me, why is this day a rare one? Has a goose finally laid a golden egg?"

"There are no geese here, and you'd know it if you paid any attention whatsoever to your duties," Shirrup sniffed. Marcus had long ago marked Shirrup as a man who lacked a sense of humor and wit. He was … a keeper of birds. "*No,* today we launch the Blue Spears. His Holiness has ordered the *summons.* Tomorrow the message will go out by courier, by train, and by telegram." Shirrup's eyes welled up as he spoke, he was so moved by the occasion.

Marcus was moved as well, but for entirely different reasons. The Holy Father was calling all the Fifth Wheels to Jonah's Sword to swear an oath to the realm. It was politically motivated, no doubt. The Oath Summoning happened once a generation and it was usually a potent of war or trouble. But this didn't stir Marcus, not in the slightest. He was just pleased to be rid of the Blue Spears, which were raised specifically to be launched for the summoning.

They were handsome birds, small falcons, all with some blue in their feathers. They were also nasty and quarrelsome and many had delivered a good peck to Marcus. He knew only too well while they were called Blue *Spears.* "Hurrah," he cheered.

Father Shirrup was taken aback by the novice's sudden enthusiasm. "What? You don't mock this important occasion?"

"Why should I?" Marcus replied. "To be rid of a hundred or more troublesome birds? I can think of no better cause to celebrate."

Shirrup's face twisted in disgust. "Don't you understand the importance of this? Is nothing sacred to you?"

"Hah! What is so important about something that happens every twenty years or so? I bet you have witnessed a few launchings in your day. As to sacred … there is nothing sacred about birds taking flight, Blue Spears or otherwise. Unless you haven't noticed, it's something birds do every day. They *fly*."

"But the Fifth Wheels," Shirrup sputtered. "Surely, you are excited to know they are coming here."

"Why?" Marcus' voice was rising. "Why should I be excited?" He kicked a piece of bedding under a cage and got some birds squawking. "All it means is ten thousand or more people will descend on the city. There will be ten thousand or more mouths to feed, ten thousand or more useless duties to carry out.

"Besides, the Fifth Wheel is an antiquated order. It serves no *real* purpose. It should be disbanded. My father says so."

Father Shirrup's face reddened and his eyes smoldered. "You *insolent* novice." He raised his hand and for a second Marcus thought the old man was going to strike him. But he didn't. *Too bad,* thought Marcus, *I would have enjoyed sending you shrieking to the floor.* Shirrup lowered his hand, shaking with rage. "The Fifth Wheel represents the law of the realm and it is the law that truly binds the realm together."

Marcus snorted. "Perhaps a thousand years ago. Now, they are impotent. We have sheriffs, city watches, police, soldiers, and real courts to uphold our laws. We don't need antiquities and relics."

Shirrup stared at Marcus in disbelief. He shook his head. "It's a shame that the likes of you will follow the likes of me. There is no honor in your kind, no ceremony, no pause, only rashness and the charge."

Marcus swelled up at that, not in anger but in pride. "True. We younger souls are men of action … not words and wind. Not pomp and circumstance."

Father Shirrup visibly deflated. He was defeated. Any response abandoned him. He waved his hand dismissively. "*Go!* Tend to your duties and I will prepare for the launching." He turned his back on Marcus and moved to a set of chains and pulleys. He started fumbling with the links, his arms struggling with the weight of the apparatus.

Marcus went about his work. He filled cups with seed, more cups with water, hauled old bedding out of cages and stuffed new bedding in. He cracked an insolent old raven with rheumy eyes on the head and collected hens' eggs.

The man and the boy worked in silence. Marcus realized there was a new wall between them and any words would be wasted. Still, he preferred Father Shirrup's croaking to the sounds of the birds. By the Giver, he hated the birds. A rooster with a wattle covered in warts gave a *cock-a-doodle doo*. Marcus tossed some seed in its face. It shut its beak and blinked its eyes.

Finally, Father Shirrup shuffled over. He was pink and covered in sweat from exertion. "It's done. We're ready," he wheezed.

"And so we are," Marcus looked at him, having no idea what would happen next.

"I sincerely hope this sight will bring some joy to you," Shirrup said.

"Proceed. I am all attention." Marcus nodded toward the pulleys and chains that Father Shirrup had so laboriously untangled. Shirrup moved forward and grasped the heavy but now well-oiled chains. Marcus moved close to the aviary door.

"Prepare to be amazed," the old man nearly shouted in his enthusiasm. He hauled on a thick chain and a large door above began to open. Marcus looked up and saw the deep blue spring sky. In less than a minute the door was fully clear. Breathing heavily, Shirrup then moved to a smaller but still impressive chain and pulled on it. There was a clattering as the doors of the Blue Spear cages opened simultaneously. All the Spears gave out their calls. It was a chorus that exuded power. Marcus' heart beat rapidly. The first of the Spears poked their faces out of their cages and into the open air. Father Shirrup moved to the centre of the aviary. And then in a rush the Blue Spears took wing.

Shirrup cried out in triumph, his face to the sky above him. Marcus realized that in his excitement the old fool had forgotten a crucial point about birds preparing to take flight. As the birds rose up to freedom they released their ballast.

Smiling gleefully, Marcus watched the comedy play out before him. He laughed as a rain of white shit fell onto Father Shirrup and his upturned face.

"Yes." Marcus yelled over the sound of the birds. "You were right after all, Father. I *am* amazed. This is a joyful and fortuitous day and it's one I shall never forget."

And it was true; it was a day the novice would remember for the rest of his life.

Four

The Lady of Seawall — Genevieve Goodregard

Genevieve Marie Goodregard, Lady of Seawall, wrung her hands, looked down at them, and immediately stopped. After all, hand wringing was a sign of anxiousness and weakness. Her husband had been engrossed in conversation with his council for hours and by now their meeting would be over, the decision made. The wheels were in motion and there was no turning back. They were committed and *she* was partly responsible. Her mother had always said she was overly ambitious, but then she came by *that* honestly. Her mother, too, was an ambitious creature; one who ensured her daughter married the Marshal of Seawall.

The Lady of Seawall went where she always did when she needed to think at night, when she needed to be alone, away from the twittering and idle gossip of her ladies-in-waiting. She went to the High Gallery. There was no one in the gallery at this hour and little chance of disturbance. Outside the windows was the comforting darkness of night.

She saw only the hint of her reflection in those windows, a willowy specter cast by the dim light below. Her long, dark hair appeared darker, her face reduced to a pale oval with nearly no features, her tall, slender body a ripple in the glass.

Genevieve walked slowly, her slippers making no noise on the glass floor. She looked down past her feet. Sixty feet below was the Grand Gallery, the mammoth room where her husband, the Marshal of Seawall, held court.

Day or night, few women walked the High Gallery's glass floor. It was no secret that lewd men used opera glasses to peer up the petticoats of any belle who took to the High Gallery. The gallery was a man's place and the impressive vistas its large windows offered in the day were reserved for men. Convention and propriety demanded that women stay clear of glass floors, if for no other reason than to guard their virtues.

Convention and propriety be damned, Genevieve thought, *and virtue too, for that matter.* She was neither conventional nor proper and her virtue belonged to her husband alone. Chastity was for ugly women and affairs were for the foolish.

She heard the bell that signaled the changing of the guard, and moments later came the sound of tramping boots. She looked down and saw the duty officer, a dashing young fellow who wore the Seawall uniform well, enter the Grand Gallery. Two subordinates accompanied him. The subordinates relieved a pair of bored–looking men, each of whom saluted the officer before retiring. The officer left with the relieved guard, their steps echoing off the granite walls.

Suddenly, a soft hiss came from the shadows of the High Gallery, startling Genevieve. Even though she was expecting a visitor, she jumped instinctively and nearly screamed. "Bastard," she whispered in the direction from which the hiss had come. She heard some chuckling as *he* slid from the shadows near the eastern door.

"My lady." Bishop Michael emerged from the shadows, his black cassock whispering as he did so. A smile played on his lips, "Your language is not fitting for one of your station." He walked over to Genevieve, his hands in front of him with his fingers interlocked.

"You may be my confessor, but my language is of no concern of yours at the moment," she said.

In the weak light she could see the whites of his eyes and the flash of his teeth. He was short and plump, but Genevieve knew his appearance was deceptive. Bishop Michael was strong and had amazing agility. He chuckled again but quickly became serious. "I am always concerned when it comes to such an important member of the faith."

She ignored the comment and his tone. "You met with my husband tonight." It was not a question. She would not dally with this man. She was not a dallier by nature and neither was Bishop Michael, unless it suited him. "And you told him the wheels are in motion."

He stood silent for a moment and then nodded. "I did, my lady."

"And how did he take it?"

"I sensed … apprehension." The bishop cleared his throat. Genevieve could smell the wine on him. Despite his piety, the bishop was fond of food and drink. He continued. "But apprehension is due. It is no small thing to usurp a High Marshal and claim the entire realm as your own."

"Hush!" She looked around quickly. "There's no telling what rats scrabble in these walls."

Michael smiled again. "There are no rats here, my lady. We are too high up. Bats maybe, but not rats."

"This is not a matter to make light of," she snapped.

"No, it's not, my lady." His tone was devoid of humor. "Rest assured the only rat of note that I know of in the palace has been removed."

"Oh, really," Genevieve arched a delicate eyebrow, but in the darkness Michael could not see it. "Who was it?"

"A nobody."

"What happened to him?"

"He … fell." The bishop's eyes flashed in the darkness. "Down a flight of stairs. Poor fellow snapped his neck and broke his head all in one go." He added, "May the Giver mind his soul more carefully than he minded his own step."

"How unfortunate." Genevieve turned, walked a few steps, then turned to face Bishop Michael again. "My husband. You said he was apprehensive. But now he's committed, you can be sure he will act quickly and ably."

"I have no doubt he will. He is a capable man. He is the Marshal of Seawall." Michael's tone was straightforward. There was no false ring to it.

"He has already sent the order to the Metropolitan to summon the Fifth Wheel," Genevieve said.

"So I heard," Michael replied.

That startled Genevieve somewhat. The message was hand-delivered by courier, not telegram. Jonah's Sword was over two hundred miles away. The Bishop had to have excellent sources to know that the Blue Spears were released this day. He seemed to read her thoughts. "When it comes to information regarding the Church, it is the Black Bishops' duty to know, my lady."

"*Black Bishop*," she let the words roll off her tongue with effect. "You use that title rather freely."

"When your husband sits on the High Seat my Order will be restored," he replied. There was a slight bitterness to his tone.

Genevieve's confessor was part of a Holy Order that had been officially dissolved over three centuries ago. Still, it existed in secrecy, and its members — the Black Bishops — dreamed of the moment when they could restore their precious Inquisition. She was not an overly religious person. Certainly, she said her prayers and confessed her sins, but only because it was required of her. She found attending church services incredibly dull and frequently dozed in the front pew as one holy man or another droned on. Sometimes it was Bishop Michael who droned on. Her husband, though, was devoted to the Faith. He was quick to kneel to the Giver — as quickly as one of the landed folk kneels to the High Marshal. *He also kneels readily to men like Michael,* she thought. She said, "That's been agreed upon, yes."

"It has, my Lady of Seawall," the bishop said. His gaze was fixed on her and even in the gloom she could see the energy in his dark eyes. *All lit up with holy fire,* she thought. "The faith grows weaker with each passing season," he continued. "Men and women turn away from the Giver and embrace the debaucheries of the Enemy. They cast away their souls for science, ingenuity, and commerce. This is especially true among the landed folk."

Let him prattle on. "You are right," she said, "and I am glad my husband has such able agents in the Church to aid him in *his* cause." She reached out and laid her fine white hand on the bishop's plump arm. "*You* have been an able agent, Michael."

"I know, my lady," he said with a touch of arrogance. "I am happy to serve your husband. The realm *needs* a strong and faithful man sitting in the High Seat, not a man whose lack of interest in the Church and the faith as a whole is as *apparent* as it is *disturbing*. The realm *needs* your husband. We all agree on this and are fully committed to his claim."

The man was working himself up, his plump lips waggling and his wine-breath washing over Genevieve. *Oh, how the holy love the contents of their cups. The more pious a man, the more drunk he is apt to be.* She removed her hand from his arm and nodded, pretending to share the same convictions as her confessor. "Yes, yes." *Two yeses are better than one.*

"And once your husband sits the High Seat and restores the Order and we restore the Inquisition, he will carry out *our* work in cleansing the realm of its rot," the bishop declared. "Lord Seawall has been and will continue to be the chief agent of our Church."

You have that all wrong, little man, she thought. *It's actually the reverse. The Church will do its part to give my husband the High Seat and I shall do my part to see that the Order of the Black Bishops is never restored. My lord husband might kneel to men in gowns, but it's my gown he lifts at night.* Genevieve decided at that moment that Michael and all of his kind must come to an end. These bishops and holy men had grown too big for their cassocks, as Bishop Michael's plumpness made plain. They presumed too much. As soon as her husband sat in the High Marshal's seat, she would see Michael and the other Black Bishops planted in the soil, even if she had to plant them there herself.

"My lady?"

Genevieve snapped out of her reverie. "I'm sorry. I was just thinking of the future." She reached out and patted Michael's arm.

"Yes," he said quietly. "The future…"

Five

The Fifth Wheel — John Gray

It's good to be back on the trail, Gray thought, as he rode south down Short Cut Pass. The weather was unseasonably cool and he wore his duster to keep off the chill. He felt the comfort of a gun at each hip, a pair of well-oiled .44 longs with lots of stopping power. In the scabbard on his saddle was a Fairburn carbine. It was a gift from his father, a weapon of pure function that had served Gray well. All his weapons had been used to kill before. *And, in a way, killing is my business,* Gray admitted to himself.

Gray didn't consider himself a good man. He prayed seldom to the Giver above, loved little, and he had killed more than his fair share of men in is day. It was true that they were evil men and he had the law on his side, but in his eyes that didn't quite settle the account. He had lost track of how many men had died at his hands. Many of their faces, most of them ugly, blended together. But not the face of the first man he had killed.

In truth, Pete Dawlsley, or Pine Cone Pete, was little more than a boy. Still, that boy was a killer and a wanted man. He was seventeen when he took three bullets to the chest, one of which went straight through the boy's heart. And Gray had personally delivered each of those lead slugs with a steady hand, all things considered.

Gray was the same age as Pete at the time — boys playing at being men in a very deadly game. Pete had lost that day, and the so-called good guy had won, but it could have just as easily have been John Gray.

It had rained hard throughout the night. The storm had wiped away the late spring heat and water had collected in pools on the path. Dragonflies and other insects were taking advantage of the water while it lasted. The clatter of raindrops, mixed with the crashing of thunder, had kept Gray awake half the night in the room he had rented at the Greenberry. Now, the rising sun was climbing over the low hills in the east.

Short Cut pass ran through a valley, green and bursting with wildflowers. The hills to the east were all that separated civilization from the wilds of the Range. Civilization? Gray found humor in that. He was surprised by how little he liked what most would refer to as civilization. In his childhood and early youth, urban areas excited him. Now, he preferred the wilder areas of West Marque, and even the Range, to bustling towns and cities. The wilderness, in its way, was safer. Even a small place like Dead Tree perturbed him and he was glad to be putting some distance between himself and the dirty town.

A thought ran through his mind. *Maybe I just don't like people.* As he mulled that over, he studied his two traveling companions. Sheriff Croft he had already measured and found lacking in substance, personality, and grit — but what about the other one?

Irwin John Kawfee was an interesting character well into his fifties. While he was a drunk and lived hard, he was also affable and possessed a certain quickness of mind. He ran the Dead Tree Livery & Stable and was a third generation freeman. "My grandfather gained free status in some gun fight," he explained as they rode along. "He did some heroic thing and by account saved the life of the current Lord Hawkins' father." John Hawkins was the Marshal's Man of this particular region, Frontier Edge. This much, Gray knew. "Is that so," Gray said.

"Aye, it is." Kawfee took a slurp from a tin flask, wiped his mouth with the back of his hand, and offered Gray a snort. Gray declined. The sun was just peeking over the hilltops. It was too early for a drink.

The morning rays were warm, promising another hot day. The sun would cut through the cool wind and burn away any respite the storm had offered. Croft was quiet and his face bore a sullen look. His eyes shifted nervously as he scanned the surrounding countryside. Gray ignored him and focused his attention on Kawfee. "You ride down here frequently?" He waved a hand in the direction they were heading.

"I do enough," Kawfee nodded. "I reckon I make about a dozen trips a year, sometimes more. Going to Jersey's Spit to get fresh horses for the stage mostly, but occasionally I purchase a private horse or two for the townsfolk."

Gray examined the trail. It seemed well traveled and wide enough. Most of the underbrush and hedge grass was cleared well away from its sides. "It appears a decent enough track," he said. "Why isn't it a primary road? I mean, if it cuts off near a day's travel, it only makes sense."

Kawfee cackled, gave Gray a wink, and spat. A smile tugged at the corners of Croft's mouth. "Up ahead, when we get past the outlying farms, the road gets rough," Kawfee said as he adjusted his hat. "There are lots of rocks, streams, fords and the like, and a brief climb through some hills. No stagecoach or wagon could make it, that's for sure. I admit though it's excellent for horse and mule traffic."

"Maybe in time they'll dynamite out the rough bits and make it a proper road," Gray suggested.

"Umm, maybe, but I doubt it," Kawfee replied. "Not much stock, rolling or otherwise, is put in the Edge — and Dead Tree is about as east as civilization, such as it is, gets. But when more people lay down stakes it might play out as you say."

"I hear the railway is bypassing Dead Tree," Croft interjected.

"That so?" Gray squinted at the sheriff.

"Yep. There was talk of a spur line coming off the east-west trunk and running down through Dead Tree to Jersey's Spit. But seeing as these hills are barren with not a bucket of ore in them, they decided not to." He scowled at the hills around them, as if they were conscious creatures somehow to blame.

Kawfee took another swig from his tin. "So I reckon Dead Tree ain't going to be much more than it is now."

"I'll drink to that," Croft said, extending an open hand in Kawfee's direction. Kawfee looked at his whiskey tin, then the sheriff's hand, and then back to the tin again. He scowled and passed it over. Croft took a minute sip, nodded his thanks, and handed the tin back. "I prefer the small town to any bustling city."

"And what do you know of bustling cities?" Gray asked.

"I was born in one," Croft returned without missing a beat. "A place called Steeplestone. Ever heard of it?"

Gray nodded. It boasted sixty thousand citizens or so.

"So you saw the arches?"

Gray had, but what visitor to Steeplestone hadn't? The victory arches were the most notable things about the city. "Yes, I saw those arches, and quite frankly, I wasn't impressed. I was more impressed by the water fountain in the center of town."

"That wrought iron thing." Croft laughed. "We used to piss in it as boys." Gray winced. He drank from that fountain. He gave Croft a weak smile.

They rode along in silence. It was a sullen silence for Gray as he thought about the pissy water that he had guzzled down like some fool eight years ago. Now he knew why the local boys had grinned at him like idiots. They weren't idiots. They were only grinning at one.

They stopped for breakfast around mid-morning. They chose a spot where a stream ran close to the track. Gray noted that the track was wide in this area. The streambed had moved in time and the track with it. They ate black bread smeared with raspberry jam, biscuits, and some dried beef. It was simple fare, but welcomed. The horses pulled at tender shoots near the edge of the stream. When they finished tucking away their food, Croft produced a flask of strong nettle tea. After he filled their cups, Gray asked, "How much farther to the spot where the bodies were found?'

Croft squinted and looked down the trail, his hands wrapped around his tin mug. "Not too far now. It's just down the road apiece."

Gray sipped at the tea. It was bitter, but it would help keep him alert. The ground had a noticeable roll to it now and large rocks were pushing their noses through the earth. The trail was bending slightly to the west and soon enough it would take them into the hills. The stream, chattering away nearby, came down from those hills. Kawfee saw where Gray was looking and said, "There are a lot more water courses farther along. None of them of any size though, even in high spring. The deepest wouldn't get much past your knee."

Gray nodded and drained his mug. "Let's get moving."

After pulling their reluctant horses from the shoots they were enjoying, the men saddled up and continued their trek. Gray was alert, scanning the hills, the undergrowth, and searching the trail for any signs of the ... demon. He spied a couple of deer, a few birds on the wing, but nothing else.

A short time later, Croft glanced about and announced, "We're here! This is the place."

Gray dismounted. "Keep an eye out." He doubted the murderer or murderers would still be about, but all the same he was cautious. As a breeze moved through the tree branches, he sensed something disturbing about the area. He could see signs of recent activity, which was no surprise. He could only guess how many people were in Croft's posse. He assumed a lot. "Where were the bodies?"

Croft looked around. "The man was over there." He pointed at a patch of bare earth near a yellow bush. "And the boys were scattered down the trail, all fairly close together."

"And all four were shot?" Gray swatted away a fly that buzzed close to his ear. Croft nodded. "Well, a demon wouldn't shoot anyone," Gray said, "but an outlaw or dirt rider sure as hell would."

Kawfee spat on the ground. "It's demon's work, I tell you." As if in response, a strange wailing call came from the east, close by. A shiver ran down Gray's spine and the horses immediately spooked. Gray's horse nearly struck him in the head with one of its hooves as it reared.

Croft hauled out his carbine, a Fairburn Cub with a weathered stock. "What was that? Was it a Range wolf?"

Kawfee's eyes were wide, like a pair of large marbles. He had a double barrel shotgun in his hands. "That isn't a Range wolf, it's a damn *demon*."

The wail rose up again, even closer. Gray drew his .44 longs, taking comfort from the smooth grips. His horse skittered to the right and then it happened. Croft struggled to say something as he brought his rifle up, pointing it in Gray's direction. Gray felt, rather than saw, something suddenly loom over him. The stench of earth and decay was thick in the air. Gray's head swam. Croft's carbine cracked. The rifle fire rang in Gray's ears and was accompanied by searing pain and a burst of fireworks in his eyes. Something struck his head with elemental force. *Was it a bullet from Croft's gun? Had the damn fool shot out of panic?* Everything started to go black and he felt himself falling to the earth.

Now he'd never bring whatever killed those boys to justice. And he'd never catch the Gambler or his wife.

Six

The Gambler — James Gallant

Exeter was a wharf town near the Arbor-Frontier Edge border. As such, it was a rough place, drawing crowds of miners with pockets full of gold dust and silver marques. With the money-packing miners came the riff-raff, the dirt riders, and outlaws who wanted their piece of the miners' pull.

Half the town looked like it was falling into the river, and the other half crawled up the side of the muddy riverbank. A crowd of shacks crowned the top of the bank. It was a town that slept little, if at all, often getting wild in the middle of the night.

On the quay, which was a dock, really, Gallant stood with his bags beside him as the toot of the departing riverboat echoed on the water. His wife, Lucille, sat dejectedly nearby on the old steamer trunk they had recently acquired. Even in this state, he was struck by her beauty and attention to detail. Her golden hair was up, kept in place by a feathered hairpin, featuring a marvelous white plume. Her fine facial features and ample red lips were accented by a nearly undetectable application of rouge. Nothing was needed for her eyes, though, which were such a deep brown as to appear almost black at night. Her cream and gold dress was all frills and fancy embroidery, accentuating her natural charms. And she *was* a natural beauty — a bright light that outshone any common candle put beside her. Gallant knew that she could do without all the decorations that many other women relied upon, but on certain occasions she chose to paint her trim to make an impact. Entering a new town was such an occasion.

His recklessness had caused her grief in the past and their present predicament was just another example. He could tell by her expression that she was frustrated and annoyed.

"Well, well," he said, staring at the lamp-lit dockside saloons, rickety hotels, doxy houses, and the rough-looking revelers who crowded their porches and spilled out from them onto the street. He could see his breath in the cold air. As a young boy on a night like this he would hold a bit of straw in his hand like a cigar and pretend he was a big boy, a man, a smoking man.

"Why do you have to *do this* to us," Lucille snapped, her fists coming down on the trunk.

He looked at her and gave her his most charming smile. "Darling. Be careful now, or you will damage our trunk." He stepped forward and gathered her hands in his. "Even worse, you'll damage your beautiful hands." He brought her hands to his lips and kissed them.

She did not snatch away her hands, but her look was one of disapproval. Gallant sighed and gently let her hands go. "If you had been there, if you had *seen* that insufferable hog Gregory Dent and heard him call me a cheat, you would have killed the lout yourself *before* he drew iron on me. And then we'd be in a worse predicament than the one in which we currently find ourselves."

Her expression softened and she sighed. "I suppose you're right." She looked toward the town. "Let's find ourselves a room, shall we?" She stood. Gallant went to retrieve the trunk but she stopped him. "Leave it! There isn't anything in there anyway, save some old trail clothes."

Gallant gathered up his battered leather valise and put an arm through hers. Arm-in-arm they started toward the buildings.

They stopped in front of the first semi-respectable hotel they could find, a place called the Blind Trout. Three gunshots in rapid succession rang from somewhere inside the hotel's common room. Seconds later, a man stumbled through the batwing doors clutching his chest. His shirtfront was covered in blood. A large, hairy man followed behind, helping the grievously wounded man along with a heavy boot. "We don't want *your* kind in here," the brute said. As he said it, he gave the man one last kick. The man stumbled down the front steps and fell to the ground at Gallant's feet, his life pouring out of him. He gave a final gasp and expired. Gallant turned to Lucille. "Well, this looks like a fine establishment."

"It's the Blind Trout," said the hairy fellow, ignoring the now dead man at the bottom of the step. He gave a brief nod to Gallant and offered Lucille a leering smile. "Ma'am."

"What sort of name is that for such a *charming* place?" Gallant asked with heavy sarcasm, "an establishment with such *fine* company." He looked down at the dead man. The man stared back with unseeing eyes.

The brute looked at the body and dismissed it with a wave of his hand. "Don't pay no mind to him. He's had it coming a while. Raped a whore, they say, and shot up a room over at the Clover. He drew iron tonight and someone proved the faster." He stepped down to Gallant and Lucille. "Name's Higgins." He extended his hand to Gallant. Gallant shook it and felt the raw power there. The man's hand felt like one big callus, like a lump of rough granite. "I'm the manager of this establishment," Higgins continued, chucking his thumb over his shoulder at the hotel. "We got a few empty rooms and we don't take to *overly* rowdy folk."

"Well, Mister Higgins, we aren't *overly* rowdy," Lucille replied, giving him a charming smile, "and we'd certainly *love* a room."

Higgins chuckled at that and Gallant could have kissed his wife. While Gallant nearly always won at cards, *she* nearly always won in social situations. Higgins went to gather up Gallant's bag, but Gallant stopped him. "I'll carry this," he said. There was hardness to his tone, so he softened it, by saying, "If you don't mind?"

Higgins gave Gallant a look and shrugged. "Suit yourself. A man's belongings are a man's belongings. I reckon he can carry them himself if he's so inclined. If you want, come inside."

"I think we will," Lucille said, lifting her skirt to step over the corpse before offering her hand to Higgins. Higgins grinned and led her up the mud-splattered steps. She looked over her shoulder at her husband, gave him a quick wink, and then stuck out her tongue. Gallant sighed and followed them in.

The crowd at the Blind Trout was loud and rowdy (but not overly so), and the common room was full. The company consisted mostly of miners. There were a few whores working the room as well, and Gallant expected the doxies were tied to the hotel. A handful of locals crowded a table close to the fire, others leaned on the old bar, threatening to bring it down with their weight, while some rough-looking men sat next to a scrawny fellow seated at an out-of-tune piano. He was playing poorly, but no one seemed to mind. The card-players, Gallant noted, stuck to several tables at the back.

Higgins led them up a narrow stairwell to the hotel's upper floor. The upstairs hallway was poorly lit, but Higgins knew the way. He stopped at a door near the end of the hall, produced a key, and presented the room.

They were dingy digs, but they would serve. They settled in, lighting the single oil lamp and coaxing the nearly extinguished fire in the small fireplace back to life. Gallant put his valise on the bed, opened it, and sifted through the clothes. He plucked a small book from the bag and casually dropped the bag on the floor. The book was a weathered leather-bound copy of poems. It fit easily in his hand.

He studied the cover. In the lamplight the faded lettering was nearly invisible. It was a cheap book, but its contents were invaluable. He opened it and leafed through its brittle pages, as he had many times before. He could smell old leather, paper, and something else — a hint of the exotic spices of Far Reach.

He snapped it shut. There was something sinister about it, he decided. He had read a few of the poems. All of them were dull and ordinary, but somewhere in those plain words there was a coded message, *but what?* He had ruminated on it from time to time. He had carried the book across a thousand miles of hostile country. He had risked his life for it.

Maybe it's best I don't know its secrets.

He turned it over in his hands, the light of the room glowing dull and orange on the worn cover. *What if I flung it in the fire?* He looked hard at the flames that were now crackling nicely, and then back at the book. He sighed and carefully tucked the book into an inside pocket of his vest. He thought about the Fifth Wheel who had pursued him to the edge of the world and back. *If he got his hands on the book would he know what it was about? Probably not.* In truth, Gallant didn't know what it was about. Not really. *The destiny of the realm,* he had been told. But that could mean a hundred different things.

He wondered what had happened to the lawman. Gallant had a feeling he was still around somewhere. He might have lost Gallant and Lucille's scent, but he would nose it again soon enough. Gallant wanted to put this adventure behind him and move on to something new. He wanted to be safely across the Seawall border with his wife. But that wasn't possible. They had leapt off the skillet and were heading into the heart of the flames. *All because of the book.* His hand went to where the book lay over his breast. They were heading right into the heart of civilization, to High Hall, the realm's capital. The lawman was tenacious, Gallant knew. There were too many narrow escapes. As they moved deeper into West Marque, the Fifth Wheel's net would grow tighter and stronger. If he caught up to them and it came down to gunplay, Gallant was certain the Fifth Wheel would best him.

Seven

The Fifth Wheel — John Gray

Gray hit the ground and for a moment swam on the edge of consciousness. Suddenly, the blast of Kawfee's shotgun, ugly and sharp, hammered the inside of his head. Something wet and slick covered the side of his face. *My brains*, he thought. He didn't want to move.

Kawfee screamed. It was a primal scream, born of instinct. Something howled. The howl played on all of Gray's nerves. He spasmed as searing pain coursed through his body. Kawfee's shotgun banged again. *Stop shooting,* Gray wanted to shout. But he couldn't even crack open his lips. *Just let me die in peace.*

Another howl rang out, but whatever was doing the howling was retreating. Gray heard Kawfee plugging two more shells into his double-barrels. "Aw, shit," Kawfee said. Gray could tell the man was scared. Gray was scared too, and fear was an unfamiliar companion. Usually, Gray went into life-or-death situations with a certain resignation. He would either live or he would die and there was nothing he could do about it. This, however, was different. Something about that unearthly howling struck him to the core. He must have moved because Kawfee gave a sudden yelp and called out. "You alive?"

It took all of Gray's effort to turn his head and look in Kawfee's direction. He tried to give a simple response, "Yep". But it came out as a croak. Kawfee scurried over, shotgun ready. He knelt over Gray, looked down, and said, "You don't look too bad."

That surprised Gray. He felt horrible, but he could sense he was starting to feel better. *But … my brains.*

As the thing retreated, Gray's strength started to return. He could wiggle his fingers and his toes.

"Hold up," Kawfee said, his eyes darting this way and that. He scurried over to a fallen horse — it looked like Croft's — plucked a canteen from the saddle, and came back. He sloshed some water onto a hanky and wiped at Gray's face and brow. *Wiping away my brains*, Gray thought. But when Kawfee pulled away the kerchief it looked like it was covered in mud, not blood. The pain in Gray's head subsided. It was not gone completely, but he felt much better. He sat up. His head swam a bit, but he steadied himself, keeping his hands behind him on the ground. "What happened?"

"A *demon*, that's what happened," Kawfee snapped. He was looking around wildly. "I *knew* it was a damn demon, but nobody *listened*." He glanced at Gray, "'Cept you."

"What about Croft?"

"Dead as doornail. Thrown from his horse and cracked his neck."

Gray nodded. He surveyed the scene. His horse looked like it was missing most of its head. *Damn, he would miss that horse.* Croft's horse was down, too, although there was little immediate sign of injury to the animal. Croft was sprawled out a few feet from his horse, his carbine still in his right hand, his head twisted grotesquely at an unnatural angle. Gray hauled himself to his feet, with Kawfee lending a hand.

"You steady?" Kawfee asked.

Gray nodded but he still felt light-headed. He choked down the feeling of nausea. "I have to gather my guns."

"Well, be quick about it," Kawfee said. "I think that thing will be back."

As Gray gathered up his pistols, carbine, ammunition, and gear, he tried to recall the lessons he had learned at Posting House, the academy where they trained boys hoping to become FiFth Wheels. He tried to remember the things he was taught about sorcery.

He examined his horse. The poor creature's head was nearly severed at the neck. He realized that the horse had taken the brunt of the blow aimed at him and shuddered when he thought what such a blow would do to a man. Around the massive wound were splatters of dark earth, almost like mud. It was the same stuff that Kawfee had wiped from his face. He touched the mud. It was warm. He sniffed at his fingertips and immediately recoiled, pulling them away from his nose. There was a heavy smell of decay and something else. Blood. It *was* a demon, *maybe*, and a big one by the looks of it.

"Hurry it up, will you?" Kawfee clutched his shotgun tightly.

"One sec." Gray padded over to Croft's body and plucked the tin shield from his coat. Demons did not spring from the earth, he knew. They were summoned and bound for a purpose. *And there's only one thing that keeps company with a demon*, Gray thought. *A Dead Priest.* Dead Priests were the mortal enemies of the Fifth Wheels, and all of peaceful humanity for that matter. They were more than outlaws. They were sorcerers from the Range. They turned the pages of the Black Book and practiced the dark arts of the Enemy.

Gray looked around, expecting something — demon or Dead Priest perhaps — to jump out of the undergrowth at any moment. He listened hard and heard only the gurgling of the stream and the returning buzz of insects. He scanned the ground for tracks that might show where the demon had come from or where it went. There were none, which didn't surprise him. It was said demons seldom left a sign of their passing. "Let's go back to town," He said to Kawfee.

Kawfee nodded. They turned tail and ran, crouching low. "My horse spooked and got away," Kawfee said. "She might be around somewhere. We should keep an eye out. It'd be quicker to ride than run and I figure she'd carry us to safety quicker than we could carry ourselves." Gray heeded the man's words, but stayed quiet. He was too intent on his surroundings to put together a response.

A few hundred paces down the trail, Gray caught sight of movement in the bracken. It was Kawfee's horse. He stopped and pointed.

"Cover me," Kawfee wheezed.

Age and hard living had caught up to Irwin Kawfee. Gray realized the importance of reclaiming that horse. Kawfee would never make it to Dead Tree at any pace faster than a walk. He kept his carbine at the ready as Kawfee crept into the undergrowth.

Kawfee clicked his tongue to get the horse's attention. "Easy girl," he said softly. "It's old Irwin here." Gray could see the horse was scared, but it took several tentative steps toward its owner. "Come now, girl," Kawfee soothed. "You and I need each other to get out of this in one piece." In truth, the horse didn't need the men. Its hooves would carry it fast and far from danger. The mare snorted once and whinnied. It shook its head and eyeballed Kawfee as he took a step forward. It stood its ground, its mood somewhere between trusting and flight. Kawfee took another step and reached into a pocket. He produced a bit of raw carrot. "I have something for you." He stepped in close to the horse and took the reins. The horse panicked briefly, but Kawfee held fast and soothed it. He patted its nose when it finally calmed.

Twenty paces away, Gray kept a keen eye out, focusing on the countryside around them. The sweat was pouring down the back of his neck. Kawfee mounted the mare and rode over to Gray. "Let's get the hell out of here." Gray needed no urging. He vaulted onto the horse behind Kawfee.

Kawfee started to turn the horse's head toward Dead Tree when they heard it. The kind of howl that turns a man inside out. The birds in the undergrowth took flight. The horse panicked, but Kawfee kept it under control. He put his heels to its sides, but it needed no encouragement. It shot off like a bullet toward Dead Tree, with Gray clinging desperately to the man in front of him.

Eight

The Dead Priest — Quentus

From a distance he saw two men ride away, double-mounted on the remaining horse. They were heading north down the valley, leaving the wreckage of a man and two dead horses behind them.

He was kneeling on his right knee and it was bothering him. *It's an old injury, reminding me of my youthful stupidity,* he thought as he stood up, rubbing the joint. He was tall, with broad shoulders and a large chest. His skin was a natural rich brown. His face was all angles, with high cheekbones, a strong jaw, a sharp brow, and a wide nose with a sharp bridge. He had full lips and liquid brown eyes. Like all Dead Priests, he wore the black cloth, head-to-toe, although his clothes had faded to grey in some places and his elbows were patched with un-dyed rough-spun.

He shut his telescope, sliding the brass tubes carefully to make as little noise as possible. A wasp buzzed past his ear, hovered for a moment in front of him, and then settled on his hand. The insect's wings caught the light. Its antennae twitched and it took flight. The man smiled and whispered to himself, "Yes, take to your wings. There's no life or sustenance there."

He heard the howl of the golem nearby. Its earlier cry had prompted the two men to leave in a hurry. They knew what it could do. He saw the golem loping out of the brush, branches cracking as it lumbered along. It was wounded, but by no means destroyed.

The golem, he decided, was none of his concern. He had little control over those things; others who wore the Black Cloth did. The creature ran down the hill, but the men's mount was much quicker. The golem slowed and gave a mournful cry. For now, it had lost its prey.

The Dead Priest's horse was settled in a hidden ravine. He decided it was time to make his way back to his horse and move on.

He had only entered West Marque a week ago, through a hidden path, on a self-appointed quest to find out what one of his fellow *brothers* was up to, and already he had doubts. He cursed and pushed aside some braches as he climbed the hillside on his way to the hidden ravine.

His native land, the Eastern Range, was civilized, but it was ancient and the customs of his people were alien to the men of West Marque. They saw his people as primitives and his Order the scourge of the land. Perhaps they were right, at least on the last count.

He skidded down the side of the ravine, the soles of his boots stirring up loose pebbles. Instinctively, he kept one hand on his gun to keep it in place and held the other hand out for balance.

"Quiet, Quentus," Salene hissed from the shadows of the ravine. "You make enough noise to wake a stone." She spoke in the desert tongue of her people, a singsong language that lacked the cutting edge of his own tongue. Hers was an eloquent language, a rapier to be used with precision. His, on the other hand, was a tongue forged by millennia of war. It was a heavy, cleaving weapon that left no doubt when it was being used to wound or kill.

"My apologies," he said, when he reached the bottom. The last of the upset pebbles and earth clinked around him. "The golem is after two men who are sharing a horse. I am sure it will pursue them."

In the green gloom Quentus saw Salene nod in understanding. She held the reins of both their mounts. Even in the off light of this hidden recess he could see her beauty, and her power. Her power came from speed and accuracy, not arcane arts and brute force. She was like a cat on high alert, always ready to pounce on some unsuspecting prey. He had witnessed her in action many times before and the quickness and precision of her attack always startled him. There was a beauty in the way she moved when she killed a man.

His mind drifted back to the day he first saw her on a slave block. She was tanned, dust-covered, her black hair a ragged nest. But he saw the beauty that lay beneath the grime and the abuse of a slaver's harsh hand. He had purchased her on a whim, expecting her to be some plaything or toy, but he was a different man back then. She, on the other hand, had remained the same.

Now, as a free woman and more than his equal, Salene stood before him and handed him the reins of his horse. He said his thanks as he took them from her.

"How is the girl?" he asked. He looked at the dirty little urchin hunched down a few feet from them. Her clothes were torn and grass-stained, and her chestnut brown hair tangled. Salene had tried to comb the girl's hair, but she had moaned in terror and had tried to flee. It had taken a few hours to calm her after the incident.

Salene shrugged, her eyes sad. "She is still the same."

The girl had fallen right at his feet a day after they entered West Marque, crashing down the side of the deep ravine in which they were traveling. Quentus had just finished urinating and was buttoning up his breeches when it happened. His hand snapped down and he drew his gun, thinking some Range cat was about to disembowel him. Instead he stared into the frightened eyes of a child, her blue eyes wide, her cheeks dirt- and tear-stained. The girl had screamed, a shrill, terrible scream. Quentus was dumbstruck and didn't know what to do. Salene, though, moved quickly and gathered her up, embracing her and stroking her hair, soothing her until the girl's screams gave way to moans, then quiet sobs.

Salene led the girl from the ravine and Quentus followed. They made camp that night in a small clearing. All attempts to communicate with her had failed. Quentus tried to speak to her in the language of West Marque. When that provoked no response he tried a dozen different tongues, but the girl said nothing. She just sat and stared at him, frightened. Instinctively, she shied away from Quentus and gravitated toward Salene, but Salene had no more success than he in getting her to speak.

"We should leave her," Quentus said that night. The girl had finally fallen asleep after drinking a bit of water and nibbling on a heel of bread.

Salene fixed him with a cold stare and shook her head. "No. She comes with us until we know her story and can deliver her safely to her family."

"And how do you propose we do that?" Quentus asked. "The girl is dumb and cannot speak. And even if we get words from her and know where to deliver her it is not like we can trot up and hand her over. We are *not* of the realm. We are children of the Range. We are their *enemies*."

Salene shrugged. "We will find a way." She reached out and stroked the sleeping girl's hair.

"Salene, there is no *way*," Quentus said, perhaps a bit too harshly. "She will slow us down and hamper us in our pursuit. The girl has undergone some hardship, that is all. There are probably people looking for her. If we let her go, they will find her."

"And what if there are *other* people looking for her?" Salene shot back, anger and determination rising in her, "people who have evil designs for her? I *know* what it is like to be in the hands of brutal men. I cannot abandon her to that fate. Even if I don't know her, I know her story."

"You know nothing of her story because she doesn't speak." Quentus threw up his hands.

"She comes with us or I will leave and return to the Range and take her with me." Quentus knew Salene never made idle threats, so the girl remained.

In truth, besides being an extra mouth to feed, the girl was no bother. She didn't speak, despite continued attempts to get her to do so, and she did as Salene asked her to without a struggle.

His eyes left the girl and he mounted his horse. Salene extended her hand to the girl, led her to her horse and helped her mount. Salene mounted up behind her. They started off slowly, letting their horses find their way through the stones and branches.

After a moment, he said, "The abomination down in the bottom of the valley, the golem, it killed a man before scaring off the two others."

Salene nodded with no expression. She had been around Quentus and his kind for a long time and was well familiar with golems. *Demons.* That's what her people called them, like the people of West Marque. "Do you think the creature is Paulus' work?"

"Of course. It has his mark all over it. It is a powerful thing. A lot of blood was spilled to create it."

The girl trembled and Salene put an arm protectively around her. "This talk disturbs her. We will speak about this later."

Quentus was aggravated because he wanted to talk about it *now*. He *needed* Salene's counsel in this. Salene's people, the desert folk, often rode in silence, but Quentus was used to speaking his mind on the trail. She would let him talk and only add words when needed. He envied her ability to ride in silence, content with the thoughts in her head, having no need to share them until they needed to be shared.

As they picked their way along the ravine his mind turned to Paulus and he recalled their time together, years ago, on Blasted Rock. Paulus was young, too young, perhaps, to have taken the rite of initiation. What was he? Sixteen? But he was one of the chosen, like Quentus. They were brothers in blood, the blood coming from others, many of them willing, but some not. The old man who gave Quentus his eyes seemed willing, at first. He had smiled and lain steady on the ground, preparing for Quentus' knife. When Quentus started to carve into the man's chest, however, he had flailed, screamed, and begged for mercy. Clouded by the rite of initiation, his stomach full of potions administered to him by the hags of the Blasted Rock, Quentus had no mercy to give. The voice of the dark god rang clear in him. With methodical precision he listened to the voice and worked the knife until the man breathed no more. Then he plucked out the man's eyes and ate them both. After that … well that was over twenty years ago. A lot had happened since then. *Too much*, he thought.

It was easy to become intoxicated by the power of the dark god, and it was understood by his Order that many would do so. That's why newly initiated Dead Priests were sent out Ranging immediately after they had undergone the dark rite. It was hoped they would overcome their brief period of madness in the wilderness (where they could do little harm) and they would return sober and sane. *It took me ten years to find my sanity again*, he thought. *My past crimes are many, and my present guilt is great.* He glanced over at Salene. *I owe her much, and more. I owe her everything.*

They followed the ravine for most of the morning. It grew wider and deeper, and so did the stream in its bottom. As it neared mid-day the horses grew nervous. Quentus knew what it was that was bothering them. He could sense it. "Let's move out of here," he said to Salene. She nodded. The girl was asleep in front of her. Salene was nervous, too, her instincts warning her of some danger ahead. They carefully steered their mounts up the steep side of the ravine, through the trees, and onto the valley floor. Quentus slowed his horse and dismounted. He gave Salene an anxious look. "Stay here."

He moved through the bushes and high grasses, reaching out with his power, feeling ahead. The thing that unnerved the horses was nearby. It was no golem. No spirit. It was nothing as tangible as that. It was residual magic, Paulus' influence on the land. A few more steps and he smelled ash, blood, and decay. It would gag others, but a Dead Priest was used to such smells. Paulus' presence whirled around him. It was invigorating and *dangerous*. He pushed it away.

Beyond a thick tangle of brush he found the hollow where Paulus had made camp. Paulus was a skilled trail rider and had covered his tracks well. This site would be difficult to spot and he would have hobbled his horse some distance away.

Quentus rooted around the campsite and found the remnants of a fire under a cover of scattered earth. He sifted through the cinders, looking for something of interest. He found the end of a cigar, made from the black leaf that Paulus liked to smoke. It would suffice. He picked it up and scanned the surrounding underbrush. He found a dead mouse, its head eaten by a wildcat. He ignored it and continued looking. He came upon a mouse nest under the overhang of a rotted branch. He removed some of the bedding to expose the mouse pups. He plucked one up. It was pink, warm, and naked. He bit into it, the blood rushing raw into his mouth. Blood, both fire and water, was a potent mixture. He swallowed it and focused on the cigar end.

In his mind's eye he saw Paulus mounted on a large chestnut. He was miles away, traveling a narrow trail through twin faces of jagged rock. He looked vibrant and healthy, his usually thin frame somewhat fuller. He was dressed in black broadcloth, and was riding easy. A heavy pistol hung at his hip and a rifle was tucked safely away in a scabbard at his side.

Quentus let the image fade and he was back in the valley. The cigar end was now nothing more than dust on his fingertips. He spat out the remnants of the mouse and carefully replaced the bedding over the others.

He returned to Salene. She had dismounted and was tending to the horses. The girl was squatting in some bushes nearby, making water or emptying her bowels. The sunlight seemed to glow off Salene's skin and her dark hair. She truly was a creature of the desert, a creature of the sun and a harsh yet beautiful wilderness. "He is in the hills to the west, moving toward the interior," he said. "He is heading to civilization and danger."

She nodded and gestured at his face before quickly glancing at the girl who was still busy about her business. "You will need to cover your eyes."

"Yes, you're right." He reached into his coat pocket and pulled out a pair of smoked glasses. He put them on, their dark lenses concealing the rheumy white orbs that now rested in his sockets. They were dead eyes, the eyes of an old man who died two decades ago to give Quentus his power. That was his curse — farseeing through those eyes revealed their true nature. It would be several hours before his eyes returned to normal.

The girl came out of the bushes and gave Quentus a curious and frightened look. "My eyes," he said to her. "The sun hurts them sometimes." She said nothing, of course. Instead she held out her arms to Salene, who hugged her.

Quentus watched as Salene assisted the girl back onto the horse. The girl looked at him and there was more than fear or curiosity in her expression. There was something that bordered on recognition. *Maybe she knows what I am,* he thought. *But that is impossible. Unless...* He shook the thought away and mounted.

As they continued their ride north the thought returned and started to nag at him. Constantly his gaze was drawn to the girl sitting silently in front of Salene. She stared at the world around her with frightened and tired eyes. If those eyes happened to meet his, hidden behind his smoked glasses, she quickly averted them. He started to put the pieces together and mere speculation become possibility. A lost girl running alone in the wilderness, miles away from civilization. Her bedraggled appearance. Her fear. She was certainly running from something. Why not someone? Why not Paulus and his golem? It was possible. He would find out when they stopped and made camp for the evening. He would force her to look into his eyes, his dead eyes, and then he'd see.

Nine

The Novice — Marcus Dawn

Marcus was feeling full of himself, and a little drunk, as he walked along the cloister. It was a sunny day and a refreshing breeze blew about him. They called it the Red Walk, and while the outer pillars were made of rose-colored granite, he knew there was some significance to the name other than the pink stone, but he couldn't remember what. His pockets were stuffed with mince pies that he had stolen from the kitchen and he had a half-consumed skin of wine hidden under his cassock.

The afternoon was his and he had no intention spending such a fine day locked up in his cell, studying like a good novice. *Hume can study for the both us.* He chuckled to himself.

Father Goodleaf was ill and the afternoon lessons were cancelled. There had been genuine groans of disappointment from some of the other novices when they heard the news, and Marcus had struggled to hide his smirk. He hated history and geography nearly as much he hated Father Goodleaf's droning voice.

Marcus heard a hacking sound coming from the gardens on his right. Curious, he stopped and looked to see what was making the noise. It turned out to be a huge orange tomcat choking on the feathers of a bird. The cat was a ragged-looking thing with a torn ear and mismatched eyes, one blue and the other green. The novices called this one Swashbuckler on account of its long sharp claws and ability to use them.

"What's that you've got there, Swashbuckler?" Marcus said to the cat. The tom gave the novice a nasty glance as it continued to crunch on bones and cough up feathers. A brilliant blue feather stuck out between its lips. *The thing's caught a Blue Spear,* Marcus realized. He was surprised and a little shocked. Blue Spears were hawks, and scrappy and dangerous besides.

Swashbuckler gave up munching and turned its full attention on Marcus. He started groaning and growling. Then it spat angrily.

Marcus threw his hands up in front of him. "Don't worry, cat. I don't want any of your nasty bird. Actually, I hope you choke on it." He scurried off, not checking to see if the tom was following him, and not really wanting to know if it was.

He went through several gates, down more cloisters, crossed a few small squares, until he came to an area of the Holy Citadel with which he was unfamiliar. He stepped into a small, out-of-the-way courtyard. There was a woman in the corner with a broom, sweeping the stone flags that were the color of dark sand. Her back was to him, and then she turned. She was young and pretty, dressed in a blue peasant's dress, her blonde hair poorly tucked under a linen cap, strands of it falling down into her face.

Intrigued, and feeling lusty from the wine, he approached her. "Hello there, pretty maid," he called out. She was close to his age, maybe a year younger. Her round face was flushed from her work, her cheeks rosy, and her lips moist. *Lips for kissing.* "It seems you have pulled an easy duty here," he drawled. He looked around the tidy courtyard that seemed to serve no purpose. It was empty but for an old monument in its center, surrounded by some white marble benches.

The girl looked at him with frightened eyes and said nothing. He half-wondered if Swashbuckler had got her tongue, but then remembered that novices were not supposed to talk to the younger female servants. He assumed the reverse applied to them. Marcus thought it was a silly rule, perhaps only a caution, to scare simpletons such as Hume into compliance.

"I'm s—sorry, holy sir," she finally managed, "I'm not supposed to talk to you."

Marcus cocked his head and smiled. "Me specifically?"

"No, not you specifically," she said, casting down her eyes. "I meant all novices."

Marcus laughed and waved a hand. "An antiquated rule for more antiquated times. No one enforces it anymore. Trust me." He gave her what he hoped was a reassuring smile. "What's your name?"

"Annie," she said shyly. "If it pleases you, holy sir."

Marcus laughed. "It does please me. Although Pretty's a name that would serve you better." Inwardly he groaned at the comment, but she blushed. "Come, let us sit on one of those benches," he continued, "and you can tell me the story of this courtyard." She looked hesitant. "It is for my education. It's important for a novice to know the history of the special places in the Holy Citadel, and I'm certain that if you have been assigned to care for it and keep it tidy, it *must* be a special place."

"It is, holy sir," she said quickly.

"And stop calling me 'holy sir'. It sounds ridiculous. Hume is my name, Henry Hume." The lie came easily and it made him grin. "But you can call me Henry." If she decided to blab to some priest or bishop that a novice had talked to her, it would be delightful if she said the novice's name was Hume. "So, shall we sit?"

She looked around, as if expecting a dozen sets of eyes to be on them. But the courtyard was empty, as it probably was nearly all of the time. "Very well." She smiled at him, and what a beautiful smile it was. She had all her teeth, and they were straight and white.

"Thank you, my lady. You are doing me a service." He gave her a bow. *It always pays to make the landed folk feel like nobility if you are planning to take something from them,* his father often said. *They'll grin and serve and give everything away. And they'll thank you for it after.* She beamed at him. *You see. I did learn a few things from you, Father.*

He held out his hand and she took it. Her hand was warm and damp with sweat. Her palms were also calloused. He was used to the rough hands of landed-folk girls, though. He had felt them enough against his skin on his father's estate.

As he led her over to a bench, he pictured her sprawled out naked on it, her plump breasts on full display, her legs apart, and a sultry smile on her lips, all for him. He ached for her, but he knew better than try to take her. She was no servant of the Dawns. She was a servant of the Citadel. *Still, I might steal a kiss or two, or even get a squeeze if I am charming enough.*

He sat on the bench and patted the spot next to him. The marble was richly veined, — with gold, silver, pink, and blue rivers running through it — and warm from the afternoon sun. *And it will be warmer still when she places her beautiful backside on it.* Tentatively, she sat beside him.

He pulled the wineskin from his cassock. "Drink?" he asked her. She shook her head. Marcus shrugged and squirted some into his mouth. He swallowed and then smacked his lips. "How about a mince pie?" He took one from his pocket. She nodded at that and smiled, saying thanks, before taking a nibble from its corner.

"So, tell me about this place, then." He fixed his eyes on her, taking in her smooth complexion, her light brown eyes with golden flecks, small nose, and perfect little chin. *No hairs on it.*

"It's called St. Lyonel's Court, holy sir. I mean, Henry. But many call it the Silent Court."

"I can see why," Marcus remarked.

She ignored his interjection and continued. "St. Lyonel is one of the forgotten saints, I'm afraid."

"*I've* never heard of him," Marcus agreed with a nod. He took another squirt of wine, and felt some dribble down his chin. *Maybe she will lick it off.*

"He lived three centuries ago, at the time of the Second Conquest. He brought the word of the Giver to the people of Far Reach, and helped convert many of them to the faith.

"Unfortunately, one of the Far Reach princes at the time … I forget his name … didn't like what he was doing. He said that St. Lyonel had a golden tongue and he meant to have it. He seized the saint and threw him in prison. He gave St.

Lyonel a choice, keep his golden tongue and go back home to West Marque, or lose it and stay in Far Reach."

"If my tongue was gold, I think I'd want to keep it," Marcus grinned and took another swallow of wine.

Annie gave him a small smile of her own. "Not St. Lyonel. He told the prince that he could have his tongue if he wanted it, but he would remain in Far Reach. He still had the Giver's work to do. The prince said fine, and had his tongue torn out.

"The prince thought that regardless of Lyonel's words, tearing out his tongue would break him. But it *didn't*. St. Lyonel remained and continued to convert the people and do holy works. He even made frequent visits to the prince who maimed him."

"To ask for his tongue back?" Marcus giggled at his own joke. He was feeling quite drunk now.

"No." She slapped him lightly on the arm. "To *convert* him; to bring him over to the true faith. And he did. The prince was so impressed by the saint's commitment to the Giver that he renounced the false gods he followed and entered the faith. Even more, he assisted St. Lyonel in his work and together they converted the other Far Reach princes, which led to Far Reach becoming a part of the realm."

She folded her hands on her lap and looked solemnly over her shoulder at the monument behind her. Marcus glanced at it and saw only a polished block of marble, with a poorly carved effigy of a skinny bearded man at its top.

She sighed and idly toyed with a strand of her hair. Marcus leered at her. *Such dainty little fingers. I bet they could unbutton my breeches quick enough.* "When he died," she continued, "the Far Reach prince, who was very old at the time and had become his friend, saw that St. Lyonel's body was preserved and shipped to Jonah's Sword for burial. He paid great expense to have the saint's body interred here. Some of that money paid for this courtyard. It is said that he replaced his friend's tongue with a golden one and it was buried with him."

I imagine the holy servants of the Citadel who buried him plucked out his tongue first, Marcus thought. Still, he smiled, as genuine a smile as he could muster. "It's a nice story, and I think I should kiss you for the telling of it."

He was about to do just that, when he heard voices echoing through the courtyard.

"The old man is still ill," a deep voice said. "The last dose they gave him nearly did him in."

"Tell them to be more careful," another male voice replied. "We can't push him over the edge and into oblivion just yet. We need him for a bit longer. There are certain duties he must carry out before he can head off to the Giver."

"Yes. And then he can die as —."

The voice broke off as two bishops came walking into the courtyard. Marcus stood up quickly and tried to strike a pious pose as he pretended to examine the monument. He gave the bishops a quick glance. One he didn't recognize, but the other he did. *Bishop Horace.* His heart skipped a beat.

Bishop Horace was large, with broad shoulders and a belly that hung out in front of him, letting everyone know how much he loved his food. He had a long, solemn face for one so fat, and dark expressionless eyes. Cold eyes. The top of his head was bald and the hair on the sides was the color of steel. All novices knew better than to cross this one. His only pleasure it seemed was meting out cruel punishments for even the most minor offences. Worst of all though, the novices whispered that he was a Black Bishop.

The Black Bishops were part of an officially extinguished Order, once the shadowy agents of the Church and the Inquisition. The rumors though were that the Order was very much alive, thriving, and plotting in secret.

The bishop at Horace's side was a small man, with wispy ginger-colored hair and a thin moustache that was lighter in color than the hair on his head. Altogether he was handsome enough, but his brown eyes were close-set, his nose somewhat pointy, and he had a downward turn to his small mouth. *A handsome rat.*

Horace looked at the girl and then his gaze fell on Marcus. He felt a chill run down his spine. The smell of wine was pouring off him. "Novice. What are *you* doing here?" His voice was deep and booming, the voice of the one who had spoken first earlier. "Shouldn't you be at your lessons, rather than staring at a statue ... or enjoying the charms of one of the Citadel's servants?"

Annie was on her feet, her face a chalky white, her eyes downcast. She gave a clumsy curtsey. "I was only telling him the story of St. Lyonel, Lord Bishop. I m—meant no harm. All we did was talk."

Stupid girl. Marcus wanted to scream at her. Her stumbling admission, true as it was, made them sound guilty as sin, like they had been rutting against the holy monument itself.

Bishop Horace looked sternly at the girl. "You know you are not to talk to the novices," he thundered.

A sob escaped her lips and she curtseyed again. "I am s—sorry, L—Lord B—bishop. It was innocent. It w—was only a s—story I told. I p—promise." She rushed forward and fell on her knees before Bishop Horace, who recoiled a bit, as if she were some dirty creature that crawled up out of a sewer to flop itself before him. The other bishop seemed amused by his reaction.

Is she going to stick his manhood in her mouth? Marcus wondered. But she was only there to plead and whine more. "P—please, Lord Bishop. Don't tell the m—matron. I need this job. My family needs the m—money."

"Lord Bishops," a familiar voice cracked across the courtyard. Father Shirrup came strutting out of the shadows. *This yard is busier than a city market,* Marcus thought.

"How long have you been here, Father?" the other bishop asked, flattening the ends of his moustache with a hand.

"Long enough," Shirrup replied. The two bishops exchanged a quick glance.

"Come, young lady, on your feet," he said gently to Annie. He helped her up. "I'm sure the Lord Bishop will let you off lightly, this time." He wiped the tears from her cheeks with his spindly old fingers.

Bishop Horace raised an eyebrow. "Will I?"

"I think you will," Shirrup said, narrowing his eyes as he looked at the much larger man.

The bishop thought about it for a moment and then he shrugged. "As you will, Father Shirrup." His cold eyes shifted to Annie. "You will *not* engage with one of the novices again, young lady. I will not go easy on you, if I see you doing it again."

"Thank you, Lord Bishop," she said quickly, giving the cassocked tub another curtsey.

"And *you*," Shirrup spat out as he rounded on Marcus. "I am not surprised to see *you* lazing about, stinking of wine, with crumbs on your cassock." He swiped the flakes of mince pie from Marcus' collar.

"You know this one?" the handsome rat asked.

"I do," Father Shirrup said, with a quick nod. "It's Lord Dawn's boy, Marcus Dawn."

Marcus groaned inside. *Old fool. Why did you give my name to these two?* He gave a clumsy bow to the two bishops.

"You said your name was Henry," the girl said to him, opened-mouthed and looking somewhat shocked.

Marcus gave her a guilty shrugged. "I lied."

"Away with you, girl," Bishop Horace snapped. She scurried off, red-faced, leaving her broom behind her.

"Dawn, is it?" Horace said after she had gone, letting the name slide off his tongue. "Your *father* is a good man." Marcus felt his face flush, from embarrassment as well as the wine. And the way the Bishop's eyes bored into him made him feel very small.

"The father may be," Shirrup snapped, his face twisted up and sour looking, "but this apple, I fear, fell far from that noble tree."

Bishop Horace looked down his nose at Shirrup, saying nothing. Then he turned slowly back to Marcus. The warm effects of the alcohol were cooling off. Fear was making Marcus sober, and he felt a headache developing behind his eyes. "Be on your way, novice."

Marcus couldn't believe his luck. He wasn't about to stick around to see if he had heard right. He sped away as quickly as his weak knees would allow, stumbled around a corner, and vomited into some bushes, a great red fountain of sour wine and un-digested mince pie spilling from his mouth "You and I must talk, Father Shirrup," he heard Bishop Horace say, as he retched up the last of it. A cold sweat covered his brow. He closed his ears, not caring about what conversation the old gowned fools were having, and stumbled off in the direction of his cell, hoping to forget everything about this day but the girl. *I hope I dream of her, and I hope she's naked in my dream.*

Ten

The Fifth Wheel — John Gray

It was clear to Gray that Irwin Kawfee knew horses. As they double-rode to Dead Tree the man paced himself perfectly, coaxing everything out of his mount without blowing her. The beast still had some energy when they hauled into town. The Fifth Wheel slid off the horse and rushed to the Greenberry Hotel & Saloon. The demon was after them and he would have to muster some men to face it.

Mayor Brook and a few others were in the common room, playing cards and eating a late lunch. They looked up as Gray burst in, the batwing doors flapping behind him. "Where's the sheriff?" Brook said, with a half-eaten chicken leg in his hand.

"Dead," Gray replied. The mayor lost some of his dignity as his mouth dropped open. The chicken leg slipped from his fingers and fell to the floorboards, landing with a greasy smack. Gray continued, "It looks like you're the sheriff now, at least temporarily. I need some able-bodied men, men who have some mettle and are handy with a gun."

"Wh—what do you m—m—mean?" Brook stammered.

"I mean hell is coming down the road to Dead Tree and we have to stop it."

Kawfee entered the saloon, shotgun in hand. The men in the room looked at him and then back to Gray.

"Let's *go!*" Gray barked. "We are pressed for time." The company scurried into action, their eyes wide and startled, their faces pale.

—— 《》 ——

It was a shabby gang that Mayor Brook managed to coddle together. Gray had thought a town this close to the frontier would be made of tougher stuff. The civilized world, he realized, was growing soft.

There were about twenty men assembled around Gray in the town square. Some, the younger ones, looked eager, but most were scared. Nearly all were armed with muzzleloaders, antique weapons handed down from generation to generation. A hunter and his two sons who happened to be in town visiting relatives were the best of the lot. They were armed with levered rifles and had a seasoned look about them. Kawfee stood beside Gray, gripping his shotgun, his knuckles white, his lips tight and his pointy chin thrust out with determination.

Gray explained his plan. The hunters would hunker down in the large barn that overlooked Shortcut Pass. Their shots would signal when the demon arrived. They would pour as much lead into the creature as they dared, then fall back to the small stable behind the inn. The main body, which included Gray and Kawfee, would be waiting at the stable where they would take the fight to the demon. If the creature survived and took that position, then everyone would retreat to the Greenberry for a final stand. Brook, along with a few old veterans of the past war, would hole up in the inn and cover them as they retreated.

"Any questions?" Gray looked from man to man.

"You're sure this is a demon we're facing?" said a white-faced Brook.

"Damn sure," Gray replied, and Kawfee nodded.

"And we can stop it, destroy it, with guns?" Brook held up his pistol, a .32 short. *A ridiculous pistol*, Gray thought sourly, *only fit for in-close fighting. But, then again, it may come to that.*

"Yes, its physical form can be destroyed and that's all we're concerned about," Gray said. "Kawfee here put some shot in it and scared it off." He nodded toward the old man.

"I ain't never fought a demon before," the hunter said, "but I reckon it will fall like any beast if you punch enough holes in it."

Gray nodded, but was unsure. He was witness to the creature's power.

—— ⟨⟩ ——

Daylight was dwindling, the sun was setting, and there was still no sign of the demon. Small bats and birds were zipping around, feasting on the insects that were drawn out by the moisture on the ground. The sky was clear and a mixture of rose and purple, smeared with orange and amber. It would have been a nice evening, if circumstances were different.

The apprehension was thick, and Gray was as full of worry as the rest of them. As the hours slid by, worry gave way to doubt. *Was the creature coming?* He'd look a fool if it didn't. Still, he was starting to think that looking the fool would be a small price to pay. Aside from Kawfee and the hunters, the quality of the men around him was negotiable at best. He glanced over at the boy next to him. He had a mop of flaxen-colored hair, a wide face covered in freckles, and he looked *bored*. His small game rifle was leaning against the wall of the adjacent stall. He had a finger far up his nose as he idly dug deep for treasure. He pulled his finger out and stared at it. He had come up empty.

If it doesn't come, I'll handpick some men and we'll hunt it down, Gray decided. He looked out again at the field beyond and saw nothing. It was dusk now and soon it would be night. He suddenly noticed there were no birds or bats in the air, and then he heard it, as did all the residents of Dead Tree.

A queer long howl filled the air. It sounded like the broken whistle of a train, mixed with the terrified screams of a crowd of men, women, and children. Gray felt the hairs on the back of his neck stand up, and the flaxen-haired nose picker next to him let out a low moan, which he followed up with a prayer.

The demon howled again, this time closer, the howl echoing off the walls of the town's buildings. From his vantage point in the stable, Gray could not see the creature. He squinted hard, scanning the dimming horizon, the bushes and trees that were now darker shapes in a darkening landscape. "Oh, Giver protect us," he heard some old voice croak in a corner.

Another howl, this one sounding like the demon was almost on top of them, and a shot rang out from the barn where the hunters were lying in wait. It was followed by two others and then silence. "It's gone to ground," came a voice from the barn. "We can't see it." Gray strained his eyes and saw nothing. He cursed and slammed a fist into the old barn wood, making the dust fly and the boy next to him jump. The demon let loose a mournful howl. "It will wait until it's completely dark," Gray muttered. The men near him cursed and moaned.

The last light of dusk quickly gave way to night. Stars blanketed the sky, but the moon was nothing but a sliver, leaking a paltry yellow light over the ground. Gray was happy when he saw the fires come to life. All around town, they had set up stands of brush to burn. Suddenly, he could see well out into the field, but there was no sign of the demon save another howl, louder and more unnerving than the last.

"We gotta get out of here," the boy next to him squeaked.

"Stand your ground or I'll shoot you," Gray growled. Panic could spread like spilt water over stone among men such as these.

The demon let out a low, mournful howl and then went silent. Gray could hear the cracking of the dry wood in the fires. A man coughed and somewhere inside the village a tomcat yowled.

Suddenly, a volley of shots rang out from the barn where the hunters were hunkered down. Gray looked and saw the twisted, giant form of the demon as it suddenly lurched up and struck the barn with great force. It cast a long, grotesque shadow across the ground. Wood splintered as the rear wall was shattered and the creature entered. He heard the hunters scream and they came out a rear door at full sprint. The demon followed.

"Fire," Gray yelled, and there was a crash of many guns fired in a closed space as the men in the stable unloaded their weapons. The boy next to him sent his panicked shot into the ceiling above. Some bullets, though, did hit their mark. The demon shivered from the impact of the lead, clods of earth flying, but still it came on. It swatted one of the hunter's sons aside like an insect, the boy screaming, his guts springing from a great wound like dark, wet rope as he pin-wheeled through the air and off into the night. "Son," the hunter cried, bringing his weapon to his shoulder and firing two quick rounds into the demon's head where its eyes would have been, except there were no eyes, only dark holes. The demon swung and knocked the man's head off his shoulders with a lazy swipe. A man whimpered in the livery and another vomited. The air around Gray smelled like a privy as men had shit and pissed themselves. Kawfee put two rounds of buckshot into the creature. It stumbled back, giving time for the last of the hunters to escape through the stable door. The door was slammed shut and barred. Gray fired his carbine, rapidly and accurately, tearing away bits and pieces of the demon. Still it came.

He turned around to steady the men, but they were gone. Only Kawfee and the young hunter remained. Kawfee was calmly reloading his weapon. The hunter breathed in the stable air in deep gasps, weeping, half in relief at having made it so far and half in sorrow for the loss of father and brother. The firelight coming through the windows danced weirdly about. Their shadows curled and twisted on the livery walls, forming bizarre patterns. The demon, now weakened, hammered on the door. It cracked but held. "Give it some lead and then retreat to the saloon," Gray said.

He dropped his carbine and pulled out both his pistols. Another blow and a splinter flew past Gray's head, nicking his ear. A drop of blood fell onto his shoulder. The demon struck the door again and it gave way. It stood in the doorway, red mud dripping from its flanks onto the ground. It looked around with its empty sockets and let out a roar. The smell that poured from the demon's mouth was ancient decay, mortification and rot, like a hundred bloated bodies that had roasted for days under a high summer's sun. Gray's stomach flip-flopped and his throat closed. He gagged, but stood firm. Kawfee gave the creature a blast from his shotgun. A great chunk of its face was blown away. It stepped forward, lashing out with its muddy arms, the mud flying in all directions. Gray dodged the debris and started opening up with his pistols. They were all aimed shots, tearing into the demon's head. It rushed forward with great speed, the young hunter backpedaling desperately away. But he wasn't quick enough. The creature lifted a foot and squashed the boy into the floor, his organs shooting this way and that, blood jetting from his mouth with his dying cry. It was a choking cough.

The demon stopped to examine its handiwork, pawing at the remains of the boy. "Now's our chance. Let's go," Gray said to Kawfee. Both men re-loaded as they retreated from the stable to the inn. The demon followed.

They entered through the back of the building, the door left open by the men who had fled from the stable earlier. They found themselves in the kitchen, the fires in the fireplaces banked, with only an orange glow coming from the iron stove. The candles had been snuffed and the lanterns were gone. There was no one around. Brook had fled with the others. Gray and Kawfee stood alone against the approaching horror.

Gray slammed the door shut and drew the iron bar to bolt it. Kawfee was wheezing, the sweat on his face apparent in the glow. "Are you going to make it?" Gray asked. The man nodded. "Just catching my breath. At least, what's left of it."

Gray heard the demon outside the door. It was shuffling around, gathering its strength to batter its way in. It was weakened now, its form seriously damaged by all the gunshots. It was a war of attrition, bullets versus mud and blood bound by sorcery. "I think we can do this," he said, more to himself than Kawfee. He finished reloading and faced the door, pistols at the ready. Kawfee was beside him, his shotgun at his shoulder.

With a roar the demon crashed through the door, sending splinters in all directions. The creature stood there, quivering, smaller than before. It was, Gray decided, less impressive. The fear that the demon invoked in him was diminished along with its power. Still, he knew that a single swat from the monster would kill him. Kawfee unloaded a barrel into the demon's leg, the shot tearing away a large clod of mud. Its leg buckled. Gray started firing shots into its head, chipping it away. The demon lurched forward. It took some erratic swipes as its form shivered from the impact of the shots. Kawfee unloaded the second barrel into the remainder of its leg and the leg gave way completely. The creature fell to the ground, howling. Gray unloaded his pistols into its face, the last shots tearing away whatever remained of its head. The demon's form collapsed entirely into a pile of mud. A bubble burped in the midst of the sludge. The creature was destroyed.

But Gray knew its maker was not.

Eleven

The Gambler — James Gallant

Gallant and Lucille spent only a night at the Blind Trout. In the common room they had overheard a bit of news that spurred them on. A group had gathered around one of the inn's better-dressed bumpkins. He had a pipe in the corner of his mouth and a copy of the town's newspaper, the Exeter Advance, open in his hands. "The Blue Spears have taken wing and the Church has made the Call," the man read aloud in a slow and measured voice. "All Fifth Wheels are to travel to the Holy Citadel in Jonah's Sword to take the Oath. If unable, either because of duty, health, age, or other circumstance, they may have one of their fellow knights take the Oath in their place." If the story was true, and Gallant had no reason to believe it was not, then the game was moving quicker than he realized.

The sun was just coming up when they settled their bill with the bleary-eyed innkeeper and started toward the train station.

"While it might not be the most secretive way to travel, it is assuredly the quickest," Gallant said to Lucille as they walked down the muddy street. The air was crisp and he was feeling refreshed. He was filled with the restless energy that fueled him. The evening before, he and Lucille had shared a bath (the wooden tub was cramped but the water was clean and warm), and then a surprisingly filling and well-cooked meal. Afterward, he had flopped down on the feather mattress, ignoring the smell of mildew that came off it. He had looked at his hands, suppressing a burp, thinking, *there's dirt under my nails*. He had shrugged and closed his eyes, and did not open them again until morning.

He looked over at Lucille and he saw faint shadows under her eyes. She had *not* slept well. *She worries for the both of* us, he knew. She was wearing a pretty little straw bonnet that she had found somewhere and her hair was down. It flowed over her shoulders and caught the morning sun. *Spun gold*.

"Yes, hardly discreet," she agreed, with the slightest nod. She let go a small sneeze.

Gallant looked at her. "You are alright, darling, I hope."

She waved a hand to brush away his concern. "I'm fine. Can't a women sneeze?"

"Not when she has such a desirable little nose," he chuckled, tweaking the facial featuring he was complimenting. She playfully slapped his hand away and smiled. They linked arms as they continued on their way.

Anyone observing the pair would have assumed they were new lovers, caught up in discovering each other's charms. In truth, they had been married for over a decade. Still, the love they felt for one another was as strong as it was when it first bloomed. Gallant could not put his finger on what it was that maintained their bond so strongly. He knew many couples whose love waned or became a love of necessity — either because of children, family, finances, or other commitments. But it was not that way between him and Lucille. Their love was always fresh.

He remembered the day he first met her. He was a young buck, one of many, going to a society ball. She was a young doe, doing the same. The ball was in Rickard's Hall, that grand place belonging to Marshal's Man "Iron" Ron Rickard, Gallant's onetime lord and master. The young bucks were full of drink and swagger. Some hoped to land wives or prospective wives at the ball, Gallant only wanted some excitement. Marriage was the furthest thing from his mind.

While his friends were drawn to the beautiful belles on the ballroom floor, Gallant was drawn to the green-topped card tables. The snap of the cards, the stern older faces, the cigar smoke, and the glint of coin pulled Gallant in and he settled at a table like a fly settling on a pile of fresh horse dung. Among the older men and withered women at the table was a pretty young creature near Gallant's age. They were playing Attrition, a game popular amongst the nobles of Seawall at that time. Each player played with a full deck of cards. The pile of coins in front of the young lady was indicative of her skill *or* her purse. If it was the former, he felt the challenge. If it were the latter, he would be happy to lighten her load, regardless of her looks.

Even back then, Gallant was a skilled player and a skilled cheat. It did not take long for the players at the table to let him in because he put on the expression of a loser. But while he suffered considerable loss at the start of the game, he soon turned things around, or so it seemed to the other players. And soon he, or rather the pile of coins he had collected, was drawing a crowd. It did not surprise him that it was the pretty young lady at the table who kept pace with him. It came down to the two of them. Together, they had artfully fleeced the other players.

Gallant was aware that, like him, she was cheating and loading her deck. She used her charms, which were plenty, to distract the other players. When it came to cards, however, Gallant was not distracted by such charms. All that mattered to him was the game. *And winning.*

He did not let on that he knew she was cheating. He let it play in his favor. He even let her have the advantage on several occasions, only to rally when all seemed lost. As the final showdown advanced he wondered if he let things go too far. His deck was awfully small compared to hers. Still, the cards he held back were strong ones and he felt confident.

Sure enough, he began to whittle down her deck, to the point where only a few of her cards remained. And then she looked at him and smiled. The look said, *I know your game and I am going to beat you.* Usually confident in games of chance, Gallant's heart missed a beat. She engaged a fat old gentleman in entertaining conversation and used the opportunity and distraction to load her deck again. Just a few cards, but it was enough. *She'll sting me now*, he thought. Surprisingly though, he had the stronger cards, much stronger cards.

Then it struck him. She was purposely throwing the game. That made his blood boil. She was going to let him win, as if he was just some titmouse.

I can beat you at that too, missy. But try as he might — to *lose* — he knocked the remnants of her deck down and cleaned the table. He was as angry as a hornet. *She* had bested *him* at *his* game. Even on the best of days, he was sore loser.

A cheer went up from the onlookers as he raked in the coins. The cheer would have pleased him under ordinary circumstances, but it only stoked his anger. Had she been a man he would have put a glove across her cheek.

He managed to keep his composure. He got up stiffly, gave a bow to the woman and said, "Thank 'ee." Then turned and left. Her titter followed him, digging under his skin like a sharp nail.

He stalked over to a punch bowl, shaking off the pats on the back and congratulations from old friends and new admirers alike. He poured himself a glass, sloshing half of it over his hand in his anger and haste. He downed the spiked punch in one go and poured himself another.

"A sore winner, that *is* new," a women's voice, *her* voice, said from behind him. He spun around and waggled a finger under her nose. "You purposely lost," he hissed, "which goes entirely against the grain when it comes to card play."

She gently pushed his finger aside, smiled and replied, "And, you sir, were trying to do the same."

"You...," he looked around and kept his voice very low, "you … cheated."

"And so did you. What is good for the stud is sometimes good for the mare."

He sputtered. It was one of the rare times when he had struggled for words. "You're exasperating," he finally said. He threw up his free hand and downed his punch.

"People are only as exasperating as we allow them to be," she chuckled. "I find you, for example, not exasperating in the least, only amusing."

"Amusing!" He stuck out his chin. "How so?"

She smiled. "You strut in here and cheat old cotton heads out of their coins thinking you have accomplished something. I think *that* is rather amusing, is it not?"

"I beat *you*," he sounded like a child when he said it.

She laughed. "Only because I *let* you win."

"Or did you?" he countered, suddenly having a thought. His cool composure was retuning and he smiled. "Maybe you *let* me win because you *knew* you were going to lose. You realized that your charms, such as they are," and he gave a titter, waving his hand in front of her face and breasts, as if to indicate her charms were limited, "were not working on me."

Her cheeks flushed. He laughed. She slapped him. Despite how the slap stung and drew the attention of the other guests, he laughed louder.

For a moment, there was murder in her eyes, and Gallant would not have been surprised if she had pulled out a derringer from some hidden pocket and shot him dead. But the anger evaporated and she started laughing as well. Soon they were both laughing and holding each other so they would not fall down. The confused expressions on the faces of the guests around them only made them laugh all the harder, until tears were streaming down both their cheeks.

After a minute had passed, they regained their composure. Gallant straightened up, handing her his kerchief so she could dab away the tears. "Would you care to dance, Miss…?"

She took his kerchief and gazed up at him through her long lashes. "Lucille. Lucille Belle. Most certainly, Mr…"

Gallant was suddenly struck by the deep brown brightness of her eyes, the flush of her face, the golden strands of her hair that fell, ever so artfully, down onto her delicate white shoulders and neck. His head was light, there was a fluttering in his stomach, and his heart was pounding like it had never pounded before. He realized she was staring at him, waiting for an answer, and recovered. "Gallant. James Gallant." He gave her a bow, which she returned with a curtsey.

And with that, they had entered each other's lives.

Rickard Hall burned down several years after that ball, but the relationship that had kindled there between the two of them continued to burn hot and bright.

— ⟨⟩ —

At the station, a picturesque little building made of fieldstone, and far removed from the mud and dirt of the rest of the town, they purchased tickets to Steeplestone. From there, they could get a train to High Hall. The trip to the capital, the wrinkled old stationmaster ensured them, would take several days at least. *Was there enough time?* Gallant wondered. He hoped to hell there was. A great deal was now resting on his expediency. *The damn book.* His hand moved instinctively to his breast pocket. He could feel it there under his coat, a simple and maybe malevolent thing that would not surrender its secret to him.

Passengers were already gathering on the wooden platform — miners and prospectors with dried mud on their clothes and their business on their backs, picks, shovels and the like; a knot of businessmen in faded suits with grimy collars, talking trade and trying to look important; their squat wives (looking like turnips in peasant dresses) behind them with their squalling children. Loafing on the benches and leaning against the station's wall were the peddlers, desperados, and failed adventurers.

Gallant and Lucille went to the end of the platform where the vendors had set up their stalls. They were selling food and drink, along with some bric-a-brac. A fat fellow was selling whole roasted squabs, next to him a rail-thin man was selling salted fish and canned vegetables, and at the end two women (who might have been the wives of the other two) were selling baskets, cutlery, cloth napkins, and bottles of wine. The squabs had little meat on them, the fish were small and bony, and the baskets fragile, the cutlery cheap and poorly made, and some of the cloth napkins were stained. The merchants looked as suspect as their wares. The fat one had a slimy smile, the thin man couldn't look anyone in the eye, and the two women stank of cheap wine as they puffed away on stubby clay pipes tucked into the smirks they wore on their faces.

"One has to eat," Gallant said apologetically to Lucille. Everything was over-priced, but he bought a basket, along with some wine and food, including the largest of the roasted squabs, which was still a sad specimen indeed. "At these prices, I expect to be as fat as you after I eat this," Gallant drawled, flicking a copper tithe to the plump purveyor of scrawny squabs. The man caught the thick copper coin with a meaty hand, letting loose a *har-har* as he did so.

The train came chugging up from the riverfront shortly thereafter, the long black locomotive hissing steam and spitting hot coals. Three passenger cars were behind the wood-stuffed tender and further back were cattle cars, carrying bawling, stinking cargo, and other cars loaded with freight. "Looks like a charming ride." Gallant said, as the train lurched to a stop in front of them.

A stoker leapt down from the locomotive. He was powerfully built, his arms, cheeks, and clothes covered in soot. He wiped his face with a dirty red kerchief, spat on the platform's wooden boards, and hauled a small tin from his pocket. He took a swig from it and looked around, muttering to himself. When he saw the station hands come strolling lazily out of the building he bellowed at them. "Get yer asses movin'. We need water and the passengers aboard. We're runnin' behind schedule." Gallant and Lucille looked at each other. He grinned and she rolled her eyes.

"Passengers aboard," a station hand yelled.

The crowd moved forward, with the miners, prospectors, peddlers, desperados, adventurers, and other riff-raff pushing toward the first car. It would be a rough ride up there, where the passengers would have little more comfort than the livestock riding in the boxcars near the back. Bare wooden benches, a lamp or two for light, all coated in the soot deposited by the engine smoke. It would be lively though, and cheap.

The businessmen, their families, and the better-dressed passengers crowded the steps of the second and third cars. There would be padded benches with goose-down cushions waiting for their soft backsides, oil lamps overhead for light, a cast iron stove for heat if it got chilly, and wallpaper and well-worn carpets for décor.

Gallant wouldn't have minded riding up front, but Lucille would have protested and she had been through enough already. It had cost a full silver marque for both of them to ride in the third car — a deal compared to the price they had paid for their squab and other miserable food.

An argument broke out between two of the riff–raff as they tried to squeeze up the steps at the same time. One was a crack-faced man in prospector's rags, with a ragged beard and mouth full of broken teeth. The other was tall, dark-haired, in a worn blue coat and pants. Harsh words soon gave way to blows. The crowd moved back to give them space. The dark-haired man was giving more than he was getting, and crack-face's beard was soon soaked in blood. Some of the rowdier sorts were placing bets and cheering them on while the businessmen were loading their families onto the train as quickly as possible. Then dark hair was about to put an end to it when he slipped on a gob of blood. He went down with a howl as his ankle buckled under him with a sickening crack. Crack-face looked at him, shook his head and cackled as he clambered aboard, leaving his opponent rolling on the ground and clutching his boot. Money was changing hands, with scowls on the faces of the losers and grins on the faces of the winners.

"Alright," yelled the stoker, as he wiped his face with his kerchief. He looked at the injured man. "Pick this one up if he is coming or leave him here if he is staying. Damn fool." He spat to show his contempt. "Everyone aboard now."

"I'm thinking this is going to be an *interesting* ride." Gallant checked the gun at his side, a Seawall Thunder with smooth wooden grips, and Lucille let out a quiet groan.

"We should go." He placed his hand reassuringly on her shoulder and then slipped it down to the small of her back. She smiled and tucked herself under his arm. The train whistle blew long and hard to let everyone know the train was about to leave the station.

Twelve

The Privileged Girl — Lara Mainhouse

Lara Mainhouse preferred the company of her father to that of her mother, and as the High Marshal's granddaughter she was free to do what she pleased.

She was unlike most young ladies of her age. She was fifteen, nearly a woman, *and* a potential steward of the High Seat. She was expected to learn the parlor game, which consisted of dancing, lessons in etiquette, courting, gossiping, and preparing for marriage and motherhood. None of that appealed to her, however. She preferred to ride horses, shoot game, hunt, chase — and bed — what men pleased her.

Her father had left Hunter's Croft, his hunting lodge and his preferred refuge from the rigors of duty, and traveled to High Hall. She had gone with him rather than returning to the family's main house, Ivy Pillar. Her mother was there, after all.

She was sitting in the viewing gallery of the Great Hall along with a hundred or so other spectators. Down below, the gray-headed lords of the Realm carried out the affairs of state. They sat around the Ruling Table, a huge slab of wood cut from the trunk of some great tree nearly a thousand years ago, during the reign of the Great King Avangar I. There were nine chairs around the table. The oldest and grandest was the High Seat, a wooden throne older than the Ruling Table itself. That was reserved for the High Marshal, her grandfather. Seven chairs represented the seven Seats of the

Realm. Before her grandfather's time the Seats were called kingdoms, and the more romantic still referred to them as such.

The seven Seats were Shieldgate, Seawall, Wood Helm, Lang'Arc, Stone Anchor, Far Reach, and Axefell. Each chair was unique, made from materials found in the Seat it represented. Axefell's looked most uncomfortable because it was made primarily of whalebone and polished granite. Only its seat was wood. There was another chair as well, across from her grandfather, but it was empty. It was an elegant chair with a tall back, golden inlays, and a plump red cushion. That chair was reserved for the Metropolitan, the head of the Church, or a bishop he appointed to represent him. Bishop Dawes had died recently though, and the Metropolitan had yet to appoint another bishop to replace him.

Despite the importance of these special chairs and the people who sat in them, for the most part all Lara saw around the table were old men in their autumn years, collecting splinters in their backsides, with their best harvests behind them. Her grandfather was one of them. *How* does *he suffer through this*, she wondered as she picked another black cherry from the small basket on her lap and bit down on it, enjoying its soft flesh and flavor.

She sat near the back of the gallery with her leg dangled over the polished oak rail in front of her, something she could not have done had she been wearing a dress. She wore soft leather riding breeches and a black riding coat. Her blonde hair fell loose about her shoulders. Judging from the approving looks and leers of many of the young men sharing the viewing gallery with her, men preferred their women wild as opposed to cloistered. Or perhaps they just preferred their women pretty — because she *was* pretty, with fine features, full lips, high cheekbones, and bright blue eyes — regardless of the clothes they wore. She ignored them all. They were the boys of High Hall, the sons of privileged families, predictable and boring in every way imaginable.

She stared down at the privileged few seated in the front row of the gallery. Her father was there, Arthur Mainhouse. He was still young enough, affable and daring, with dark hair and striking blue eyes. He had rakish good looks, which included a small dagger-tip beard and moustache. Around him were his cronies — free-spirited fellows all — *and his mistress*. Lara pulled the cherry pit from her mouth and dropped in on the floor. She thought little of her father's choice in mistresses.

Heather Shield was a minor noble, but from a family that boasted great wealth. She was pampered and soft, very beautiful and sharp-witted. She was also presumptuous. Lara had been stabbed by her sharp wit more than a few times. Still, Heather Shield was what most at court would call good company — and few would say that of her, the *wild* Lara Mainhouse. Or of even Lara's mother.

Lara's mother was beautiful; it was true. But she was poor company, quiet and pious and dull, dull, dull. There was a time — before Lara was born — when her mother was said to have been fire itself. But the death of her lover had extinguished her spirit. Even Lara's father could not console her; try as he might, even suggesting other lovers for her. No, she loved but one man and that man was not her husband.

Lara had seen a portrait of her mother's lover, the man people called the Panther. He was from Stone Anchor and had the black hair and dark skin common of the people from that part of the Realm. In the portrait he wore an easy smile, and there was something devilish about his eyes. His entire look excited Lara. He held the promise of adventure — the very thing that got him killed, as she was told he died in some tragic accident. When he had died, Lara's mother had screamed and wailed for days. By the time she was ready to face society again she had become more holy than the Metropolitan, her fiery personality replaced by the flames of the many candles she lit in the family chapel in memory of her Panther.

Next to her father's small party was the party that belonged to her uncle, Henry. He was the heir and would one day sit in the chair that her grandfather now occupied. The thought made her sad. While Lara's father was carefree, and well–liked because of it, Henry Mainhouse was stiff and severe. He had few friends, but as heir to the High Seat was surrounded by many cronies hoping to earn his favor. He had a flat, spade-shaped beard — in contrast to her father's sharp beard — and heavy-lidded eyes full of judgment that looked down on the world past a long, hooked nose. His wife — Maude — sat next to him. She was dressed all in black, as was her want. She was as stony as her husband, and plain-looking, with a face like sour dough. She already acted like she was the High Marshal's Lady and had done so since she was first married over a decade ago.

Beyond Lara's uncle was her natural aunt, Corrine, the eldest of the siblings. Her striking good looks were overshadowed by her nature. She was prim, proper, and domestic. No rouge for her, on either cheeks or lips. No beads, no baubles, no frills. Seated next to her was her husband, Donald, who was presently dozing. He was fat, friendly and very fond of his books, boasting the largest known library in the Realm.

Behind them all sat Lara's cousins, a healthy brood of nine children, five belonging to Corrine and four to Henry. They ranged in ages from three to ten and didn't interest Lara in the slightest. Nannies, tutors, and servants struggled to keep the bored youngsters in line.

Lara's Aunt Alice was absent, which was no surprise. Alice was sixteen, just a year older than Lara, and she rarely made public appearances. She only did so when she was *healthy* enough, which was seldom. Alice was an embarrassment to the High Marshal's family and was rarely talked about. She lived in the country somewhere on a secluded estate.

Lara was just three or four when Alice first went away. It was after the death of her other aunt, Margaret, who was Alice's twin. It was said Alice was driven mad by her sister's death. But there was more to it than that, although Lara was never privy to *that* dark secret.

In truth, Lara was glad Alice was not here, as her aunt unsettled her. Alice had a tendency to smile knowingly at her niece and seemed to stare into Lara's soul with her feverish eyes. Once she had painfully twisted Lara's breasts when they had first budded. Lara had screamed and ran off, chased by Alice's mocking laughter. *Now I'd knock her teeth out*, Lara thought, still stung by the memory.

She chewed on another cherry and focused on what was going on around the Ruling Table below. Lord Happichance of Wood Helm, the Realm's Lord Treasurer, had just pushed his hulking old body up from his chair. He held an official looking piece of paper, decorated with blue ribbons. Lara tried to recall some details about Happichance, other than the fact he was very old, but could only think that her father's mistress called him Lord Flatulence or Lord Shat-his-pants. Heather Shield could be crude and sometimes she used low speech, which was fine with Lara as Lara sometimes used low speech herself. Lord Happichance *did* have a tendency to break wind, frequently and loudly. Lara giggled and was quickly shushed by her Aunt Maude, whose tight lips were pursed even tighter than normal.

Lara leaned forward to hear what Happichance was saying. His purple lips quivered in his craggy old face as his quavering voice drifted up softly from below. *Apparently his backside speaks with more conviction than his mouth,* she thought.

"As you know, the Metropolitan has made the Call," he said. "Several thousand members of the Order of the Fifth Wheel are expected to answer. They, along with family and retainers, will be encamped around Jonah's Sword. Many noble families across the Realm will also travel to Seawall to take in the ceremonies.

"This will put a strain on the host Seat, and Seawall is asking for compensation to host so many guests. Expected are the traditional tournaments and usual entertainments."

"This is a matter for the Church, not the Realm," injected Hugh Talbot, with a dismissive wave of his hand. Talbot was Shieldgate's representative at the table and the Lord Councilor of Territories and Holdings. He sat in his chair comfortably and was no friend of Seawall's. He fought against Seawall in the last war and lost two sons in the conflict. He was fat, red-faced, and bald-headed, save for cotton-like tufts of hair above each ear. "The Church has made the Call *independent* of this council's authority. The Church has money in its coffers. It should compensate."

As expected, Seawall's representative Brian Carr, Lord Councilor of Defense and Munitions, responded. "I should remind Lord Talbot that the Call goes out in the name of the *Realm,* and the Fifth Wheel is an expense that we *all* share. I don't think the Church should be responsible to care for *our* agents." At forty-six, Carr was the youngest at the table. He was tall and gangly, with black hair that was probably dyed. He looked down his long nose at Lord Talbot.

Talbot's face reddened more than usual and his jowls quivered. "Regardless," he barked. "We were *not* consulted on the Call. If the Church wishes to be cavalier in its actions then let the Church pay for that privilege."

Carr's eyes crinkled in the corners as he chuckled. "But we *were* consulted."

Talbot drew up out of his chair. "No sir, *we* were not." He jabbed a finger in Carr's direction. "Perhaps Seawall was consulted in this matter, but the rest of us were kept in the dark."

Lara spit out a pit and quickly grabbed another cherry. Things were getting heated. Her grandfather broke in. "Lord Talbot, sit." The old lord did so, like an obedient dog. The High Marshal of the realm was old and grey like the rest of them. But even at seventy, his powerful physique was still apparent. He turned his attention on Lord Happichance. "We will compensate Seawall. Send them fifty thousand in gold. That should suffice, should it not?" Happichance nodded.

Carr smiled and then leaned forward. There is another matter, High Marshal. As the honorary head of the Order of the Fifth Wheel, your attendance is required at the Oath swearing."

The High Marshal turned his gaze on Seawall's representative. "I am well aware of my obligations, Lord Carr. I intend to leave with my family in a few days time and we should arrive within a fortnight." The man from Seawall nodded at this and smiled, but the oily smile disappeared when the High Marshal added, "I am glad to see this meets with my *servant's* approval." Talbot guffawed at the jab.

The talk continued, but Lara stopped paying attention. If her grandfather was taking his family to Seawall, that meant she might be going as well. She had never been to Seawall but had read it was beautiful, full of adventure and *very handsome* men.

She knew the Blue Spears had been released and the Call had gone out, but she didn't pretend to understand the implications. The Fifth Wheel was an old Order and its agents were seldom at court or the capital. The older gentlemen of the realm thought the Order important and so too did her father, but they were nearly alone in that. Most of the younger nobles and the commons thought the Order should be dissolved. Lara was uncertain. She did, however, like how some of the young Fifth Wheel looked in portraits — all gunned and spurred — venturing off to become dirty frontier riders. Her heart started beating faster. Perhaps she could meet some of these young men if she went to Seawall. And then ... she'd be able to judge them for herself.

Thirteen

The Fifth Wheel — John Gray

Gray stood in the crowd of mourners. He was kitted up and ready to leave town, but before he left he would pay his respects to those who had fallen fighting the demon. A preacher with a pale, pinched face intoned the words that Gray knew well. He half-listened as his mind wandered to another funeral he had attended several years before.

He had been a veteran of the trail, spurred and gunned, for many years when he buried his father next to his mother, who herself was many years dead. His brother was at court, too busy to attend to planting their father in the soil. So the job fell to John Gray, as most of the ugly jobs did where his family was concerned. All the same, he loved his brother and didn't blame him for not attending the funeral. Their father was an unlikable man — at least in the eyes of his sons.

As he stood at the edge of the hole that would serve as his father's final resting place, Gray noted the human vultures circling the corpse. They were there to feed on the dead man's wealth, not his memory. Some were business associates, others the sons of those who served alongside his father during the war. And to the latter, Lord James Gray — father of John and Jessop — was nothing more than a name mentioned in the tales their fathers told.

Gray smiled bitterly as he looked around at the *mourners*, their eyes and heads down as the old priest labored through the words. It was an autumn day and the weather was fine. It was the sort of day that a man of means spent in easy leisure, perhaps hunting or fishing or riding. Standing by a graveside was the last thing any of them wanted to do.

After the funeral, cups would be raised in James Gray's memory. Barrels of fine wine from the fine man's cellar would be consumed. Laughter and chat, as befit the custom, would accompany the funeral feast, the kind of laughter and chat that James Gray reserved for friends, not family. And John Gray would suffer through it all at the place of honor, the head of the banquet table; although Gray knew that honored place was not his by rights but his brother's, the one with the busy court life.

"Into the soil we go. From the soil again shall we be reborn in the eternal spring of the Giver's garden," the priest said, as he cast a handful of earth down upon the casket of Lord James. Gray wondered how his father was faring in the Giver's garden, *if* he was even there. He suspected his father was more likely wearing the yoke of the Enemy in Hell.

"So be it, so be it, so be it, sirrah," intoned the mourners. A long moment of silence followed. Gray stood there staring down at the casket, at the wooden box that encased a man and his life's tale. He felt no remorse. Nor did he feel satisfaction either. He felt ... nothing. That did not surprise him. The last time he had talked with Lord James was two years before the old man's death and then only at a public function they were both forced to attend. Lord James was seventy-two and showing his age. His hair was gray, his beard unkempt, his clothes out of fashion, and he walked with a stoop and the aid of a cane. Father and son exchanged few words.

Lord James died of some chest flux. His servant, Steven, was with him when the end came — loyal Steven, who had served James Gray for more than fifty years, himself an old man now. He was weeping openly at the graveside. Gray would make sure he was taken care of, that Steven got his fair share *before* all the others.

The mourners were looking at him. They were waiting for him to toss a handful of dirt into the hole, so they could follow suit and get to the drinking, the eating, and the business of the will. Let them wait, Gray thought.

In due time he walked to the priest. He kissed the man on both his sagging wrinkled cheeks and said, "Thank you, sir, for this final service in honor of my father. Thank you, sir, for sending him off to the Giver's garden. May he earn favor in the Giver's eyes and so taste the fruits of paradise."

"And so he shall," the priest replied, looking Gray full in the face. He was a sour old man who liked his whiskey and was a staunch drinking companion of James Gray, handpicked by the lord to make his final bed. Gray bent down before him and picked up a handful of dirt from the pile that was placed there for that purpose. He cast the soil down on the coffin lid. The dirt rattled loudly on the wood. His part done, he turned and walked away.

— «» —

Gray eased out of his revelry as dirt rattled on the coffins of the late Sheriff Croft, the hunter and his two sons — the *heroes* who had died slaying the demon. They would be remembered for many years in these parts, even the useless Croft. Next to the graves of the townsmen were three graves for the fallen Fifth Wheels.

Gray sighed and turned away as the gravediggers put their backs into their shovels. He looked up at the overcast sky. The ceiling of clouds was high and there'd be no rain. It was easy weather in which to travel.

Next to Gray's new horse — gifted to him for his deeds — was the new sheriff in town, Sheriff Kawfee. Kawfee wore the shield proudly. He had been off the booze for several days and didn't look to be tempted by it any longer. Deadly encounters with demons can do that to people. Only time, of course, would tell. Sink or swim — it was up to Kawfee now. Mayor Brook had protested, but Gray had persuaded him that Irwin Kawfee was the man for the job.

Kawfee extended his bony hand when Gray walked up. "Be seeing you around," he said.

"Not likely," Gray returned. He shook the man's hand. "Take care of yourself — and this town. It's yours now to guard."

Kawfee nodded. "Be safe on the trail, wherever it takes you." Gray tipped his hat to that, mounted up, and rode out.

He was happy to leave Dead Tree and its demon behind him, but what of the man or woman who had created it? Gray was certain that it was no mere sorcerer or witch that had brought the demon forth. He was sure it was a Dead Priest.

Dead Priests were practitioners of the dark arts. They were servants of the Enemy — servants of the dark god. This Dead Priest was out there somewhere, moving farther into the realm, bringing corruption with it. The unholy man or woman had a good lead and it would be difficult to pick up the scent, maybe impossible, but damn it, he'd try.

Rather than skirt the hills through Short Cut Pass, Gray decided to take the longer route that would take him into Jersey's Spit — another small town, still close to the Range and the border. He tried to convince himself that he needed time to collect his thoughts and regain his focus, but in his heart he knew he wanted to avoid the path that led to where he first encountered the demon. Still, he'd have to face the Dead Priest soon enough, that was certain. And he knew that pride would conquer fear when that moment came, but there was no need to face that fear yet.

Gray had had a run in with a Dead Priest before. Predrag Landry was his name — a strange name for a strange and evil man. He had not thought of Landry in several years, but fighting the demon had brought back many disturbing memories — memories that Gray had worked hard to bury through hard trail riding and diligence to his duty.

The village where the final showdown with Landry took place was Feather's Cap. Thanks to the Dead Priest that place was now nothing more than dust and ruins. But Landry had learned a fatal lesson that day; that bullets could beat magic.

He wondered what magic the sorcerer he was now chasing would try to use against him. Landry had lorded over human minds, not demons born of earth and blood.

He shook his head and touched spurs to his horse's sides, urging it into a trot. The dark gifts that the Dead Priest possessed did not matter. What mattered was that the man or woman who wielded them had to die, preferably at Gray's hands.

Fourteen

The Lady of Seawall — Genevieve

"What news, Patriarch?" Genevieve asked. The Lady of Seawall was wearing a white morning dress, airy and comfortable, a pair of silk slippers on her feet. She was lounging on a settee in her chambers, a newspaper beside her, and a cup and saucer on her lap. The settee, which was a deep burgundy, had a hunting scene embroidered on it, played out in silver, gold, and green thread. It was tucked into a niche under a window and the sunlight was warm on her skin. She could feel it on the back of her neck, as comforting as a lover's kiss.

Bishop Michael sat on a large cushioned chair at the dining table. *The chair reserved for my husband*, she thought peevishly. He was wearing a rich red gown this morning, fringed with silver. He was looking regal. *Too regal*, Genevieve thought. He took a sip of wine before answering. "The Metropolitan's ill-health continues," he said. "The usual stomach complaints. I think it's the rich food he eats."

Genevieve considered that as she took another sip of her tea. "Well, he *is* old. It's to be expected. I hope he will be well enough to perform his duties when the High Marshal arrives."

Michael shrugged, a slight smile on his lips. "I'm sure he will be fine, my lady. He always seems to muster his strength when he has a chance to be the center of attention."

"I hope he doesn't *die* on us." It was a sudden thought that she spoke aloud.

Michael tittered. "No fear of that. He's taken frequent naps in the sickbed for nearly five years now and always rises for the occasion when necessary. For good or ill, I think we'll be stuck with our Holy Father for quite some time yet."

There was something in the way he said it that niggled at Genevieve. Her brow furrowed. There was a knock on the door. "Enter," she said. Several servants came in carrying covered platters of food. The aromas held promise for a hungry person, but Genevieve was not hungry. She seldom was. Her appetite for food had never been large and it had grown smaller following the birth of her first child, Roland, some fifteen years ago. Three children followed her firstborn. She lost only one of them, a tiny thing who died a few days after her birth. Still, she was blessed with a strong, healthy son and two vibrant daughters. Her duties as the Lady of Seawall though meant that her children knew their governesses, tutors, and the house staff better than their mother. Roland had left for High Hall three years ago to study at Tilting Yard, the military academy for young officers there. He seldom came home and was now man enough to consider his mother a nuisance. But he would be home to witness the Oath Swearing and would be forced to endure a mother's meddling. The middle child, Susan, was twelve and becoming a proper lady. She was a ward of her husband's uncle. Lord Goodregard's younger brother, on the coast. Lady Seawall had not seen her in a year and would be glad to see her again, too. Only young Jane still remained hers. Tender Jane. She was just ten and Genevieve was determined that she would remain by her side. Lord Goodregard *and* Bishop Michael wanted to ship Jane off to Jonah's Sword to become a lady of the Church. *Not in my lifetime,* Genevieve thought.

The servants uncovered a dozen dishes, steam rolling from most of them. When the servants left, she got up and joined the bishop at the table. She gestured at the food. "Please. Eat."

When it came to the consumption of food Bishop Michael needed no urging, but he had the good grace to restrain himself and pour both of them a glass of chilled yellow wine before digging in. He offered to serve her, but she waved the offer aside. "I had a large breakfast, but you go ahead."

He shoveled the food onto his plate, but left the choice bits for the Lady of Seawall. He ignored the cutlery as he plucked up a chunk of springhare, dripping with sauce, and popped it into his mouth. He chewed rapidly, swallowed, and looked up at her. "You're certain you won't join me?" He dabbed at a bit of grease at the corner of his mouth with his napkin. "This rabbit is most delightful." She shook her head.

As the bishop plowed through his dinner — slurping up soup, tearing through meat, cracking open crab legs and enjoying chunks of warm bread — they talked about pleasantries, the upcoming tournaments, whom would best whom on the field, what man was pursuing what lady and vice versa. It was only when the bishop was finishing his dessert, a trifle of cream, custard, and berries that the discussion turned to important matters.

"What news of the High Marshal?" Genevieve asked. "When will he arrive?"

"It took some coaxing to get the old bear to leave his den, I am told," Michael replied, sucking at his teeth to remove something stuck between them, "but even he must answer the summons. He is after all, as ruler of the realm, a member of the Fifth Wheel and the honorary leader of that Order. He is leaving High Hall on the morrow and is traveling by private train."

She nodded. High Hall was the castle-fortress that housed the High Marshal, his family, retainers, and personal guard. It was also the name given to the city that surrounded it — the capital, the focal point of the entire realm and, if things played out properly, Genevieve's future home.

Genevieve recalled the first time she visited High Hall with her family. She was only six at the time, but the vastness of both castle and city impressed itself on even her young mind. It was truly the greatest city in the realm. *And it should be mine.* The Great Avangar, the very first High Marshal (who would have been called the High King back then) supposedly erected the original keep, called Old Keep, that was at the heart of the castle and that might have been true. The rest of the sprawling complex, however, was built over the centuries, some of it in recent memory. The bastions of the First Fort that surround the High Marshal's castle seemed to reach to the sky. "And what of his sons?"

"They come as well, of course." The Bishop brushed crumbs from his robes. "And his daughters."

"Even *Alice*?" Genevieve couldn't keep the shock from her voice. The girl had not been seen in public for years.

Michael looked up from his robes and nodded. "Yes, but I suspect we won't see much of her." She nodded.

Already she was thinking of the cost of housing the High Marshal and his retainers. The sons, the daughters, the accompanying families, and their lackeys would tax her household. More to the point, the presence of the High Marshal's sons was troublesome. She bit her lip in worry. "Could the presence of his sons pose a problem for us, foil our plans in some way?"

"No," the bishop said calmly. "In fact, it is to our benefit. The heir and the spare are as a different as fire and water and very quarrelsome; the more people who see that, the better. When the old bear is removed, the cubs will roar at each over the carcass."

Genevieve cocked her head. "And how does that benefit us?"

Bishop Michael looked at her. "It's quite simple, really. I will fuel their dislike for one another."

"And?"

"And I will undermine any loyalty that Arthur Mainhouse might have toward his older brother Henry, subtly pointing out Henry's obvious flaws — his rigid way of thinking, his stony nature, his lack of humor, his disregard for Arthur's *obvious* talents.

"In turn, I will remind Henry that Arthur is a frivolous fool, a loose cannon, who needs to be as far away from any court as possible," Michael smiled. "And an enemy's house that is divided is easily defeated. Even if it's a Mainhouse." He giggled at his own joke.

There was a long moment of silence before Genevieve asked. "How exactly is the High Marshal going to accommodate us with an easy death?"

It was a direct question and she was hoping for a direct answer. The bishop, however, disappointed her. "The matter, as you know, is very delicate. It has taken time and a great deal of effort to ensure that all the pieces of the puzzle are gathered. We are now ready to assemble it and once it starts assembling itself we can't stop it."

"I know," Genevieve whispered. She started to wring her hands, then realized it and pulled her hands apart. It had taken all of her efforts, obstinacy, and charm to make her husband agree to this crucial part of the plan. "He is old and will eventually die of natural causes, and then we can make our move," he had said in that stubborn way of his that told her to leave it alone. "No," she had slammed her foot down. "These Mainhouses are long-lived and that could mean waiting another twenty years. You'll be an old man by then, and I'll be an old woman. We must do this *now*, or not at all." He had seen the wisdom in that.

Her own doubt now was starting to creep in. "Is … this … the wisest course of action?"

Bishop Michael stared at the High Lady for a moment before answering. He leaned forward and looked hard into her eyes. "It is the *only* course of action, High Lady. If your husband wants to sit the High Seat then the person presently occupying it must be removed. It will be *good* for the realm. *Good* for the Church."

Genevieve sighed. She was resigned. She was *not* weak. She had risen high and proven her strength time and again, going beyond even her mother's expectations. She was the Lady of Seawall and soon she would be the High Lady of the entire realm.

Fifteen

The Gambler — James Gallant

Gallant usually enjoyed riding on trains — the click-clack of the iron wheels rolling over the rails, the gentle sway of the carriage, the towns, forests, and farms scrolling by in relative comfort. It suited him. It meant civilization, and all the promise that civilization brought with it. The rigors of trail life and strange foreign places had a certain appeal, but the appeal was short-lived.

He remembered when he was a boy standing with his grandfather and father as they watched as a gang of men lay down a rail line across the family's land. "And so the modern world continues its advance," his grandfather had commented bitterly. Then he had cursed and spat on the ground. He saw steam-powered locomotives as *unnatural inventions* and had been only a boy himself when they first started to appear. Gallant's father, who was less frivolous and not a waster when *his* father was alive, had added a curse and a gob of spit of his own. Gallant, though, was excited by it all, but he was careful to keep the excitement to himself, hiding it behind a boy's scowl. *My father learned to love those trains though,* he thought. *They made it easier for him to keep ahead of his creditors.*

Gallant loved trains, just as he loved the steamboats that powered their way up and down the rivers of the realm.

For a while, the train traveled through a wilderness of brush, forest, and hills, broken up only by miner's camps and the shacks that were next to cisterns to feed the trains'

boilers with water. By mid-day, though, the wilderness started to give way. He saw farms and fields, small villages and
wide tracks. The wood and plank structures of the frontier
gave way to stone walls and thatched and tiled roofs; the
tracks became roads. And everywhere spring was starting to
surrender to summer. Flowers of a hundred colors covered
the meadows, the woods and forests were filled with rich
greens, and the landed folk men had stripped off their shirts
as they worked their land, while their women wore light,
airy dresses.

The Gallants ate their squabs, bony with little meat, and
drank some of the wine, which was sour. He opened a can of
"summer greens", but grimaced in disgust when he took the
first bite. It tasted as though the vegetables had been soaking
in vinegar for over a year. He meant to toss the can out the
window, but Lucille stopped him. After her first bite, though,
she threw it out herself with a giggle.

It was an easy ride. They were well away from the riff-raff
and the people in their car, which were few, had settled into
the silence of travel. Some had even fallen asleep. Gallant
was dozing himself when the train came to its first main stop,
Allstone. It squealed into the station, the waiting passengers
lining the back of the platform to avoid any cinders. Gallant
peered through the dust-covered window at a modest-sized
town of primarily stone buildings with slate roofs.

As the clouds of smoke and steam drifted away, Gallant
saw the crowds of passengers — men in fine suits, women
in gaily-colored dresses, children in whatever their parents
could afford, and two others; two who were gunned and
spurred. They wore pistols on their hips and they carried
swords. They also wore the badges of their office – eleven-
pointed stars - proudly on their breasts. Fifth Wheels — the
knights of the Realm.

Lucille had drifted off to sleep, so he gently nudged her
awake. He gestured with his chin to the two men outside the
window. "It looks like there's some wonderful company out
there."

Lucille stared at them and her eyes narrowed. "Do you
think they are looking for us?"

"I highly doubt it, but I don't know for certain," he admitted. "If they are, we are more wanted than I thought. Nevertheless, it's always best to assume the worst and be prepared." He plucked the small book of poems from his breast pocket and stuffed it into his right boot, then he eased his hand down to the pistol at his side.

The stoker was off the train now and bellowing at the passengers. Some of the riff-raff spilled out as well, stretching their limbs before disappearing into the town. Bag boys and servants were wrestling with travel trunks, bags, and other luggage. The two Fifth Wheels were smiling and chatting as though they were heading out on a hunt or a picnic. The older of the two, now well into middle age, was fat of face and had a large gut. The other, who bore a striking resemblance to his older partner, was equally soft and was carrying a fancy basket. Neither of these men appeared hostile or determined. Instead, they wore easy expressions, the younger man even tipping his hat to an old lady next to him. They started to make their way to the train. Gallant tensed and he felt Lucille tensing beside him as well. *Please don't enter this car,* he thought, and then groaned inwardly as they did just that.

The older man mumbled to his young friend as they sauntered into the car and scanned the empty benches. *Please don't sit beside us* or *across from us,* Gallant thought. He inwardly groaned again as they plunked themselves down in the empty bench across the aisle from Gallant and Lucille. Seeing Lucille, a charming smile spread across the older Fifth Wheel's face. "My lady," he said, with a tip of his stiff hat.

She beamed back at him. "Good sir."

Gallant was now certain that the Fifth Wheels were not looking for them, *or anyone else apparently.* A creeping suspicion started crawling up from his gut. Without thinking or really caring at this point he decided to pry into their affairs. He leaned across the aisle and asked, "Good sir, where are you bound?"

The man didn't seem to mind Gallant's question and quickly replied, "To High Hall, of course, and then to Seawall.

The Call has gone out. All Fifth Wheels that are able are to make to Jonah's Sword to take the Oath."

Gallant smiled. "Yes, yes, of course." They were answering the damn Call. The Call that had gone out *months* before it was supposed to. He felt the disturbing presence of the book in his boot, and the comfort of the pistol at his side.

Lucille chuckled and put a hand on Gallant's arm, squeezing it gently and reassuringly. "You must excuse my husband's prying," she said to the Fifth Wheel, giving him her most winning smile. "He has been very busy with his enterprises of late and as a result has been quite forgetful."

"It was just a question, my lady. No harm done." The man laughed, his double chin wobbling as he did so. He patted Gallant's arm reassuringly with a plump hand loaded with pudgy fingers. *Can he even get one of those through a trigger guard to shoot?* Gallant wondered. "I can be quite forgetful myself," the fat Fifth Wheel burbled. "When I am busy I sometimes forget that my boots go over my stockings and not the other way around." Lucille shrieked with laughter as though the man had said the funniest thing she had ever heard.

"We need some introductions," she said. "I am Missus Lucille Slate and this is my husband," she turned and gave Gallant a mischievous look, "Earnest."

Earnest Slate — a damnable name and one that Gallant hated. It belonged to a relentless suitor of Lucille's who was Gallant's chief rival for her affections. Gallant cleared his throat and Lucille winked at him. He smiled at the Fifth Wheel as he said. "While my given name is Earnest, my friends call me by my middle name, Rupert. Feel free to do the same." Lucille's claws dug painfully into his hand, turning Gallant's smile into something of a grimace. Rupert Hardwood was the name of another of Lucille's suitors, but he had been a swindler and cheat, robbing her of both her affections and some expensive jewelry.

"Very pleased to meet you, Mister and Missus Slate. I am Edward Poke — you can call me Ed — and this is my nephew Arnold. You can call him Arnie." Young Arnie said hello.

— ⟨⟩ —

Like it or not, Gallant and Lucille were stuck with Ed and Arnie Poke as traveling companions. In truth, they were good company. Ed had a fat purse and liked to lighten it to prove he was somebody, which was welcome to Gallant because he starting to feel the leanness of his own. The money that his employer had given them to cover their expenses was starting to run out. He was down to a single golden crown, three silver marques, a few silver quarters (which the landed folk called winks), some copper tithes, copper commons, and a handful of copper pins (or pinnies, as they were called).

Poke frequently instructed his servant, a dull fellow indeed, to grab bottles of claret from the luggage, which he freely shared with his nephew and his new friends, the Slates. Arnie's whicker basket turned out to be filled with meat pies, hothouse fruit, and pastries, and Arnie was as a generous as his uncle. They stuffed the food and wine down and let their secrets out. It was easy for Lucille and Gallant to pump this pair for information.

While the Call had gone out only a week prior, the Pokes were intent on getting ahead of the game, traveling early before the trains and carriages became overloaded with other Fifth Wheels and the nobility of the Realm.

That they *were* Fifth Wheels shocked Gallant. The pair patrolled the rivers around Exeter, which Gallant assumed was a frontier at one time — perhaps over a century ago. They lived easy lives, spending more time fishing and managing horses than assisting local sheriffs in bringing outlaws to justice. Gallant guessed that neither had pulled a pistol from its holster in anger or even self-defense. The weathered Fifth Wheel who had pursued him so doggedly for the past several months would have little time for the Pokes of the world. They were a disgrace to the Order. And as Gallant listened to Ed and Arnie windbag away he started to realize that they were typical examples. They called themselves *knights of the realm* and *keepers of the law*, but they were in truth just comfortable rich men and keepers of good wines.

The man who is pursuing me is a relic, he thought, as Edward Poke toasted Lucille one night, a ridiculous white napkin embroidered with his family's coat-of-arms stuffed in his collar. *And if he is a relic then what am I?* He wondered. *Just the other side to the same coin, I suppose.*

For three days they traveled, the train rolling along and the passengers sleeping when they could on their benches. There was some gambling between the gentry, but Gallant quickly got his fill of cards with this lot, as there was no challenge in it. The Pokes and other soft men were poor players, with Ed Poke frequently questioning the morality of "games of chance" as he flopped his losing hands down on the table. The winnings were meager because they played only for copper commons and pinnies. By the end of the third day, Gallant's pockets were bulging with copper coins. "I am starting to jingle like a carriage bridle," he complained to Lucille.

As they got close to the realm's capital, the car filled with comfortable men, highborn ladies in feathered hats, bawling children, and stressed retainers.

Finally, they reached the great city, High Hall. Gone was the green countryside, replaced by blocks of brick houses, ancient stone arches, wide thoroughfares and crooked alleys, crowded warrens filled with tenements — with laundry hanging like multi-colored sails from rooftop to rooftop — factories with raging furnaces, tall chimneys, and iron stacks, churches with tall steeples, market squares filled with vendors hemmed in by shops and storefronts, and wide green parks with statutes and fountains. Ancient stone structures rubbed shoulders with trim brick buildings and pillar-fronted monstrosities. The train crawled through all this, past a sea of humanity — of men, women, and children of all shapes, sizes, and stripes, poor, rich, and otherwise. Finally the train chugged into the city's main station, a great golden stone palace of a building where the Realm's main rail lines converged.

Gallant nearly vaulted from the train carriage, hauling on Lucille's arm, dragging her along, as he shouted good-bye to Ed and Arnie Poke. He dove into the crowd, pushing his way through, ignoring Lucille's protests to slow down.

Flocks of pigeons crowded the rafters. The light that came through the grime-covered windowpanes and glass ceiling above was sickly and grey, but the light outside the large entrance arches was golden and inviting. Gallant made for the nearest exit.

— «» —

They stayed the night at the Angel & Bell, a small inn on the western fringe of the city. It had been a farmstead once and some enterprising fellow — perhaps the current owner — had turned it into what it was now. The main house was white stucco and blue trim. The outbuildings were made of solid fieldstone, covered with rich green moss. It was a quaint place with little in the way of pretension and it pulled most of its custom from the immediate area. They had arrived at night and the small common room was filled with the local farmers, stinking of soil, manure, and sweat, and their wives stinking of the hearth. The proprietor's name was Robert Bell. He was small and grey, with a pointy little beard as white as the stucco on the side of his house. Little hair remained on his head, but what he lacked in hair he made up for in liver spots. With beady eyes and a long pointed nose he reminded Gallant of a rat. He proved to be a pleasant rat, though.

As he ushered them up a tight staircase, the walls of which were lined with family portraits — rat-faced men and women — to a room, Lucille asked, "Is your family originally from Seawall?"

"Might be," he gave her a smile. "Back about four or five generations, maybe more. Why do you ask?"

"My maiden name is Belle."

"Huh," he grinned. "Perhaps we're related."

Lucille giggled. "Perhaps, although my name is spelled differently than yours. My name has an 'e' at the end."

Bell chuckled. "I'm not much of a man for letters, leaving those to my wife. Figures are my thing, sums and such. Give me a number over a letter any day, I say, and give me a big number if its money we're talking about." He cackled. "Anyways, it is good to meet you, cousin." Lucille grinned at him.

"Only four rooms here," he said, as he stopped before a door, candleholder in one hand and key in the other. "My wife can cook a hardy meal if you want food, and the local beer is the best bitter for miles around."

He unlocked the door but had to put his shoulder into it to get it to open. When it opened, it opened with a pop. "The old house sucks up moisture and it swells the wood," he said, with a shrug by way of apology.

He led them into the room, which was large, but sparsely furnished with a bed, good-sized wardrobe, a small nightstand, and a fireplace that looked like it hadn't been lit in a year. There were two large windows, one that faced the front of the house and the other the side. "If you need air, you'll have best luck getting that one open," Bell said, gesturing with the candle toward the side window. "There's a Good Bush under the window that can freshen up the smell." Gallant sniffed. At the moment he could smell bacon, but there *was* the hint of mildew underneath.

He handed Gallant the candle and the key and then fetched a tin basin that was on the nightstand. "I'll have my daughter bring some water, so you can freshen yourselves up. She'll also bring some oil for the lamp," he pointed to a dusty little thing that was on the mantel. "I don't expect you'll need a fire tonight, but if you do, she can set you to rights.

"You need anything else?"

"No." Gallant shook his head.

"Thank you," Lucille said.

"You're welcome, cousin," Bell cackled again and left.

"I like him," Lucille said when he was gone.

"Well, you should. He *is* your cousin after all." Gallant smiled and she gave him a playful slap. His stomach rumbled. "I could go for a plate of that bacon I smell." He patted his stomach.

"Be careful, James Gallant, or you'll become fat." Lucille said with a smirk.

Gallant tossed their battered bag onto the floor next to the bed. "Me? Fat? Never." He took Lucille in his arms. "Would you leave me if I became a tub?"

"I'd be tempted," she smiled, "especially if I couldn't put my arms around you."

"I see how it is then." There was a smirk on Gallant's face now. "If I am to be careful about my weight, then *you* must be careful about your age."

Lucille's mouth opened in a shocked 'o' of surprise. She slapped his cheek lightly.

"I know a way to work up an appetite." Gallant kissed his wife and glanced at the bed.

"So you'll eat more bacon?"

Gallant scooped her up off the floor. "We best get to it now before I grow a gut and you turn gray." Lucille giggled and the door popped open. Robert Bell's daughter stood there with a basin of warm water in her hands and fresh towels over her shoulder. "Hello," Gallant said.

"I'm s—s—sorry, sir and l—lady," the girl managed to get out, averting her eyes as best she could. She was a scrawny thing of sixteen with a red face and chicken neck. She'd make an exceptional farmer's wife in the near future.

"You can just set that load down," Gallant nodded toward the nightstand, "and we can take care of the rest."

Timidly the girl made her way around Lucille and Gallant and set the basin down. Her hands were shaking and she spilled a bit of water in the process. She placed the towels on the bed and then scurried out quickly.

Lucille burst out laughing. "I forgot what prudes these Shieldgate maids are, especially the landed folk," Gallant observed. "Imagine if she caught us naked under the sheets. Imagine if we asked her to *join* us." Lucille laughed again and slapped him lightly.

Gallant tossed his wife onto the bed, dove gently on top of her and they worked up an appetite.

— 《》 —

At one of the four small tables in the common room they ate a good meal of peas porridge, bacon, and bread washed down with the beer that Bell had boasted about. "If this is the best for miles around, I'd hate to taste the worst. Bitter it is," Gallant said dryly. A few of the locals overheard and they scowled at him.

"Hush," Lucille cautioned. He looked at the farmers and noted their large arms and thick chests. He smiled and nodded at the men, who nodded back but continued to scowl.

He ate a lot and soon regretted it. The food sat heavy in his stomach and he made his way to the outdoor privy where he emptied his bowels with a great rush.

When he returned he said to Lucille, "I am afraid my stomach thinks little of Mrs. Bell's peas porridge."

There were no cards played in the Angel & Bell, just two old gaffers hovering over a spotted tiles board with some of the farmers around egging them on. They sat for a bit and then went up to their room with a handful of tallow candles. They had learned that Robert Bell's candles burned down quickly. When they had finished their frolic the one he had left them was half gone. "I'm not that hardy of a stallion," Gallant had joked, pointing at it. Lucille had looked at the candle. "No, but you do give a lady a good ride, especially at the gallop."

He stripped and clambered into the bed with his wife. The mattress was stuffed with feathers and was a delight, despite its stale smell. Lucille wrapped her arms around him and kissed his neck. "I'm afraid to go again," Gallant said. "I might soil the bed." He rubbed his stomach and Lucille wrinkled her nose.

An hour after they had blown out the candle, Gallant was still awake and so was Lucille. The room was stuffy, but it was more than that. His stomach had settled but he was agitated.

With a huff, he rolled off the mattress and went to the side window. With great effort and a good deal of cursing, which got Lucille laughing, he managed to open it. The evening air rolled in, cool and refreshing. He breathed deeply, and as Robert Bell had promised he could smell the Good Bush. The bush was in full bloom and it let off a pleasant, heady scent that bordered on the exotic. It reminded him of Far Reach.

It had been months since they had left Far Reach, that place with customs so strange it seemed it could not be part of the same realm.

He had been delivering diplomatic papers to the princes. When he had finally met them he was disappointed. He had heard tales of handsome men with wicked, curved swords and ornate pistols. Instead he was greeted by fat, simpering fellows with smooth faces and many chins. They wore light silks that their fat spilled out of, and covered their stink with perfumes. Behind the plump lords were not the exotic beauties that were promised, just spry women with dark and dusky skin.

He had sat with the princes in an open-air courtyard. The mist from water spilling from ornate fountains cooled them, as did the shade from several orange trees. Their wives had served them silently and the more powerful the prince, the more wives he had. One prince, a great tub of a man, had seven wives in attendance. They had laughed when they realized that Gallant had only *one* wife and they had frowned when Lucille refused to sit behind him and serve him.

With the princes there was always a feast. There were carafes of sweet, iced liquor and silver pots of spiced tea, and there were mounds of spiced rice that the princes loved to shovel into their faces, often served with thick, sweet bread. They had bath-sized tureens of soup and a never-ending supply of spiced meats and fish that made one's fingers sticky and lips warm.

The princes had cooed at him and hummed and hawed, while the ladies fussed about them. Their voices were soft and feminine, their language strange. Still, they had delivered. They pledged Far Reach's support for Seawall in the event of war. They had each signed and sealed the document that said it was so, which Gallant had turned over to the captain of a Seawall packet bound for home. He wished now that he had gotten onto that ship as well.

Outside of the princes' halls, the excitement that followed was something to remember. The lesser lords of Far Reach knew a great deal about hospitality. They knew how to entertain their guests by means other than feeding them.

He *did* get to see exotic beauties and handsome men with wicked swords. Many of those men favored him as much as they did Lucille. There were men in Seawall who were the same, but Gallant had never felt any inclination to lie with a man. Lord Eldham was one who enjoyed the company of an ever-constant supply of young fellows who sought his affections, or, more likely, his gold. He was a soft, fluffy-haired fellow with a large paunch, bandy legs, and a woman's mouth — and he was as carefree as a lark. Eldritch Carver, another man who liked the company of men, was a different sort altogether. He was dangerous and a notorious duelist. His lover, David Bonn, was the only man spared his ready wrath. He loved that man to death quite literally, taking his own life after David was killed as an act of revenge against Carver himself.

It was strange that in Far Reach the Eastern Range was in the west. Still, they called it the Eastern Range.

"What are you thinking of, James?" Lucille asked.

He turned from the window to look at his wife. The moon was bright and there was enough light that he could make out her shape. "This and that," he said, "but mostly that I love you."

"Come to bed," she ordered, holding her arms out to him. He did as she bid.

Sixteen

The Privileged Girl — Lara Mainhouse

"No! I will not!"

Lara stamped her foot on the polished wooden floor. It was a childish act, but one that was warranted. She knew she had those annoying creases between her eyebrows, the ones that formed when she was really displeased or being obstinate.

She glared at her mother, at her mother's sad expression — the expression that spelled disappointment. It was written all over her pale face, a face like marble worked by a master's hands — the perfect cheekbones, the perfect chin, the perfect nose … and blue eyes that were twin pools of sorrow, a sorrow her mother had drowned in long ago.

Mother never got angry, not even when she was being yelled at. Not anymore. Not in Lara's lifetime. Not since the death of her beloved Panther.

"Your place is not at a tourney. It is here, in Shieldgate, at High Hall, following the affairs of court," her mother said, matter-of-factly.

"My place is where *I* choose it to be," Lara snapped back.

"As a steward of the Realm and your father's heir –" her mother began, but Lara cut her off.

"As my father's heir, my place is at *his* side, *not* in a bench in the gallery at High Hall listening to old men drone on and on about *nothing*."

"Lara—."

"I *am* going to Jonah's Sword with father! *You* cannot stop me!" Her voice echoed off the high, rose-colored parlor walls. Rose was her mother's favorite color. She hated the room, nearly as much as she hated her mother at this moment.

"*You* don't want me to go because you don't want me to have any joy in my life," she continued. "Your joy was ripped from you and you want to deny others any joy that you can, *especially* me." She could see the tears filling her mother's eyes, but the words had to be said, the words that everyone else was too weak to say. Lara was not weak. She was not her mother.

Her mother turned away from her. Her hands came up to cover her face. Her back shook from the quiet sobs that were racking her. *Let her weep,* Lara thought. *That's all she ever does.*

"I *hate* you," Lara screamed, her voice so loud it rattled the windows. "I am *going* and I am *not* coming back." She strode past her mother and out of the room toward the main doors. She was seething now, not just in anger but also in shame.

Suddenly she heard quick footsteps behind her. She turned in time to receive her mother's open hand to her cheek. The quickness of it startled Lara. The sharp sting startled her even more. Her mother's eyes were daggers of fury and pain.

Lara was dumbstruck. Her parents had never struck her before. Her nanny, yes, her tutors as well, and on occasion a few servants had gotten licks in for good measure. But never Mother, nor Father.

She felt a tear roll down her cheek, which was warming because of the slap. The tear felt good. It felt cool on her hot skin. It meant there was more to mother than sadness, there was some fight left as well. She managed a smile. "Thank you, Mother." There was a slight tremor to her voice. "That's the first time you've shown me any real feeling."

With that she spun on her heel and exited her family home. She was off to Jonah's Sword, off to the tournaments and festivities that marked the Call, which culminated in the swearing of the Oath.

It would be a grand occasion. Already the newspapers were full of accounts of the preliminary goings on. And the actual affair promised to be much grander. Lara would immerse herself in it and forget this recent angry exchange. She would see her mother again in a few months time it would be like this had never happened. Just like many times before — they would argue, Lara would rebel and storm off, Lara would return, and the thing they argued about would be forgotten. That cycle defined the relationship she had with her mother.

A carriage was waiting outside. It was polished to the point that Lara could see her warped reflection. The trees in front of the home were tall and old, with new green leaves replacing those that had fallen and now lay in thick mats on the ground. The four horses attached to the carriage had coats nearly as shiny as the carriage. The sky was overcast, and she heard a few fat drops of rain hitting the dead leaves on the ground.

The coachman had stepped down to open the door for her. *Had he heard Lara's yelling?* She did not care. He was there to open carriage doors and lift her baggage. What he heard was of little concern to her. So he might have an amusing tale to tell some of the other servants over their cups tonight.

She settled into her seat as the coach door closed. Mother was not standing on the steps. She had remained inside. *Had she done that before?* Lara could not remember. Their fights were too frequent to recall the details of all of them. They had been fighting since she could talk, or so it seemed. She gravitated naturally to the wilder instincts of her father. And that was part of it. Lara was both a wedge between them and a link that bound them. She kept them apart through her stubborn nature and she kept them together just by existing. If she hadn't been born they would have divorced and gone on to live very different lives. Her father counted her a blessing and said so often. An unhappy union, he said, was a very small price to pay for that. She was unsure about her mother's feelings toward her — resentment mostly, she thought. Hatred maybe. It would have been different if she had been the Panther's bastard.

Lara wondered why she was conceived. Duty perhaps, or a single night of passion between her mother and father when the Panther was away? She became the little mistake in her mother's belly that grew and came bawling out, demanding attention that her mother didn't care to give her — demanding feelings that her mother couldn't feel. Lara was not, after all, the Panther's cub.

The driver snapped his reins and the carriage lurched forward. She took one last look at her home and then settled back in her seat. She was on her way to Seawall.

Seventeen

The Old Lord — Lord Everisle

Lord Axel Everisle felt the urine leaking out of him before he smelt it. The smell was strong. He was dying, but he had been dying for years now. He was closing in on his ninety-fifth birthday and he was determined to make it.

He stared out the grimy window at the estate grounds. So green, so beautiful. Tears watered his deep blue eyes, but an angry scowl was on his thin, bruised lips. *Part anger, part sentimental fool, that's what I am.*

He waved a hand of dismissal at the scene outside and then pulled the blanket up around him. His hands were thin, fragile, and covered in liver spots. *Just like the rest of me.*

His chest, once broad and muscled, was sunken, with saggy old breasts tipped with long grey hairs. Sitting, and he was always sitting, he was so stooped it appeared he was hunched over his large paunch, fat and filled with gas. He farted as if to prove a point. His legs were useless things that dangled beneath him. He could manage only a few steps, even with the pair of canes. *My sticks*, he called them. Most of time he spent in his wheeled chair, being pushed around like a babe by the nurses.

The room was sparse and *cold*. There was a bed, a chair, a wardrobe and nothing else. The wallpaper was peeling off the walls and the threadbare carpet was turning up in the corners and spotted with mold. Even a pane in the window was cracked. And it stank. *Piss and shit, mine.* Such common vulgarity would never have sprung to his mind before, but time had changed and so had he. He liked using low speech these days. He had become crude and vulgar. Vile.

Half of him pitied the nurses that cared for him and the other half hated them. They had to clean him up and he resented them for it. Most of the nurses were young things. But it was hard to tell how well they were formed because they wore those shapeless grey shifts.

His breakfast lay untouched on the wooden tray in front of him. Porridge again. The Sow had brought it to him. She was a large woman with meaty hands and a hideous mole on her jutting chin. Her face looked like a banquet ham and her beady eyes like a pair of raisins placed in it. She was rough and hard-mouthed.

He wondered if he would have a visitor, but he quickly cast that hope aside. He knew he would not. His family was large, but they were grandchildren and great-grandchildren — *selfish schemers the lot.* Still, Young Skyp might come. Young Skyp had been Lord Axel Everisle's manservant for a number of years, taking over where Old Skyp left off. Young Skyp, though, was now in his seventies and his health was poor. *I'll outlive him too.*

He had outlived them all. His daughter had died when she was nine — poor little hen. So fragile. She had caught a cold and could not shake it. Both his sons, too, had passed. The older son did his duty to the realm and the younger his duty to the family. The older had died in battle in the last war. He was valiant, but a fool. The younger son had died from a burst heart several years later. He was not as valiant and he was weak. They left behind widows and packs of children who now fought over the fortune of the Everisle. *His* fortune. And there was Lizabet.

"Liz'bet," the word came out of him as a croak, his voice cracking and the tears flowing freely. She was the strong one — the true rock of the Everisle, even though she was born a Penberry. She kept them altogether.

She was long–limbed, lean and beautiful, although some men said she was weathered and wild–looking. True, her skin was touched by the wind and the sun because she loved to ride and be outdoors. She didn't have the pale cheeks of other highborn ladies or fancy hair piled on her head. Her hair was long, wavy and brown, and she let it flow over her shoulders and down her back.She *was* the strong one.

"Liz'bet," he said again, almost a whisper. She had died before her sons. *Too soon. Too damned soon.* She was thrown from her favorite horse, Dapper. In his sorrow and anger, Lord Axel had shot the beast and had its head mounted on his gate. He dug his wife's grave with his own hands, burying her next to the large oak she loved so much. *She was strong, like that oak.*

He wiped away his tears, a jagged nail scratching his cheek in the process, and spit angrily on the carpet. "What's left of the Everisle now? Weeds?" He laughed but it was a bitter laugh — nearly a cackle.

There was a soft knock on the door. A visitor? No, most likely a nurse and not the Sow either, because she never knocked. She just barged in. "Enter," the old lord barked.

The door opened and a nurse stepped into his room shyly. It was Pretty. She had some other name, but that's what he called her. A very pretty face with brown eyes, a full mouth, and plump lips stared out from the grey shift. He smiled at her, but knew his smile was more of a leer. He couldn't keep his damn mouth shut when he grinned anymore.

"M'lord," she said, as she curtseyed. Her eyes fell on his porridge. "You haven't touched your food."

"Bah, take that away." He waved his hand feebly at the bowl. "I wouldn't give my pigs that slop."

Pretty bent over to retrieve the bowl and fold the tray. She presented her backside to Everisle in the process, but it had no real shape in all that gray cloth. Still, he lifted his hand to touch her. "Let an old man feel a young arse," he said, his smile-leer cracking across the bottom of his face. She smiled and pushed his hand gently away. "Ah, nothing to fear from this one, Pretty," he cackled. "Even if you were naked and wet I couldn't service you." It was true. His manhood was now nothing more than a shriveled white worm in a grey bush that leaked piss whenever he moved. *Crude, vulgar, and vile.*

"Would you like a book, m'lord?" The folded tray was tucked under her arm and the bowl of uneaten porridge was in her hand.

"No," he snapped. "I'm tired of reading and I tire when I read. I only have so many days left and I don't want to spend them dozing and drooling and dreaming of the past."

She smiled and inclined her head. "As you say, m'lord." She started to leave.

"Pretty," he called to her. She was at the door. She turned to him. "Yes, m'lord?"

"Will I have any visitors, today?"

She smiled. "Maybe, m'lord." It was a lie, a lie told by one with a pretty face, but a lie all the same.

He waved a hand in dismissal. "Be gone and get someone in here to clean me up. I've pissed myself and I think I will shit myself soon as well." She left, closing the door behind her.

He had been locked up in the main house for several years now, and confined to his small room for a year and a half. At one time this particular estate, Blushing Meadow, had been his pride and joy. It was once famous for its willow trees. His grandfather had built the main house — and most of the grandiose outbuildings that came with it — and he was a man of exceptional taste and refinement in his day. The grounds, too, were precise in a picturesque way. But the red willows had grown twisted and large with age and were decorated with thick beards of pink moss. The house and the grounds were rundown through neglect. His grandchildren preferred to live at other Everisle's holdings, favoring houses closer to the capital, High Hall. The old lord was left to rot with his willows.

But he was not alone. He cackled at that thought, but was also afraid. His gaze fell to the floor. *She is down there beneath me, closeted in the room below.*

As it turned out, the final insult to Lord Everisle was when his family — his damned youngest son really — had turned his beloved Blushing Meadow into an asylum of sorts just before his heart popped. Of course, the old lord had enthusiastically agreed with his son at the time and signed the papers to make it so, but he preferred to overlook that.

That was eleven years ago. His health was still good and Blushing Meadows would become home to a very special tenant, an act that would further advance the already good standing and great wealth of the Everisle family. *Yes, I had signed the damned papers with delight and now I am both lord of the manse and tenant myself.*

Along with the staff, the lord shared his home with two other *guests. The girl and the boy*, he thought. The boy did not trouble him in the slightest. He was a cousin of a cousin, a big dumb imbecile as simple as a tot. The girl though ... she was dangerous in more ways than one. At times she appeared like all other children of her age. No, she was a woman now, beautiful and charming when she wanted to be. She looked more like her mother than her father, which was something of a blessing, with cascading hair, the color of folded gold, and dark blue eyes. But then she had her fits. Strange words would bubble from her pretty lips. And her eyes ... well, they were windows to her soul and whatever else it was that lurked inside her. *Something not far from hu*man. The staff would shrink back from her in terror, even the Sow. Only Raif had the courage to confront her.

Lord Axel cackled again. Raif Penberry. Another damned relative. He was a grandnephew of Lizabet, a weed that sprang from the seed of one her useless brother's brood. He was tall and thin with soft hands and creamy white skin. He had a woman's mouth and a woman's taste for men. Still, Everisle enjoyed Raif's company. The man was capable and educated. He was refined and had manners, which was more than he could say for all of his own grandchildren. His love of men, though, was his downfall. He was caught with some man's poker up his arse and had no choice but to go into self-imposed exile. Had he born in some other Seat he would have been safe, but Shieldgate frowned on men who lay with men. Now Raif was caretaker for the Lord of piss and shit, an imbecile, and *her*. He would coax *her* back into her chambers, even in her most agitated state, and then send a carriage to collect *the priest* as quick as possible.

The priest. *Another unwanted guest in my house.* Father Hans Lowman. *A fitting name.* Only the Giver knew what guided that man into the priesthood. Yes, he could speak in a fancy way and rattle off facts, but the truth was Father Lowman looked like a dirt-scratching farmer. He was extremely tall, had those broad shoulders good for carrying large loads, and the bowlegs needed to push a plow. He tried to hide his common upbringing, but under the holy robes Lowman was a blunt peasant. He would stride into Blushing Meadows main house full of holy confidence and head straight to the girl's chambers. Her mad ravings would eventually subside and peace would fall over the manse again.

The girl hadn't had a fit in a while, and that concerned Lord Axel. The longer the lapse between them, the greater the fit would be when it finally came. He shivered and looked down at the carpet again. *She is down there.* Sometimes he thought the girl could read his mind. She would leer and grin at him when he had inappropriate thoughts. She would laugh when he silently shat himself or pissed down his leg. And the words that boiled up out of her when she was raving … he knew smatterings of many languages, but she spoke in an unfamiliar tongue. *It's the tongue of madmen, I suppose, so one day my mind might slip and I might start to understand her.*

At times he pitied the girl — probably, in part, because she was a girl, but also because she was an exile, like him, cast out by her own family. *But she was cast out for entirely different reasons.* He was old and broken, no longer of any use. He was merely a barricade, blocking his heirs from the family fortune. She was young and vibrant. And she was very important. So important that her madness was an embarrassment and could not be tolerated for the sake of the realm. And there were the disturbing rumors of a crime, a crime that it was said she committed just before she was sent to this place. It was an abominable act, if true. Frightening also. He could not think it possible that a girl of five could do such a thing.

When she had first arrived those many years ago, he had wanted to see her. He was in his eighties, still proud, still vibrant and still strong even then. *But I was getting weaker and could feel it.*

It was a warm summer day ... *or was early autumn? It does not matter.* He had ridden his stallion, Buzzard, to Blushing Meadows to look at his new ward. When he was ushered into the parlor he saw her sitting in the middle of the expansive room on a carpet. She was leafing through a book with colorful illustrations. She had lifted her head, topped with golden curls, when he entered and stared at him with those strange blue eyes of hers. She didn't smile, she didn't cry — her face remained a rigid white mask. They had locked eyes and he had been forced to turn away first. *She was unsettling even then, especially then.*

He had made a mistake, coming to see her, he realized. He wanted to leave, and so he did. As he rode away from the manse, he glanced over his shoulder and saw her face in the parlor window; her eyes were two dark pools, staring at him.

Lord Axel shook his head and shuddered at the memory. A moan escaped his lips and then he cried out because he thought he heard her muffled laughter below. "Quiet," he bellowed. He stamped a swollen foot on the floor and immediately regretted it as the sudden pain stabbed through his heel like a heated knife. His eyes filled with fresh tears and he let out a quiet sob. *I have become an old woman.*

Eighteen

The Fifth Wheel — John Gray

Gray picked up the Dead Priest's trail in Jersey's Spit, a town that was several times larger than Dead Tree and many times more ugly. The Spit had all the trappings of a prosperous frontier town. Dirt riders, outlaws, and vicious people filled its many saloons. Whores leaned out windows and draped themselves over balconies while the pimps and madams looked on. Drunks fought in the streets and passed out on the plank porches that fronted the watering holes.

Coins in the right palms bore fruit. A beggar at the edge of town told Gray, through a mouthful of broken teeth, that a rider, well–gunned and wearing worn black cloth, had passed through the Spit a week before and asked which road led to Steeplestone. "That was a mighty queer question as everyone knows their way to Steeplestone 'round here," the man said. "It's the only big city of any note on the southeast road, the biggest place on the map from 'ere to High Hall."

From the Spit, the Dead Priest had headed north and west, deeper into the realm. His trail was easy to follow as he was dressed in black, head to toe, and stood out like a sore thumb. More than that, Gray could sense the man's taint on the land. He left a feeling behind him. And some of that stuck to the people he talked to — it was the same with Predrag Landry. Memories of Landry came surging to the surface, slamming around inside Gray's head. He had forgotten the faces of most of the men he had killed, but Landry's face was burned into his mind; the sallow skin, black hair, pointy nose, and chin that ended in a stab of black beard. The eyes. They were deep brown, almost black, and full of malevolence.

Was *this* Dead Priest like Landry? Would his evil be apparent in his eyes? By all accounts he was a handsome fellow and people said he was friendly enough. *But they had not faced the demon in Dead Tree or met Predrag Landry, who was also friendly enough until the time came for him to display his true nature. Deceivers.* He had been taught that a Dead Priest's deadliest weapon was his ability to deceive, to make people believe and see things that were false.

He wished he followed a simpler kind of foe, a more straightforward and nobler enemy, like the Gambler. There was honor in the Gambler. He was from the realm. This Dead Priest had slithered out from under the Blasted Rock on the Eastern Range. He had snuck through the realm's back door, a poisonous monster filled with poisonous purpose.

When Gray arrived in Steeplestone he heard the Call had gone out.

As he approached the town, a dandy in a buggy asked him if he was heading to Jonah's Sword. "What the hell for?" Gray snapped in response, his mind occupied. He was thinking about the report he planned to forward to Posting Host about what occurred in Dead Tree.

The man was taken aback. Gray assumed it was due to the roughness of his tongue. He had forgotten that the interior of the realm was a place of refinement and good manners, especially among the gentlefolk.

"I apologize," he said. "I've been riding the frontier trail for too long. Why would I go to Jonah's Sword?"

The man chuckled. "No need to apologize for your tone, sir," he waved it away. "I'm just surprised you haven't heard. You must have been far away if you don't know the Call has gone out. Your Order is migrating in large numbers to Jonah's Sword to take the Oath."

Now it was Gray's turn to be surprised. "*When?*"

The man thought a moment. "It's been two weeks or more."

"Well, that bears some thinking," Gray said, more to himself than to the man in the buggy.

"Yes," the man was smiling. "It should be quite splendid. There'll be tournaments no doubt, banquets, and balls." Gray thought little of tournaments, as he deplored wearing armor and was a poor jouster. He thought less of banquets and balls.

"I'd go myself," the man continued, prattling on. "But I'm too busy with affairs of my own."

"You're no Fifth Wheel," Gray observed.

"No, but much of the nobility of the realm will attend, sir, and I have *some* noble blood in my veins. It's a grand occasion worth attending."

Gray didn't think so, and he avoided grand occasions as best he could. He had first taken the Oath when he was first gunned and spurred at Posting House. He was just a boy then, one of thirty or so Fifth Wheels, most with fuzz on their faces rather than beards.

The words came back to him.

We are the knights of the realm.
Our shields are truth, our swords are justice,
And our armor is the law of the land.
We are the Fifth Wheel.
Unwanted, until we are wanted,
Not needed, until we are needed.
Always faithful, always serving,
With our hearts, our minds and our hands...

Gray nodded at the man and tipped his hat. "Thank 'ee for the news."

The man nodded in return as Gray turned his horse and set off at a trot toward Steeplestone. In the distance he could see the great arches at the entrance to the city and the tall ornate steeples of the churches near its center.

— «» —

The telegraph office was located in a magnificent stone building in Silver Flag Square, the same square that held the iron fountain that he was fond of before he heard the local boys pissed in it. There were several gangs of urchins lingering at the fountain's edge, splashing in the water, laughing and horsing around. Gray eyed them warily, wondering if they had pissed in the fountain recently. He hitched his horse to the rail in front of the office.

Inside, it was all old oak — oak furniture, oak trim, and large oaken beams blackened by the smoke that came from a stone fireplace on the wall. Even the men behind the desks seemed made of wood. They were rigid men, old and proper, all dozing at their desks when he entered.

He showed his badge of office and one of the operators snapped to attention. Gray pulled a note from his pocket and handed it to the man. "Get this message to High Hall — Posting House right away," he snapped.

The operator gave a curt nod and got to it. Gray watched as he tapped away at his switch. He wondered if the operators actually read the messages they were conveying or if they simply went through the process mechanically. It didn't matter. There was no mention of demons or Dead Priests in the message he was sending. All those details were in his written report, which he would trust only to one of the High Marshal's couriers.

"Is that it?" The operator looked at Gray expectantly. Like many operators he wore spectacles. *They all go blind eventually,* Gray thought. He grunted, handed the man a handful of pinnies — a pinny a word — and left.

An old, bent-backed man had set up a rickety-looking cart near the fountain. He was selling peanuts to the people in the Square. Some of the urchins were eyeing his wares, most likely wondering if they could steal a handful or two and get safely away. Gray headed over and gave the vendor two pinnies for two handfuls of nuts, which he stuffed in his pockets. He watched the water falling in the fountain and idly worked his way through the peanuts as he thought about the Call. It was another obstacle in the way of his real duty, but at the same time it *was* his duty to attend. He cracked a shell angrily and popped the peanuts in his mouth. They were winter nuts, hard and dry. Some were even bitter. The spring crop would yield better bounty, softer and more fulfilling.

A young couple was standing next to him, admiring the fountain as he once did. They were newly married, judging by their banter and the way they giggled and clung to one another. They were happy and in love. Gray was nearly twice the man's age, but he had never found love like that. Any love in his life was short-lived. A few days here, a few days there, with whatever doxy was available in the backwater inns he stayed in along the frontier. The love lasted as long as the money and then both were gone.

Well, all but one ... *Julia*. She still held a place deep in his heart. She was skinny and long limbed, with little in the way of breasts. She had chestnut-colored hair and a hawkish sort of nose. While she wasn't pretty in the traditional sense, she was striking in her way. She was quick to laugh and slow to judge. She was good company.

Her father was a wagon driver who had driven the wagon trains east as they pushed into the Range. Her mother was a washerwoman and a whore who gave what little money she had to her husband to spend on drink. His leg was crushed in an accident and the family was forced to settle in Feather's Cap. Crippled and unable to work, Julia's father sent his wife to the town's only inn to become a doxy. And when a sudden illness took her, he sent his daughter to replace his wife.

Gray was still young when he met Julia. He was still riding with Luke and Dan — and Diggs had joined them too. Luke and Dan would give him his space when he decided to head into Feather's Cap. They knew he was smitten with Julia and they left him to his business.

The bed play was good, but it wasn't the bed play he enjoyed most. It was her smile, her laughter, and her wit. She always set all other men aside when he rode into town. Until the day that Predrag Landry arrived in Feather's Cap.

Gray rode into town shortly after Landry had arrived. He went straight to the rough, clapboard building that served as the inn. He vaulted up the steps and through the batwing doors with a smile on his lips, looking forward to a few days of Julia's company. Ed, the town's doctor, was drunk as usual and working a violin in the corner, and a few of the regulars were present, nursing their drinks and sharing some words.

Heather, another of the inn's doxies, was rubbing some liniment on her knees. Bill, the barkeep and owner, was dozing on his stool. And there was Julia on the stairs, tucked into Landry's side and under his arm that hung so easily over her shoulders.

"Well, hello, John," she said, a smile on her lips. Gray didn't know how to reply.

Landry looked briefly at Julia and then at him. He laughed, a mocking kind of laughter, and Julia joined in. It stung because Gray thought her laughter was reserved only for him.

"Predrag Landry's the name, but you can call me Pred," he said in a gravelly voice, those dark eyes of his flashing angrily, despite the smile that was on his lips. "You must be the lawman sweet Jules here has spoken about afore." Gray could not find his tongue and Landry guffawed. He pulled Julia closer and placed a sloppy kiss on her cheek. Gray seethed.

Landry's grin disappeared and his expression turned serious. "I hope you're not angry with me, boy," he said. "You two aren't married and I'm *not* breaking any law. And she *is* a whore." He stuck his lip out, pretending to pout. "Don't be mad, boy. I just got here first, that's all."

"And there's Heather there," he continued, nodding toward the inn's other whore. Heather was just finishing up rubbing liniment on her knees. She looked up and gave Gray a wink. "She's sweet enough and can service you just as well as Julia can ... well, maybe not *as* good as Julia, but good enough."

Julia giggled at Landry's side and looked at Gray not with *her* eyes, but with eyes that were strange to him. Eyes he didn't know.

"I'm not here for Heather. I'm here for Julia," Gray replied, sounding more like a greenhorn than he wanted.

"Well, that's too bad." Landry chuckled. "You'll just have to wait your turn. And seeing as I paid for a week in advance it'll be a long wait. Best take a seat at the bar."

"Julia." Gray looked at her imploringly.

"Best head out of town, John," she said coolly. "Things have changed."

Gray felt a weight in his chest and a sting in his eyes. He turned around and left.

In the weeks that followed, Gray steered clear of Feather's Cap and kept what had occurred in the saloon from his partners. He was playing at being a man and men were meant to carry their woes in silence.

There were disturbing rumors coming out of Feather's Cap, but Gray chose to ignore them. It was said the place was now a magnet for rough company. Troubles there eventually reached a point where honest farmers chose to avoid it and take their custom elsewhere.

Finally, Luke had had enough and one night while they were sitting around the campfire he urged Gray to go to town to check things out. Stubbornly, Gray refused and the argument grew heated. Gray tried to shout Luke down, but Luke held his ground. "If whatever occurred between you and Julia is going to stop you from doing your duty then it's time you surrendered your star," he yelled, pointing at the badge Gray wore so proudly back then over his breast pocket.

That did it. Gray agreed to ride into Feather's Cap — alone. But, by then, it was too late.

A wave of bitterness swept over Gray. *Buried memories always fester,* he thought. Those were words his mother used often. *I failed in my duty back then. I failed to protect the people of Feather's Cap, especially Julia, because ultimately I was weak. I was also young and ignorant.* Those excuses rang hollow now. Had he heeded the rumors coming from Feather's Cap and acted on them he might have saved the lives of many people. He might have saved Julia.

He wouldn't make the same mistake twice. Stopping this Dead Priest was more important than saying some words, repeating an Oath that he had already taken many years before. His *duty* was to protect the people of the realm. He looked over at the young couple next to him. *My duty is to protect people like them from scum like Predrag Laundry.*

The young man leaned over to drink from the fountain. Gray stopped him. "I wouldn't do that if I were you."

The man looked up. "Why not?" Gray pointed at a muddy-faced boy of about four. Other boys, older and larger, were shielding him as he happily pissed in the water. "Oh," the man straightened up. His wife looked at the boy and pursed her lips in disgust. The man tipped his hat in thanks. Gray nodded and left.

Nineteen

The Novice — Marcus Dawn

Jonah's Sword, the Holy City, was old, but not ancient. All the ancient things were swept away by time or battles, or they lay hidden like dark secrets in the expanse of the Eastern Range, the seat of the Old Ones.

Located in Seawall at the mouth of Vineyard Valley, Jonah's Sword was founded on the plateau-summit of a high hill. The city's origins were a mixture of history and legend.

It was said that Jonah, the legendary holy man, had made his stand on the hill with the faithful against a large host of barbarians, tribes that were twisted and corrupted by agents of the Enemy. As Jonah fought his battle on the hill, the faithful fled down the valley. Although Jonah fought with the ferocity of a thousand men, the holy might of the Giver within him, he was defeated in the end. He was taken alive by his enemies, boiled, and then eaten. His flesh, however, proved their undoing, as it was filled with a poisonous vengeance. The ensuing plague swept through the corrupted tribes, taking every man, woman, and child.

The faithful returned to the site of the battle and there they found Jonah's sword, nicked and scarred from the battle that ultimately took its wielder's life. They buried the sword and placed a cornerstone over top of it. On the stone they built a grand temple to the Giver. Years passed, the original temple was razed, and another built in its place. There were those who claimed to have seen visions of Jonah, sword in hand, and they further claimed the ghostly saint performed miracles. Pilgrims came to the temple to ask Jonah's blessing in the name of the Giver, and many blessings were granted.

A town sprouted up around the temple as people planted roots in the area. Merchants built shops, inns, taverns, and stables to cater to the pilgrims. The town became a city and a glorious cathedral replaced the temple, and the cathedral became the focal point of the palace-city (the Holy Citadel) that was built around it. Some said the sword was removed when the cathedral was built, because there were no longer any sightings of the martyr Jonah. But the Church remained steadfast that the sword was still in the soil.

All of this Marcus Dawn knew. He was taught those things in school, the history hammered into his skull by hard study and his father's calloused hands.

Jonah's Sword had evolved like a tree, with new rings of buildings being added to the old, the city spreading down from the hill and onto the plains below. The old city, the core, contained the Holy Citadel, which consisted of the Metropolitan's Palace, the Plaza of Prayer, the College of Sanctity — which Marcus attended, the Nuns' Palace, the offices of the Church's bureaucracy, their residences and the residences of the Citadel's many lay servants. Below that were tightly packed suburbs and merchant's quarters, the exterior rings fresher and more modern than the core. At the outskirts of the city were the rail yards and the works and beyond them the vineyards, pasture land and fields.

The wide river, Kirbin's Arm, flowed around the western side of the hill upon which the city was built. The sun was shining off it and it looked like plate steel, which was fitting. The river was named after the knight who, legend said, rode at St. Jonah's side. There were many boats on the water. A few ferried people, livestock, vehicles, and materials across the river. Pleasure barges idled down the middle. And farther away he could see small fishing boats, their crews hoping to fill nets with salmon or cages with crayfish.

Dawn felt like a giant as he looked over the southern half of Jonah's Sword from a tower window. The city was spread out beneath him, tier upon tier of slate and wooden roofs painted a hundred different colors, a forest of chimneys, stretching to the green vineyards and fields miles away. On the plain he saw a tent city going up around the tournament grounds, the temporary home of the Fifth Wheels and all the hangers-on — at least those Fivers and folk who could not afford a private room or long stay in a hotel.

How many Fifth Wheels are there? he wondered. Most put the Order's total number at ten thousand. With family, retainers, and those that followed the drum — any drum — that number would be quadrupled or more. So far, only the Fifth Wheel from Seawall had arrived. The rest, from all four corners of the realm, would straggle in over the upcoming weeks. Some wouldn't arrive at all. Instead they would send letters and telegram messages, swearing the oath *in abstentia*.

And then there would be all the nobles, who were not Fifth Wheels but had come just to see the spectacle. They would outnumber the knights of the realm ten to one.

Marcus saw it as a theatrical farce because most Fifth Wheels cared as little about oaths as he did. Saying words was one thing. Socializing quite another. Most wanted to indulge in the tournaments and festivities that surrounded the oath swearing. They wanted to drink, woo women, shoot their guns, cross blunted swords, participate in jousts, beat each other senseless in boxing rings, etcetera. Everyone loves a party.

Certainly, there would be some ancient officers too craggy to mount a horse or lift a sword or pistol. *They* would avoid the shindigs and admonish the youth under their breath. *They* would mumble about the importance of words. *They* were the Fifth Wheel's equivalent to the likes of the old crow, Father Shirrup.

The clouds moved across the sky, pushed by a wind that came from the sea that was hundreds of miles to the west. They were white clouds with only a touch of grey. The warm spring sun, now rising, was pulling the winter from then. It would be summer soon enough, Marcus' favorite season.

—— «» ——

He arrived at the aviary an hour late. Father Shirrup was tight-lipped when he entered. The pair had not spoken to each for over a week, since the encounter in St. Lyonel's (the tongue-less saint's) Court. And that was fine. Shirrup had shut up as far as Marcus was concerned. He had not seen the girl, Annie, either. *She is most likely avoiding me.*

As he was mustering the energy to go about his chores, Shirrup suddenly spoke. "I have talked with Father Allard about your transfer."

Marcus was taken aback. "What transfer? I have requested no transfer."

"It is not *your* place to make requests, *novice*," Shirrup snapped. "It is obvious to me that you are not fond of the aviary ... or this seminary."

"What do you mean?"

"I mean that you will no longer be my problem after today. You will be someone else's."

It was true that Marcus disliked Father Shirrup and the aviary, but he still felt the sting of rejection. He smiled an ugly smile, an expression to mask the barb in his chest. "That's wonderful," he said, his voice suddenly high-pitched and boyish. "I'm sick of looking at bird beaks and I'll be glad to be rid of the stink of this place. Where am I going? The stables? The vineyards?"

"No, no," Father Shirrup shook his head. He suddenly laughed, but it came out as a cackle. There was a tremor to it that Marcus did not like. "You are being transferred away from *here*." He swept his hand in a grand gesture, "Away from Jonah's Sword. You are going to the seminary in Bythesea."

"No!" The word came out with a gasp. Bythesea was an ugly coastal town, far to the west. It was a remote backwater, blasted by the spray of the Thunderwall Sea. Even its name spoke to the lowness of its inhabitants. Hundreds of years ago it was called Anchorage by-the-Sea, but that was too much of a mouthful for the so-called Sea Captain who lorded over it back then and all the peasants that made up his court, so he renamed it. "This *can't* happen. My *father* will hear of this and he will stop it."

"No, he won't," Shirrup snapped.

"You can't *stop me* from talking to my father." Marcus' bottom lip quivered.

Shirrup stared hard at Marcus and his expression softened to something bordering on pity. There was also some concern there. "That's not what I mean. Your father suggested it. It was *his* idea."

"Damn him!" Marcus squeaked, his hands tightening into fists. "Damn him to hell."

"Swearing will do you no good, novice." Shirrup said. "Bythesea will provide you with the discipline you clearly lack, and..."

"And what?" Marcus asked, his voice cracking.

"And ... and nothing. You are going, and that's that."

Tears stung Marcus' eyes. He turned his face away from the old priest. Shirrup cleared his throat. "It's done, boy. You leave in three days. Go up top and clean out the rafters."

Marcus left to get a broom. He was seething inside, hating his father, hating this place, hating his future, and hating his life. He climbed the narrow staircase that led to the walkways at the top of the aviary.

The aviary floor was forty feet below and the smell of ammonia stung his nostrils. It was hot in the rafters and hard work sweeping away the cobwebs and clearing the nests of the wild swallows that roosted here. He was sweaty, stinking, and miserable.

Suddenly he caught something moving at the corner of his eye. He turned to see a shadow quickly slip across the wall. He heard a sound. Footsteps? Was someone up here with him? And then he saw an old wooden bucket drop off the walkway.

Marcus looked down with wide eyes. The bucket was on a collision course with Father Shirrup's head. "Father," he yelled in warning. Shirrup looked up, but it was too late. The bucket slammed home with a crack that echoed up to the rafters, slicing a giant half-moon in the old man's scalp. The father squawked and fell to his knees as red rivulets of blood poured down into his face.

"Father," Marcus yelled again. Instinctively, he leapt from the catwalk to one of the pulley chains, skinning and bloodying the palms of his hands on the links as he grabbed hold. He rode the chain down to the aviary floor. Father

Shirrup vomited and wet himself. A giant flap of skin hung from his forehead like some obscene thing and beneath it was the white gleam of splintered bone. Shirrup's eyes rolled up into his head, showing only the whites. Blood leaked from the old man's ears and he was weeping red. Long ribbons of bloody mucous dangled from nose and mouth.

"Father." Marcus fell down next to Shirrup, the stone flags chewing into his knees. The old man grunted something and bubbles of blood and spittle flew. He flopped forward, his face smacking onto the stones. He gagged, made an animal noise, and flipped awkwardly onto his back. His back arched in some primal spasm. He wretched once, shuddered violently, and died.

Marcus stared at the old father's eyes, glassing over and weeping red drops. "Oh, Giver!" He started to scream. It was a nearly inhuman cry. "Haaawwwwllllllllp!"

Twenty

The Lady of Seawall — Genevieve

Genevieve had dreaded the thought of a lengthy stay at Jonah's Sword. The Holy City did nothing for her. It was two hundred miles east of the Seawall capital, Starfall, which she considered her home — far enough for her to have reason not to go there. While her husband made frequent trips to Jonah's Sword, she rarely did. *It is too provincial,* she'd say when he asked her to accompany him, *and besides I have too much to do here.* Excuses would not work this time. She had been obligated to go.

And now that she was here, she had to admit she was happy.

Best of all, her family was together again. Her son, Roland, had returned from Tilting Yard. He was taller than she remembered and the fuzz that he passed off as a moustache and the wisps of hair he called a beard were a little thicker. Susan came back acting the lady and looking more the part as well. This was hard on her younger sister, Jane, as Susan was much less inclined to play the games the two of them had loved when they were younger.

Genevieve breathed deeply, taking in the fresh air. The smell of early summer flowers filled her nostrils, intermingled with the warm smell of tall grasses fringed with the barest hint of damp earth. She sighed happily. She was glad to be outside the city walls and in the countryside. The sun was out, the air warm and the breeze cool. They had just passed the tournament grounds. The day before there had been some jousting there, but it was quiet now. Even the town of canvas tents and silk pavilions that had grown around it was quiet. The late night revelers would be sleeping off the previous evening's indulgences and the more sober would be in the city proper, seeking distractions there.

She sat astride her favorite horse, Topper. He was a blonde gelding, old, but even-tempered and sure of foot. Beside her, her husband, Sylvan Goodregard, the Lord of Seawall, sat on his black stallion, Mercurial. That horse was aptly named. It was a bad-tempered beast that would only allow her husband to mount it. *We have the latter in common*, she thought. Mercurial snapped his teeth angrily at Topper, but the gelding ignored him. Sylvan calmed Mercurial. He was dressed in the dark blue of Seawall, piped with green. The color of his coat went well with his light complexion, and the cut of it complimented his fine physique. Genevieve smiled as she secretly admired the man that she had married so many years ago. He was tall, straight-backed and well-built. His dark hair had the lightest sprinkling of grey, as did his well-trimmed moustache and beard. There were some laugh lines around his handsome mouth and in the corners of his blue eyes. *He might be getting old*, Genevieve thought, *but he is not old yet. He gets more handsome with age.*

She wondered about herself. Everyone still called her beautiful, especially Sylvan, but she was under no illusions that she was still a spring bud. Her breasts had sagged and softened, her stomach was no longer the taut thing it was when she was first married, and she bore the stretch marks of childbirth. Her face had a few lines, but her dark hair showed no gray. *Why is it men grow into their looks while a woman's beauty quickly fades?*

"Shall we picnic here, my lord?" a servant called out behind them. There was an orchard in front of them and the trees were rich with color as they had bloomed — pink, white and red. Genevieve looked back. A small host was following her and her husband. There were servants and retainers and guards, Susan and her friends were sitting pretty on their horses with their own servants and retainers, and Jane was in an open carriage, sitting angrily with her plump tutor, Helda. *She had wanted to ride like the rest of us.* Genevieve thought it would be fine for her do so, but Sylvan had told her no.

She glanced at Sylvan as he told his man the ground was good and to see that everything was set out for them. He was always hard on the girls, and always too easy on Roland. Her son was out riding with his friends, no doubt testing the racetrack that was located along the bank of the river.

Genevieve thought about her son. *He has not learned any lessons today, and Sylvan is partly to blame.* While the day was shaping up to be a glorious one, it had not started out that way.

Early in the morning the Goodregard family, with many other noble families, had gathered under an overcast sky at the railway station. There, a coffin was being loaded onto a train. In that coffin lay Lord and Lady Bellchime's youngest son, a handsome youth with golden hair. He would chime no longer, though. He was not a friend of Roland's, but surely he knew the boy. He had been killed the day before. He had tried to race ahead of a train on his horse and cut close across the tracks in front of it. It had been a dare, she supposed. He had misjudged the horse and his riding ability and paid with his life. The engine had struck them both, killing the horse instantly. The boy had lingered for a few hours, his legs severed above the knee. He had cried out for his mother. She was at his side, but he did not see her there or feel that she had his hand in hers.

Sobbing, Lady Bellchime had demanded retribution for her son's death. She had called for the life of the train's stoker, as if he was somehow to blame for her son's stupidity. Sylvan, though, forbade any action to be taken toward the man and so had spared him from a hangman's rope. Genevieve had supported him in that. *If it had been Roland, though, would I have been any different?* she wondered. *No, in my grief I would have irrationally demanded the stoker's life as well, and the outcome would have been different as my husband would not have been able to save him.*

Shortly after the train had left the station — with the dead boy on it, packed in ice as part of its cargo like a choice side of beef — Roland had asked his father's permission to ride off with his friends. Sylvan quickly gave him leave to do so, which angered Genevieve.

"He was to spend time with *us*," she snapped, "but you allow him to go and gallivant around the countryside with those young fools. One boy has died already." She did not add voice to her fear, *would you have our son be next?*

Sylvan looked at her, his face calm. "Other boys will die before all this is over, Genevieve," he said, sweeping his hand in the direction of the city and the tournament grounds. "They will be thrown from horses, they will be pierced by badly held lances, they will be struck by errant shots when they hunt, some of the fiercer ones will die in duels, and they will continue to dodge trains.

"The young cock always crows into the face of the fox. Young men are daring and they take greater risks than they should." He sounded somewhat envious of them, of Roland, his friends and the other young boys playing at being men. They had no responsibilities, not even the responsibility to appear respectable at all times.

"And young ladies will fall in love, and out of love, and back into love again," Genevieve said with a heavy sigh. "And a few of them will end up with children in their bellies."

Sylvan nodded.

Genevieve remembered a certain Lang'Arc noble from her youth. She felt some guilt, thinking about *him* while she was standing next to her husband. Especially because she could feel her excitement rising. *I was a foolish girl.* Two spoonfuls of Midnight had corrected that mistake. Even after she had swallowed the vile-tasting syrup she fretted and sweated for a month until her blood came.

It was silly cousin Jane that led me briefly down that path. Jane was a lusty girl who parted her legs whenever the opportunity arose. She introduced Genevieve to *that* man, and to the Midnight afterward. Jane had married young and she married wrong. She lived a miserable and short life, hopping from one bed to the next, never her husband's, and died a year before Genevieve's youngest daughter was born. Still mourning Jane's loss, Genevieve had named her youngest daughter after her, *and I have been ever watchful that she will not grow up like her namesake.*

Sylvan placed his hand on her arm. "The Giver will watch over Roland."

She pulled her arm away. "As He watched over the Bellchime boy?"

"Roland doesn't take such risks. He has more sense," Sylvan assured her. He almost sounded disappointed, saying it. *He wants our boy to be more daring.* Genevieve was angry with him for that, but she understood it as well. *He sometimes lives through his son, as I will sometimes live through my daughters when they become proper young ladies.* He looped his arm through hers. "I don't know why some parents must lose their children. Bishop Jerome says we cannot hope to understand the mysteries of the Giver, and –."

Genevieve cut him off. "There is no mystery in death. That is *not* the Giver's work." Sometimes Sylvan could be a pious fool. He was too influenced by his confessor, horse-faced Bishop Jerome. *Another Black Bishop, no doubt.*

Sylvan was more devout than she was, but so were most people. His devotion to the Faith was not a problem, though. It was his devotion to the Bishops, priests and other servants of the Church that grated on her. "A man cannot rule a realm if he is being ruled by a man in a cassock in turn." It fell out of her mouth. She knew she should not have said it so loudly in public. She felt her cheeks flush.

Although no one was near them and no one appeared to be interested in their conversation...

There are ears everywhere. Bishop Michael impressed that upon her. Bishop Michael — another cassock-wearing, self-serving, so-called servant of the Giver. If Michael were beside her at that moment, she would have slapped him out of spite.

Sylvan looked around, and then leaned close. There was a smile on his lips, but his eyes were serious. "No one rules me, I can assure you. I am my own man, but I am also a servant of the Giver. I have my faith, but my faith will not deny me what is rightfully mine."

He said it, but Genevieve only partially believed him.

— «» —

The morning and the disagreement were behind them, and now they could enjoy the day. The overcast sky had given way to a clear blue expanse.

Genevieve had set aside the morning's black dress for a set of light blue riding clothes and a blue bonnet, decorated with yellow flowers. Black was not her color. It was no one's color. No woman's, anyway. Some men could be handsome in black. She thought the blue brought out the color in her eyes. Sylvan had declared her very pretty. He had not called her pretty in a long time; she was always *beautiful*. To be called pretty had excited her and she had pounced on him, making the most of the moment. It took a few minutes for her to smooth everything back into place after they were done, but it was well worth it.

The picnic was laid out now. The cloth was on the ground, the baskets were down, an awning was raised to give them some shade and wooden camp chairs were being set up.

"Shall we go?" Sylvan asked her.

"Yes," she said.

"There was a death at the Metropolitan's Palace," he suddenly said to her, his voice low so others couldn't hear. "One of the fathers was killed and there's the possibility he was murdered."

She raised an eyebrow. "Oh, really?"

"That's what I've been told, my lady." He could be overly formal in public settings. He thought it made him appear more proper. *And here we are talking in whispers.* She almost laughed. "Do you have any details of the incident, Sylvan?"

He laid his hands over the pommel of his horse and let the animal come to a halt. "The Master of Birds died when a bucket fell from a height onto his head. A malicious novice is suspected of purposely dropping it on him. It is said the novice is Lord Dawn's son, but I haven't pursued the matter yet."

Genevieve gasped. Lord Dawn was a Marshal's Man, one of her husband's more powerful retainers. He was immensely wealthy and lorded over great tracts of land. "You should look into this and intercede if necessary," she said.

"No, I shouldn't," he replied calmly. "Lord Dawn has always been a faithful retainer. His loyalty is sound, and prying into his family's affairs could compromise that."

"When did this occur?" she asked, after a moment's pause. Her voice was louder than it should have been.

"A few days ago, but Bishop Michael told me about it just this morning." He dismounted and then moved over to help her down.

She took his hand, knowing that a telltale crease of worry would be between her brows. She carefully hid her face from him as she slipped off her own horse. *Why didn't he tell* me *of this?* she wondered. The bishop was always quick to drop gossip in her ears to show how clever and well informed he was. *This is not something he should have kept from me.*

She composed herself as best she could and went over to the picnic area. It was a beautiful spread, with wild flowers set about in small, decorative arrangements. The open baskets were filled with foods and sweets, flasks of sweet tea and beer, but she had lost her appetite. She quietly sat beside her husband, her mind turning.

Twenty-One

The Gambler — James Gallant

James and Lucille Gallant booked space on a morning coach at a small train station located a short walk from the Angel & Bell.

The station, a single-storey building of plain clapboard, had a small waiting room with benches for passengers and a tiny taproom off to the side. Despite the early hour, most of the male passengers were in the taproom with their faces in their mugs. The women sat in the waiting room with the luggage and many were kept busy corralling their children. More than a few shot angry glances in the direction of the taproom where their spouses talked big over their beer.

Gallant had woken agitated and in a sour mood, so he was happy to hear that the passengers were waiting for the train. He was hoping for an empty coach that he and Lucille could share alone. His hope was for naught, though. When the coach rolled up, a family of four was waiting with them. And two young gents came at the last moment to hitch a ride to a spot where they were planning a hunting excursion.

While Lucille was all smiles to the assembled company, Gallant seethed inside, hating them all for no reason whatsoever other than the fact that they existed. He usually enjoyed the company of others and many enjoyed his company in return. He was, after all, the lovable James Gallant — the happy-go-lucky rascal with the easy smile and ready laugh.

What is wrong with me, he wondered, as he scowled at one of the hunters who leaned over Lucille's fingers to plant a kiss on them. *I am just anxious to get this done, I suppose.* He reached up and touched the pocket over his breast where the book was once again tucked safely.

The driver, a dusty old codger with a weathered face and a full head of steel gray hair, ordered the gents to sit on the bench on the back. He was about to tell Gallant to do the same, but at the last moment relented and decided he could sit in the coach with Lucille.

Inside, the coach was cramped. He and Lucille shared their bench with the youngest child in the family of four. He was a snot-nosed boy who Gallant guessed was seven or eight. He whined that he wanted the window seat, which put Gallant in the middle. As soon as the coach started rolling he discovered the boy was little more than knees and elbows. He squirmed in his seat like he needed to piss, drove his elbow into Gallant's side a few times, and knocked his knee against Gallant's repeatedly. The boy shifted his gaze nervously, one minute staring out the open window at the countryside and the next staring up at Gallant. His fingers frequently found their way up one nostril or another, but once they wandered to the grip of Gallant's pistol and Gallant had to push them away. He wanted to slap the child, but restrained himself.

The father was a flabby-faced doctor in a fine red coat, the mother a tight-faced woman in a dull brown dress with eyes full of judgment— her stern expression didn't even change when Lucille flashed her a smile and wished her a good morning. The final member of this family of four was a girl of ten. She was proudly clutching a daisy that one of the gentleman hunters had given her, and she chatted incessantly and apparently to no one, as her mother never said a word to her and her father was too busy filling up the coach with hot air and idle chatter of his own. Inwardly, Gallant groaned.

The two men on the bench in the back started singing bawdy songs until the coachman caught a bar or two, craned his head around and barked at them to shut up. They laughed at that, but Gallant heard no more lusty songs from the hunters.

Shortly after they had started they stopped in front of an inn in the middle of a hamlet that was nothing more than a tight cluster of houses — with white stucco walls, thatched roofs and wooden frames — where there were four more passengers waiting. Three were farmers who apparently knew the coachman, trying to cajole a free ride out of him. After sharing a few crude jokes and slugging whiskey from the jug they carried he allowed them to sit on the coach's roof. The fourth passenger was a stout woman, dressed in the high-collared blouse and long skirt of a teacher. The coachman offered to kick either Gallant or the doctor out of the box so she could have a seat inside, but she declined, declaring in a tone that would allow no argument that she would ride on the front bench with him. He looked uncomfortable with that, but dared not say a word when she fixed him with a steely-eyed glance. And when she went to haul herself up to the bench and the coachman offered her a helping hand, she slapped it away.

The coach had just cleared the hamlet when the farmers on top decided to dangle their feet down over the side. A clod of manure dropped from a pair of boots and onto the boy's shirt. He screeched and started to cry. After a harsh prod in the ribs from his wife, the doctor thrust his head out and started bellowing at the farmers on top. The coachman stopped the coach and told the farmers to get off and be on their way, apologizing profusely to the doctor in the process. The doctor nodded acceptance of the apology, but his wife's expression showed that she was not consoled at all.

Gallant's head began to hurt. The boy was still sniffling, so he leaned down and hissed into his ear. "It's just a bit of cow shit. Wipe it off and stop your bawling or I'll *really* give you something to cry about." The boy looked up with frightened eyes and Gallant flicked his to the gun at his hip. The boy wiped away the manure as best he could and clamped his mouth shut, although his bottom lip was thrust out in a prize-winning pout.

The gambler felt immediate shame. *What in all the dark hells has put me in such a mood?* He nudged the boy with his elbow and the boy looked up. Gallant gave him a wink and a smile. Hesitantly the boy returned with a false, frightened grin of his own that made Gallant laugh. He reached into his pocket and pulled out his deck of cards. He shuffled them quickly and the boy watched with growing curiosity as the cards flashed.

"Let me show you a trick or two," Gallant said.

The boy's mother loudly cleared her throat. Gallant stopped shuffling and looked up at her. "*We* don't approve of cards," she said, her lips tight. She nudged her husband who grunted something that could have been agreement or not.

"Well, I don't approve of people who don't approve of cards," Gallant drawled back casually. A silence fell within the coach that was suddenly broken by Lucille's laughter. The little girl joined in along with the doctor and the woman's face turned scarlet. Without wasting another moment, Gallant returned to his cards and showed the boy some tricks.

The hunters were let off mid-morning in front of a worn little cottage that was backed by a wood. They yelled their goodbyes to their fellow passengers and one blew a kiss. "That's for the fair lady from Seawall," he cried. Lucille clapped her hands and smiled and Gallant faked a scowl before grinning.

Two hours later they arrived at their destination.

The town was called Twisty Lanes and one look at its streets told a visitor why. The town with its tight, crooked streets was small with less than a thousand people. Most of the buildings were made of red brick, but there were older structures in the centre of town made of heavy stone, gray with a pinkish tone. The church itself stood out, with a bell tower that rose above everything else. The surrounding countryside was beautiful, rich pasture, good farmland, high hedges, streams and brooks, and small copses of trees. There were also many red willows, many of them sporting beards of pink moss.

The Gallants were let off at an inn called the High Marshal's House. There were hundreds of inns, hotels and public houses that shared that name across the Realm, with the proprietors always claiming that a High Marshal stayed in one of its room in the past, almost always beyond living memory.

From the inn they had to walk to a house that was on the eastern side of the town. It was the town rectory, home of the resident priest, the man that Gallant was instructed to take *the book* to.

As they reached the front gate of the rectory's yard, his hand went subconsciously to where the book sat in the inner-pocket of his coat. He fought a sudden urge to spin around and leave, to toss the book into a ditch somewhere and go into hiding.

The crumbling wall was only a few feet high and beyond it, Gallant could see that the rectory grounds were poorly tended and the hedges went untrimmed. A red willow was in the front, its branches drooping down and covering the view of half the house, which looked a tidy place despite the unkempt yard. It was a red brick building, small and boxy with white wood trim. In the back, Gallant could see other buildings as well.

"Let's hope our man is home," he said to Lucille. "I'd hate to have to wait some more after traveling all this way in such a hurry."

The wooden gate swung open easily and they made their way along the path that led straight through the tall grass to the front door. Gallant reached up and pulled the bell rope. In a few moments the door was opened by a looming figure in a priest's cassock.

Gallant was taken aback and Lucille gasped. The man before them was well over six feet tall, close to seven, and he had a set of shoulders, chest, and large calloused hands to match. He had a full head of dark untidy hair that fell to his shoulders and spilled down his brow with locks of it falling into his eyes and onto his face. A thick but trimmed beard covered his chin and mouth. His eyes were a vibrant blue. "Can I help you?" the priest asked, his eyes flicking from Gallant to Lucille and back.

Gallant reached up and tipped his hat. "I'm James Gallant and this is my wife Lucille. If you're Hans Lowman, then we've traveled a long way to see you."

The thick lips that were nearly hidden in the man's whiskers curved into a smile. "I *am* Father Lowman," he said. "I've been waiting for you. Enter." He stepped back from the door. This was one of those moments when Gallant would not let his lady enter before him. He gave her a look that told her to be cautious and entered first, his hand dipping down to the grip of his gun.

They were greeted by the smell of tea, spices, and baking bread. The rectory was little more than a large cottage. They were in a sitting room with worn horsehair furniture and a sooty fireplace. Beyond a broad archway was the kitchen in the back. A staircase led to the rooms above and there were doors to two other rooms that were closed. "This way," Lowman said, ducking under a low hanging beam and leading them into the kitchen. "I am baking bread and I don't want it to burn."

The kitchen was large and open with a big fireplace and an open window on each side of the room. The smell of the baking bread was warm and homey. There was small iron door above the fireplace that was partially open, showing the dark pit of an oven where the priest was baking his bread. Off to the right, under a window, was a desk covered in papers, ink-pots, and pens. Next to it were shelves crammed with books. On the opposite side of the room, next to the other window, was a large wooden table covered in a stained linen cloth and surrounded by four sturdy chairs. On the windowsill, two pies were cooling and hungry flies buzzed around the cheese-cloth that covered them. Gallant's stomach rumbled.

Lowman gathered two thick rags to cover his hands and opened the oven door. He plucked two bread pans out, each containing a little loaf, and placed them on the brick mantel. "There's nothing like fresh bread," he said, smacking his lips to make his point. He tossed the rags over the back of a chair. "Would you like something to drink? I have a nice bottle of local wine."

I'd much rather have a loaf of bread and slice or two of those pies, Gallant thought. "Wine would be nice," he said.

The priest gathered three glasses and a bottle from a small cabinet that was tucked in a corner. He placed the glasses on the table and poured. The wine was a rich red color. He handed a glass to Lucille first and then to Gallant. He picked up his own glass. "Shall we toast to a journey ended?"

"Yes," Lucille said with a smile. Gallant nodded. They clinked their glasses together and Lowman drained his quickly, following it up with a belch. He laughed and winked at Lucille. "Excuse my manners. It's not often I get company." Lucille blushed and Gallant felt a twinge of jealousy, or discomfort, or both.

"Please sit." Lowman gestured to the chairs and pulled one out for Lucille. "We'll have some mince pie, some fresh bread, and finish this bottle. Then we'll get down to business."

Lowman was a good host, despite his earlier declaration that he got few visitors. He was a good conversationalist as well, and knowledgeable on many subjects. There was something coarse and vulgar about him and it irked Gallant that Lucille seemed to be enjoying his company. *A bit too much*, he thought as the priest refilled her glass and made some jest that brought laughter pouring from her lips. There was something hypnotic about the priest's eyes and Gallant did not like the way they seemed to crawl over Lucille, devouring her shape and form, drinking it in, like his lips drank in the wine. She was unnerved by it too, he could tell, but she got some perverse pleasure from it as well.

In the end, they finished another bottle of wine and devoured the other pie and the rest of the bread. Gallant had measured his cups carefully, so the wine wasn't affecting him. Lucille had been less cautious and was tipsy. With the food gone and little wine remaining in the bottom of the second bottle the talk finally turned to the business at hand.

"You've arrived on time," Lowman said, his gaze falling on Gallant and his expression turning serious. "We are well on schedule ... as long as you *have* the book."

"I have it." Gallant nodded. He felt an urge to smash one of the wine bottles over the man's head and drag Lucille out of the place.

"Can I see it?" Lowman made a gesture with his fingers for Gallant to hand it over.

Gallant reached into his breast pocket and removed it, the small book of poems that he had carried over a thousand miles. The book that had nearly gotten him and Lucille killed a dozen times. The book that the Fifth Wheel would have wanted. He looked at it. It was simple and worn, its leather cover was stained, and it had broken corners. He did not pretend to understand *why* it was so important. All he knew was its delivery to this priest was crucial. It was worth a thousand gold crowns to Gallant, an incredible sum, more than a common man could see in several lifetimes, which would be paid to him by his employer when he returned to Seawall.

He recalled the first time he touched *the book*. He was in an oddities shop that he had been directed to through his employer's instructions. It was hidden in the inner alleys of a sprawling market in Far Reach's capital, Sun Reach, the city that never slept and always stank. Although it was the capital, it was a city of slums and poverty. The wealth and opulence was tied up in the purses and palaces of the princes and lesser lords.

The oddities shop was one of those places that sold stuffed lizard heads, potions, spices, totems, amulets and charms, relics and artifacts of the Old Ones, and other bric-a-brac. It was stacked on shelves, spilling from open barrels and crates, and hanging from nails driven into the overhead rafters.

The shopkeeper was as strange as the contents displayed on his shelves. He spoke the realm's tongue with an accent that Gallant couldn't place. He wore a weathered grey robe and was adorned with golden jewelry — rings on his bony fingers, a thick necklace around his scrawny neck, and even a pair of large earrings pulling on the long lobes of his ears. His skin was like leather and drawn so tight over his face that Gallant could clearly make out the shape of his skull underneath. He could easily imagine this one dead and rotting, nothing but bones and dark holes for eyes. He even stank of rot. He had handed Gallant the book with a strange smile, his bright eyes crinkling at the corners, and said a few words Gallant did not understand. He made a gesture with his fingers. When Gallant asked him what the words meant, the shopkeeper had only cackled in response and continued to cackle after Gallant left, the cackle echoing off the alley's stone walls.

"Is that it?" Father Lowman pointed at the book in Gallant's hand. Gallant nodded and stared down at it. It was so plain in appearance ... but still somehow sinister. Lowman signalled to Gallant to hand it over and Gallant did.

Lowman smiled as he stared at it. He turned it over in his hands, opened it and flipped through the pages. He snapped it shut, his smile now a full grin. He turned to the fire and tossed it into the heart of the flames. Gallant was mortified. Lucille gave a shriek. Gallant wanted to shoot the man, and he would, but first he had to save the book before the fire could consume it. He dove forward, but the priest was quick and powerful. He intercepted Gallant and gathered him up into a bear hug. Lucille pulled out her derringer and pointed it at the man's head.

"Easy now," the priest yelled, flicking his eyes at Lucille. "Stop and watch."

His words were a command and Gallant and Lucille were forced to obey. They watched as the book shriveled in the heat, smoke issuing from the paper, growing thicker until flames appeared, slowly eating the book. After a few minutes it was nothing but a black husk. Lowman let Gallant go. He snatched up a poker and maneuvered the book out of the fire and onto the stone flags. He reached down to pick it up. Gallant expected him to drop it and recoil, as it would still be very hot, but he did not. Instead he carried it over to a battered desk under the window. He waved Gallant and Lucille over. "Come and see."

They edged up to where the priest was now carefully opening the book's black cover. "This," the priest said, "is a true *black book*. What novices, dabblers in the art, might call a cipher." He chuckled to himself. The pages within were black and brittle, but on them, written in white ash, were characters of some sort, letters. It was no language that Gallant was familiar with. Each flaky page had a few letters on it, or just a crooked line. Lowman, though, seemed to know the language well. He had gathered up ink and pen and was writing furiously on a paper, muttering to himself as he did so. He did not stop until he had made his way through the entire book. It was quickly done, taking only a few minutes. In the end, the paper he was writing on was filled with words. He picked up the burned book and went back to the fire. He held it in his open hands and blew on it. It disintegrated into ash that his breath sent into the fire. The flames seemed to leap up to devour all evidence of what the priest called a *black book*.

Lowman straightened up. "You have done well." He smiled at Gallant and his eyes glanced hungrily at Lucille for a moment, "both of you." He went over to the desk, rifled through one of its pigeonholes, and produced an oilskin envelope. He tossed it to Gallant. "In there, along with an address where you can get in touch with *our* friend and *your* employer, is a sworn declaration from me that you have carried out your end of the agreement. That should be all you need to receive your payment. A thousand in gold, is it?" He whistled. "That's quite a sum."

And it was, but Gallant felt no joy or elation. Instead, he felt hollow. He tried to push the feeling away. He tried to focus on the twinkling gold he and Lucille would enjoy. He managed a weak smile. "Yes, it is." Even to his ears the words sounded flat.

"You'll need a bit of money to get back, too," Lowman continued, either not registering Gallant's mood or not caring. He picked up a tiny cloth bag from the desktop and tossed it to Gallant. He caught it and heard the chink of coins inside. "There's thirty silver marques in there, or there about. Enough to get you back to Seawall, quickly and in good order.

"You're welcome to stay the night," he said, his eyes flicking to Lucille as he licked his lips. "There's a cottage out back that is comfortable enough." He turned to the desk and picked up the paper that held the notes he had just written. He studied it for a moment, his lips moving, as though he was going over the words on it in his mind. When he had finished, he nodded to himself and made sure the ink was dry before folding it and tucking it into an inner pocket of his robe.

"Unfortunately, I have to go," he said, holding his hands apart in way of an apology. "Your task is done, but now I have my part to carry out and that means travel. I might be back tonight, very late, maybe not."

He left to get ready.

Before leaving, he gave Gallant a key to the cottage. "Help yourselves to any food you can find," he said, waving a hand at the rectory. He had a wide-brimmed hat on his head and a battered leather bag hanging from his shoulder. His arm was draped over it protectively. He was holding the reins of the rectory pony, a stout brown mount with a shaggy blonde mane. It looked strong, old, and bored. "There should be several bottles of wine left, if you have a thirst. I recommend the bottle of Pale Valley Yellow. It's from Seawall, so it's a taste of home. It's a bit too sweet for me, but everyone else seems to like it." With that he shook Gallant's hand roughly, planted a slobbery kiss on Lucille's mouth, mounted the pony and left.

"I think he ran his tongue over my lips," Lucille said when he was gone. She looked disturbed as she brought her hand to her mouth.

—— «» ——

That night Gallant lay on his back in the dark, staring up at the ceiling. The small cottage that Lowman had put them up in was at the back of the rectory grounds. It had a musty smell and was little used, but it still had a rustic charm. In his mind's eye he once again saw *the book* burning down to a black husk, nothing more than ash marked by strange letters. He should be elated that the task was done, that he would soon be wealthy. But he was not. He felt ... *cheated* somehow.

If I was sitting at a table and scooping in the coins after playing a solid hand, I'd have reason to smile, he thought. *But this isn't a game of cards; it's some ugly game and everyone playing it is as dishonest and dangerous as they come, including me.* Still, a thousand gold...

He sighed. *Money owed was not money collected,* as any who lent money to his father knew. He had no reason to distrust his employer, though. He had wealth enough at his disposal and a thousand gold would mean little to him. *I should be damn relieved it's over.*

For the first time in months he wasn't being chased. Now he had time to reflect on all that had happened, all that had led him to this point. *What made me do it?* Greed, gold, a sense of adventure ... pride mostly. Yes, pride. He was full of it. Lucille reminded him of that often enough. He smiled.

Lucille let out a little moan and rolled toward him, as if she had *heard* his smile and it had stirred her. Her naked breast pressed up against his arm. He absently reached down and rubbed his sore groin. She had been a hellcat just an hour or two ago, filled with a passion — lust really — that he had never witnessed before. And he had been the same. He was surprised their rickety bed had held up.

He tried to convince himself that the hot passion had been a result of the tension they had felt, that it was a celebration of the release from the constant danger they had faced for so many months, but he didn't believe that — not for a second. The lust he had felt and that Lucille displayed was something dark and sinister. It had turned them into rutting animals and he had a feeling that Lowman, with his lecherous leers and grins (and that slimy tongue of his that had passed over her lips), had something to do with it.

He wanted out of this place. He wanted to put as much distance between them and the priest as possible, as quickly as possible. He wanted to get back to Seawall. *I'll get the gold and lose all these ugly feelings. Won't I?* He had played a pivotal part in some great plan, he was sure of that now. And whatever Lowman had pulled from the book, a "true black book" he had called it, was important.

Was this great plan good or bad? As a gambling man he knew the odds of anything good coming from a plan that included something called a *black book* were mighty slim, mighty slim indeed.

Twenty-Two

The Dead Priest — Quentus

They made camp in the heart of a dead forest, the bare white trunks of the trees surrounding them, looking like bones jutting from the earth. There was little shelter here and the horses had no desire to eat the yellow grass that grew in this place. Quentus knew they were close to civilization, too close for his comfort. They had crossed a road earlier that had two grooves sunk into it by heavy carts and wagons.

The land here was tainted, but that was not surprising. They were close to the Range and Quentus knew the Range in these parts was full of the ancient taint. The poisonous and dangerous land was part of the buffer that separated West Marque and the Range, an invisible evil line that ensured that both lands didn't meet — or clash. *Although the taint is diminishing*, he thought. *Slowly, but it is going away and one day it will be gone. What will happen then?*

He didn't linger on that question, as he had more immediate concerns. The three of them sat around a fire, the dead trees and their dry timber providing excellent fuel for the flames. The flames were bright, more yellow than orange, and the smoke was almost as white as the wood itself, interlaced with inky black tendrils that weaved their way in and out of the white clouds like thin, poisonous snakes.

Wooden plates were on their laps, laden with rice and fresh fish caught earlier in the ravine's stream. Even the girl ate with some gusto. That was a good sign. He looked at her as she tore her fish apart with her fingers. She looked at him

and almost smiled. His eyes had returned to normal and he
had removed his glasses some time ago.

He stared into the dancing flames before him and absent-
mindedly put some fish in his mouth. He chewed and then
said in the desert tongue, "Salene, there is something I must
do."

She looked up from her meal and replied in the same
language. "What is it?"

"I must cast my gaze upon the girl. I have a feeling that
she might know something about Paulus."

Salene knew what he meant. "I have been thinking the
same thing, about Paulus and the girl, I mean." She put her
plate down beside her and idly pushed a branch deeper into
the flames with her foot. "You must do it gently. She has
been through a lot."

Quentus nodded. "I know. And I will need your help.
You must keep her calm, at least until I begin, and then you
may have to hold her down. I am not sure what I'll find
inside her, but we know Paulus is a brutal and evil man. He
can bury dark things deep inside people, even a person as
small and innocent as this young girl."

"And if you find something, can you root it out and get
rid of it?" Salene asked.

"I don't know," Quentus sighed. "I could be wrong —
hopefully so — and maybe there is nothing to this. Maybe
outlaws set upon the girl. Maybe she is an imbecile who ran
away from home or fled some asylum."

"You don't believe that, though."

He shook his head. "No. Are you ready?"

Salene nodded and turned to the girl. The girl stared
back at her, flakes of white fish on her lips. Salene reached
out and stroked her hair. "Quentus must look at you, sweet
one," she said. "It will be okay, I promise you. He will make
sure you are fine and will help you if you are not." She
gestured for Quentus to come over.

Quentus put down his plate and moved cautiously over
to the girl. A look of fear came over her and she began to
moan. Salene tried to soothe her, but the girl pushed away.
Salene grabbed her tightly about the arms and the girl

screamed. Quentus moved in quickly and put his hands, firmly but gently, on either side of her face. Their eyes locked. She screamed again and closed her eyes tightly before opening them again. His eyes whitened rapidly and puss started to ooze from their corners, stinking and leaking down his cheeks like teardrops. She made to shriek one last time, but his power had hold of her.

He turned the power of his mind into something like a spear point and struck hers. He broke through her own feeble defenses and started reading her scattered thoughts. "I am Tabatha," he mumbled to no one. "I am nearly ten. My family … oh, sweet Giver … my family … Danny, little brother … mother … father … Rufus … Gran … I am little Hen Chick … the man … he betrayed us … he killed us … your kindness will get us killed…." Deeper he delved, images from the girl's mind hanging like half-completed tapestries before him. Even Paulus' face appeared grey and fuzzy, smiling, first friendly, and then malevolent. And then it was there, the dark wall he feared would block him.

"Paulus," he said through gritted teeth. The girl had gone limp, her eyes still locked with Quentus' dead ones. Puss and blood leaked from his sockets, a drop falling onto the girl's chin. *"You bastard!"* He threw his will against the black wall and it held. He smashed against it again. And again. And again.

Quentus was shaking with effort, his white eyes filling with blood. The girl began to convulse, and words bubbled from her lips. "Quentus…" A deep voice rumbled from somewhere inside the girl's chest. *"You* are not the one who is meant to use this agent. The chains remain fastened, the locks secured, the door closed."

"Fuck you," Quentus snarled, and he pushed forward, his breathing labored and heavy.

"What's wrong, Quentus?" the voice rumbled. "Are you dashing what little remains of your strength on my mighty walls?" Laughter, not a girl's laughter, resonated from her small frame as a hiss escaped her lips, spattering Quentus' cheeks with flakes of fish.

Quentus was exhausted, just clinging to the power of his god. It would abandon him soon. But he had to try again.

He hurled his will with all his might against the wall and the slightest chink in it appeared — enough for a glimpse, a peek behind the curtain. He had no time to consider whether he wanted to know what Paulus had locked inside this little girl. He *had* to look, and so he did, and was horrified by what he saw there - an angry spirit of the land, a wrathful shadow, a great ghost that had lingered over an ancient battlefield for millennia. A battle fought in the dead woods not too far from here, made of all the anger, hate and bitterness of those who died fighting there.

Paulus had pulled it from the land somehow and bound it. He had injected it into this girl and buried it into her to be drawn out by someone who had the key and means to do so. Quentus was not that person, and he didn't want to be.

Paulus' prime power was the ability to bind things, forces of nature and beyond, to even give them physical form. He had consumed the heart and blood long ago, on the Blasted Rock. It would have been considered an ambitious undertaking for any Dead Priest; it was even more ambitious for Paulus because he had been so young at the time. Others had been surprised, particularly so because he had succeeded, but not Quentus. He had caught glimpses of the arrogance and ambition that was under the mask that Paulus had worn at that time. Quentus had seen it because that very same arrogance and ambition had mirrored his own. But while Quentus had let go of those things, as best he could, Paulus had clung to them and fed them.

On top of it all, Quentus suspected that Paulus had dabbled in other...things. It was rumored he had sought out forbidden knowledge, rubbed shoulders with necromancers and the like. They were only rumors, but Quentus thought they they leaned more towards truth with each passing day.

Unworldly laughter echoed from the girl's body again, no longer the laughter of the gatekeeper but that which lurked behind the gate. "So you see me," the voice said, "and I see you. I see weakness and ignorance. I see *nothing*!" The last word was so loud that Salene winced as she struggled with the girl's thrashing body.

Suddenly, a smile turned the corners of Quentus' mouth. "I know you too," he said. "I know what you are and ... I know something you don't."

A puzzled look crossed the girl's face. "What—?"

"I know sometimes it is better to keep something caged rather than kill it," Quentus sneered. "Enjoy your prison, beast."

The voice roared in anger and Quentus screamed back. He and Salene struggled with the girl as she thrashed about. The roar became a pitiful howl, and then suddenly fell silent.

Quentus rolled off to the side, his chest heaving, his bloody, rheumy eyes rolling in their sockets. Sweat covered his brow. The girl, in contrast, lay silent and still. Peaceful. Her breathing was steady, as though she were in a deep sleep. Salene stroked her forehead once before turning her attention to Quentus. She leaned over him and kissed his brow. "Is it gone, Quentus?"

He panted. "No. It is locked up inside her," he turned his face to the girl. "Inside Tabatha. We know her name now and ... we *must* take her back with us. Back to the Range.

"We will leave first thing in the morning. She can't stay here," he continued, almost babbling now. "The thing inside her draws its power from West Marque, from the land itself. We must take it far away from here, so it can be destroyed — or cast out — and never used for its intended purpose."

"What purpose?" Salene stroked Quentus' hair.

"I'm not sure. It is waiting for something, or someone, or both. I don't know." He shook his head.

"And what of Paulus?" Salene stroked his hair.

"Forget Paulus." He sighed. "Let the people of West Marque deal with him as they deal with all of my kind. He'll be kindling for a fire soon enough. The way he's been acting, conjuring up abominations and preying upon those who he meets, he'll be caught eventually. Here, they *burn* Dead Priests, remember."

"He is reckless," Salene agreed. "It will be his downfall."

And possibly ours, he wanted to add. Instead, he said, "Tomorrow we head for home."

Twenty-Three

The Novice — Marcus Dawn

Marcus rolled onto his left side, trying to get comfortable, but it was impossible. This place was designed to torment people, not provide comfort. A piece of straw pricked his cheek. It was dark and insufferably cold. He was shivering, despite the thread-worn wool blanket over top of him. He whimpered in the darkness.

He was in one of the prison cells located deep beneath the Holy Citadel. It was a place once reserved for heretics, when the Inquisition's fires roared and the Church burned so-called unbelievers in large numbers rather than hang them from a common gallows. The last occupant had probably died a hundred years ago. The old straw had turned to gray dust, but Marcus might have preferred it to the fresh manure-covered straw he was given for bedding. Sometimes he thought he was the only inmate, but occasionally he would hear a wail from somewhere in the bowels of the prison that reminded him he wasn't.

He reached out into the black, his knuckles aching from the chill, and found the clay bowl. He brought it to his lips and sucked at the cold, sulfurous water. He coughed and nearly retched. Something was wrong with his innards. They were feeding him black, weevil-filled bread and dried beef, so hard it nearly cracked his teeth.

Justice, such as it was, was swift.

— 《》 —

Marcus had screamed himself hoarse when finally a father had heard the cry and come running to the aviary. The chubby priest, cassock flowing, bent over Shirrup and pronounced him dead. An inquiry followed. Marcus relayed the events that led up to Shirrup's death, including the movement and shadow he had glimpsed while he was in the rafters. "I think someone else was up there," he said. But few listened. Several of the fathers, including Father Allard, accused Marcus of making up the shadow. "For this one, lying is like breathing," Allard had sneered. The motive was clear — Marcus was angry about being expelled from the Holy City and, in his anger, had deliberately killed the Master of Birds.

Marcus fiercely declared his innocence, but it did him no good. There were no character witnesses to defend Marcus Dawn. The other novices hated him. Novice Hume went so far as to mention Marcus' blasphemies directed at the cardinal that day in the latrine.

Marcus was tossed into a cell after the inquiry.

Later, a pair of Citadel guards arrived and hauled him forth. They escorted him to a small, dingy hall where a tribunal sat at an ancient iron-studded table. Three men made up the tribunal — Father Allard, Bishop Horace with his big belly and cold eyes, and stern-faced Bishop Jerome (another one who the novices whispered was a Black Bishop). *For an extinguished order, it seems to have many members,* Marcus thought as he glanced at the two bishops. The guards dragged him to a black cushion in the center of the room and the one on his left indicated that he was to kneel. Marcus dropped to his knees on the cushion, then screeched. The cushion was not stuffed with goose down. In fact, it was no cushion at all. It was a block of hard wood covered in black cloth. Marcus' sob echoed off the bare walls.

The only light in the hall came from high, dust-covered windows and two tall candles on the Tribunal table. One candle was white and the other was black. When the tribunal reached its judgment a candle would be snuffed. If the white candle continued to burn, the accused was innocent. If it was the black, the accused was guilty. Bishop

Jerome shuffled through the stack of papers in front of him, his face hidden in shadow. Father Allard looked at Marcus with narrowed eyes, while Bishop Horace seemed irritated by the proceedings.

The Tribunal lasted less than an hour. Marcus was asked only a few questions, as most of the time the three men deliberated points amongst themselves, including the boy's possible execution. It was a nightmarish experience for the young novice and he remembered little of what was actually said.

After some deliberation, Bishop Jerome stared at Marcus with hooded eyes and reached to pinch out the flame of the white candle. Guilty. Marcus shrieked. Bishop Jerome was unmoved. In a voice dry as paper he declared that the tribunal presumed Marcus' guilt, but lacked the evidence to administer proper justice. Marcus would wait in a jail cell until they could agree on a fitting punishment.

The guards led him down narrow passages, through gates and chambers, and then downward, ever downward, to the cell he now occupied. The larger of the two, who had black, greasy hair and cheeks covered in pimples, told Marcus he would be forgotten and die in the dungeon. "Them fathers won't be quick about figuring out the manner of your remaining days," he had said, his horrid breath washing warm over Marcus' face. "You're a cellar root now, boy, so I hope you like your new digs." The man clouted Marcus on the ear, laughing, before roughly pitching him headlong into the cell.

Marcus met his jailer an hour later, an ancient relic, but powerfully built all the same. He gave Marcus some straw, a clay water bowl, and a bucket. "For yer fundament duties," the jailer had said as Marcus stared at the bucket. "Or soil yer straw for all I care. Makes no difference to me. You have to live in it."

— «» —

Time had passed — several days, at least. Marcus had cried for hours, but then gave up. No one cared. Only when he became extremely hungry did he eat the tainted beef the jailer had given him. Even then, he ate sparingly.

There were no rats down here, and that bothered Marcus. There *were* spiders, however; great, pale ugly things with mottled bodies and odd-sized legs, but *no* rats. When he asked the jailer about it the man cackled and said the spiders ate the rats. *No doubt they did*, Marcus thought. And in his fitful sleep he often dreamt of spiders, scurrying on long, clattering legs out of the darkness to bite him.

He heard the sound of approaching footsteps and stared at the pale line of flickering light that marked the bottom of the door. Was it time? Were the guards coming with a rope to pop his neck? Fear ran through him, up and down his spine, and icy cold in his chest and guts. The footsteps stopped in front of his door. Shadows broke up the line of light. He retreated to the back of his cell and a small moan escaped him.

The door was flung open and Marcus raised his hand to shield his eyes from the stabbing lantern light. "On yer feet, lad," the jailer growled. "You have a visitor." Slowly Marcus gathered himself up, brushed the straw from his robe, and squinted. A familiar form filled the doorway. "Father," Marcus cried and rushed forward.

Marcus' father struck him. Hard. The backhanded blow knocked him to the ground. Marcus tasted blood. "*Fool*," his father hissed. "You bring shame on our family."

The boy looked up. His father stood there, staring down. Lord Edward Dawn was powerfully built, with a wide, handsome face, hidden mostly in shadow. He wore casual riding clothes and high leather boots, the toes of which were inches from Marcus' face. "But, Father," Marcus began.

"*Silence*," his father roared. He turned his head and said to the jailer, "Leave us." The old man grunted. He left the lantern by the door and shuffled down the hallway, whistling some tune. Lord Dawn returned his attention to his son. "What have you *done*, boy?"

"I did nothing, Father. Honest." Marcus looked and sounded much younger than his fifteen years at that moment.

"Nothing, eh?" He squatted down and grabbed Marcus' face in the fierce grip of a calloused hand, one that was used to hard work. His eyes locked with Marcus'. In the shadows they were nothing more than a pair of glints. Marcus tried to shake his head, but the strong fingers held his face fast.

"Never mind your protest. I believe you. I know you well enough to know when you lie, which is often enough. He released his grasp.

"Father, I—"

But his father cut him short with a gesture. "It doesn't matter what *I* think, Marcus," he said. "All that matters is what *they* think. And *they* think you are guilty."

He stood up straight and his hands balled into fists. "I should have been harder on you, but you were the youngest and the most spoilt. I put too much stock in the Church, thinking it could somehow offer you a career.

"And now *this*." He opened his hands and closed them again, so tightly his knuckles cracked. "*Murder.* And my name associated with it, the *Dawn* name. Your guilt or innocence is no longer of consequence. The damage is done. *Fool.*" He spat on his son.

Tears rolled down Marcus' cheeks, but his father remained unmoved. He was a Marshal's Man, a lord, born of fire and iron. "Oh, don't worry, Marcus," he said. "Your life will be spared." Marcus looked up with some hope. "Yes, boy. A thousand gold crowns can buy most things in life, including *your* innocence. *Most* holy men forget their vows and forsake their faith when they see the shine of gold."

"Father, thank you." He reached out to hug his father's legs, but his father stepped back.

"*Don't* touch me," he snapped. "There is a price to be paid, Marcus, and you *will* pay it. You are exiled, but not to Bythesea as I initially planned. No, you must go to the land of ice and snow. You must go to Axefell and have your spirit tempered there."

Marcus did not know what to say. His father continued. "Furthermore, you will not be excommunicated. You will continue to wear the cloth and serve the Church as best you can.

"I don't expect you to amount to much. In fact, I suspect you will soon wither and die. But your death will mean nothing to me because I disown you. You are not fit to carry the Dawn name or benefit from the privileges that come with it. So pick a name of your choosing. Whatever you wish, but *not* Dawn. If I hear that you are claiming *my* name as your own, I shall send men to silence you, *forever*. Do you understand?"

Marcus only sniffled.

His father spun on his heel and stopped at the doorway to pick up the lantern. He did not look back but said, "Good-bye, Marcus." And he was gone.

Marcus lay in the straw and cried. The door to his cell was open. He was free to go, but go where? To *Axefell*.

Twenty-Four

The Old Lord — Lord Everisle

The priest had arrived mid-afternoon and was now with the girl. Lord Everisle was confined to his bed, but he could hear Father Lowman muttering below.

He was not surprised the priest was here. Two days ago the girl had had another spell. It was a mild thing, but enough to warrant a visit from the lummox.

Or had he come unbidden this time?

Lord Everisle wasn't sure. He did not know, nor did he much care. He had heard Lowman was taking her away — at least for a while — and that was good enough for him.

Her recent episode had resulted in the events that led to the old lord's confinement to his bed. "I want her *gone*," he snapped aloud, even though he was alone and there was no one there to hear. "I want her out of *my* house."

The pain rippled up his side and then shot over and into his guts and down his spine. He cried out. "Oh, Giver."

When he was young, pain meant little to him. Now he was old and broken, pain consumed him.

His hip was not broken, the doctor had said, only bruised. "The Giver be praised," the doctor had said, before Lord Everisle damned the man to all the dark hells, not for the diagnosis but for the rough prodding of his tender side. "I am not a horse, you fool," Everisle had barked at him.

He groaned and shifted himself in an attempt to alleviate his suffering. This only brought forth another stab of pain. He cried out again and cursed. "Shit," he yelled.

The door popped open and the Sow was there, her ugly moon face peering at him from around the door. "Get out," the lord barked. He flailed his hand, trying to grab the bowl of un-eaten porridge next to him so he could fling it at her head, and instead his knuckles slammed into the nightstand. "Giver, be good," he wailed in anguish. His fingers found the bowl and he hurled it with what strength he could muster at the nurse's head. But she was too quick. She ducked back and slammed the door behind her, the bowl crashing harmlessly against the wall. A clump of porridge hung there, gray and grotesque.

Did he hear the girl laughing in the room below?

"Quiet," he screeched. "Be gone."

He groaned again and recalled the girl's latest episode. He had woken in the middle of the night to singing. It was a strange song, with no tune or words that he immediately recognized.

He should have pulled the rope near his bed to summon one of the nurses, but he 'hadn't. Instead, like a fool, he had listened and realized the song was coming from outside.

Curious, he sat up and with great effort had dragged himself out of bed. He grabbed his sticks and made his way to the window to see if he could spy the culprit.

He peered out, his eyes adjusting to the dark, and he saw *her*. Down in the garden. Naked.

She moved in the moonlight and he couldn't make out any of the details. Her nipples were just two small dark spots, the trim between her legs a bit of darkness. "Her hair is blonde and her thicket is the same," he muttered.

Her back arched, her arms moved with grace, her bare feet carried her across the grass, and all the while she sang.

He was not aroused. His manhood hung limp, as it had for the last ten years or more. But he was … curious. And he felt sad for some reason.

It was the way she moved. Her dance brought an old memory to the forefront of his mind. It was something he hadn't thought about in over half a century. It was a memory from when he was barely a man. His first campaign. The first time he had left Lizabet, who was not yet even his bride, but was his betrothed.

He had rode out with a force from Shieldgate — five thousand strong, men from Wood Helm, Shieldgate, and Seawall, and some from Lang'arc and Stone Anchor, as well. They were all young, all noble, all riding out thinking of glory, riches, women, and adventures. *And we weren't too wrong in our thinking.* It was a noble campaign, something that couldn't be said of any campaign since. The foe was some desert tribes from the Glaze, brought together by the Sand Fox to raid the bordering Seats of West Marque.

"I had looked good in my uniform," he said to no one, "and Lizabet had cried when I left. She gave me a lock of her hair and a locket to protect it." Tears rolled down his cheeks as he continued to watch the girl dance in the moonlight.

She was singing louder now, the moonlight silver on her pale skin, and he could make out the words more clearly. His heart skipped a beat. He *did* know the song. It was the song he had heard when the desert girl had danced for him in that tent over seventy years ago. She was a brazen beauty from one of the friendly tribes, and she had filled him with lust. She had shared his bed, and so he had broken his heart's contract with Lizabet. He had betrayed his love. *And the girl danced just as this girl is dancing now in my garden.* "Why do you torment me so?"

The tears streamed down his cheeks, his heart ached from sadness and shame, and he made to hammer on the window to make her stop. Instead though, he had lost his sticks and fallen, the girl's laughter ringing in his ears like a chime.

He groaned and tried to turn onto his side with the good hip, but the pain was unbearable. He cried out and tore at his sheets.

The girl could not leave soon enough and he hoped that when she left, she would never return.

Twenty-Five

The Privileged Girl — Lara Mainhouse

Lara was seated on a cushioned bench in the lounging car of the High Marshal's train, her grandfather's train. Everything was green and gold — the wallpaper, the cushions, the forest scene painted on the ceiling above. She would have preferred to have the car to herself, but her Aunt Maude was there with Lara's cousins in tow..

Outside, the realm rolled by, green fields, greener woods, houses large and small, blue lakes, and wide rivers rolling like silver ribbons across the countryside. She saw mostly landed folk, but also a few knights and nobles. Many waved at the passing train. Some of them, the landed folk especially, had never ridden in a train, Lara knew. That knowledge brought her a strange sort of satisfaction. *I am better than them in some way*, she thought. *I should be ashamed to think that, but I'm not.* She smiled and waved out the window at a scruffy farm boy, his face dirty and his eyes filled with envy and wonder, doubting the boy could see her.

They were the realm's rails, meant first and foremost for the High Marshal. The lines ran from High Hall to the capitals of the other Seats — save for Axefell and Far Reach, which could only be safely accessed by sea.

The rails were well maintained by gangs of convicts who toiled under the watchful eyes of hard taskmasters. It was said blood lay in the rail beds, and a few bodies, too.

There were high roads for horses, wagons, and carriages, of course, a vast network of them, but they weren't all well maintained. Some of them weren't even high roads at all; they were more like low roads, just dirt tracks and miserable little trails, especially on the fringes of civilization.

But the realm's rails ran straight and true.

She saw her reflection in the window and saw her mother staring back at her. Their recent argument had been different than the ones in the past, fiercer, more direct, truer. She pushed the recollection away. Her mother was not going to ruin her experience. *That is what she wants.*

A servant came into the car. He was tall and handsome, but old. His dark hair was graying along the sides. He was pushing a trolley loaded with sweets and a glass decanter filled with iced lemonade. She took a crystal glass from a leather case fastened to the back of the bench in front of her, held the glass out, and the servant dutifully filled it. She noticed her cousins grabbing handfuls of biscuits from the plates on the trolley and stuffing them into their pockets while their mother's back was turned. Lara tried to hide her smile.

Sitting on the bench somehow reminded her of a moment from her childhood when she was at her lessons.

Father Cairn was her favorite teacher. He was rail-thin, with a head of wild white hair and a cheerful expression. He loved to laugh and tease, as well as tell little jokes.

When he gave instruction, he always stood at the front of the room in High Hall that served as the academic classroom for the noble children of the castle. Lara did not think it fair that she was forced to learn *with* the other children when she knew she was entitled to private tutors. Her father, though, had insisted. "There's much to be said for learning alongside your peers," he had told her when she first protested at age six. Her grandfather had agreed with her father's wisdom and there was no denying the High Marshal.

She took a sip of her drink, smacking her lips and relishing both the sweetness and tartness of it, recalling one lesson in particular about the hierarchy of the realm. How old had she been? Seven? Eight?

"Who is the Lord of the Realm, the protector and ruler of West Marque?" Father Cairn had asked, pacing back and forth at the front of the room. He had his hands behind his back and was staring down at the floor as he paced.

"The High Marshal." The class had responded as one.

"Who serves the High Marshal?" Father Cairn asked.

"The Marshals, the Princes of the seven seats of West Marque," came the response.

"Who serves the Marshals?"

"The Marshal's Men, the greater nobility, the small lords of the Realm."

"Who serves the Marshal's Men?"

"The landed gentry, also known as the small nobility."

"Who serves the landed gentry?"

"The landed folk, the salt of the earth."

He smiled. "And who does the High Marshal serve?"

"The Giver above."

"Yes," he had cried, clapping enthusiastically, his face beaming with his infectious smile that was quickly reflected on the faces of his students, Lara included. "Well done, my pupils."

A favorite expression of Father Cairn's was, "Keep your head in your work, your feet on the ground, your heart at home, and you will be fine."

Lara had decided long ago that that expression didn't really apply to her. It was wisdom better suited for those who served.

She should consider herself lucky that she was living in such a time and had the means to witness the Call from a private box, in a seat of honor. *No*, she decided, *it is not luck; it is my privilege, my birthright.*

She was not born one of the landed folk or the daughter of some petty noble, she was the High Marshal's granddaughter and as such the best things in life were hers, were *meant* to be hers. That thought filled her with a smug satisfaction and brought a smile to her lips.

"What are you smiling at, dear?" her aunt asked, stiff-faced as usual.

"Nothing, Aunt," she replied.

"I did not ask what your thought was worth," her aunt snapped, her mouth drawn into a peevish little line. "I asked what your thought *was*."

"Oh," Lara replied airily, waving away her aunt's sour remark with a hand. "I was just thinking how fortunate I am to be able to attend this event."

Her aunt stared at her a moment and then nodded. "Yes, you are. *We* are." She patted her niece's knee with the closest thing approaching affection in this cold woman.

Oh, for the Giver's sake! I can see why my uncle can't stand you, Lara thought. She smiled at her aunt, who nodded in return before removing her hand to return to her knitting.

The front door to the car burst open and one of her other cousins came running in. It was Benjamin, or Benny. He was the youngest of Aunt Corrine's brood. He was only five and already terribly willful. He had a smear of chocolate on one cheek and was wearing an impish grin. The grin disappeared, though, when Maude's disapproving eyes fell on him. "Clean that muck off your face," she snapped at him.

The boy reached up and rubbed the chocolate off as best he could, then sucked it off his fingers. Maude let out a loud huff and was starting to stand up to do the job herself when Aunt Corrine entered. She looked winded. Her face was red and strands of her black hair fell across her forehead and over her cheeks. "There you are," she panted. "Benny, come with me." She held out her hand and Benny ran and grabbed it. Given the child's nature, Lara knew he ran to his mother not out of obedience, but to escape the scrubbing Maude would have given him.

When they had left the car, Maude turned to her own children and sniffed. "You see that one. *That* is what comes of disobedience and lack of discipline. He can afford to be a fool, though. *He* will never amount to anything. You cannot. As heirs and stewards, all of you have responsibilities to the realm."

Lara drained her cup and put it back into its leather holder. She sighed. She was growing tired of her family's company, having seen plenty of her uncles, aunts, and cousins on the trip. Even Alice.

Lara frowned thinking of Alice. There was a calmness — even a pleasantness — about her that Lara had not seen the few other times she had been in Alice's company. Alice appeared *almost* normal. She carried herself well, spoke politely and calmly, and said none of the cruel things that usually sprang so easily to her lips. It was only her eyes that betrayed the malevolent darkness lurking within. She acted as if she had some purpose and this charade was necessary in order for her to carry it off.

I will see little of them when we finally get to Seawall, Lara thought. *Oh, I do hope we will get there soon.*

She stared back out the window. They were crossing a high bridge now, traveling over a great valley that had two rivers running along its bottom. She craned her neck to get a glimpse of what lay ahead to the west, and saw mountains looming on the horizon. They were called the Teeth and they marked the border between Shieldgate and Seawall. Some said they were ugly mountains. Lara though, who was so anxious to get to Jonah's Sword, thought they were the most beautiful things in the realm.

Twenty-Six

The Fifth Wheel — John Gray

Gray had pushed his mount, and the Dead Priest was now only two days' ride ahead. He had lost the trail briefly at Four Forks, not knowing the direction the man was heading, and had to double back several times before catching the scent again. He was certain now that the sorcerer was heading west with purpose.

The rains of early summer were light but steady, accompanied by a cool wind. In the past week he had only once caught a momentary glimpse of the sun, casting a beam on a distant meadow. He knew the farmers would welcome the rains, but they made for miserable riding.

The frontier was far behind him and every night he slept beneath a sound roof in a dry bed. The wilderness had receded and was replaced by stretches of farmland and pasture. What woods the roads cut through were small, and there were bridges to cross instead of fords. Every few miles he passed through a hamlet, if not a village or town. The buildings were older, taller, and as many were made of stone and brick as were made of wood. He even rode down some cobbled streets. The saloons — so frequent on the edges of civilization — gave way to public houses, inns and, in the larger towns, hotels. Wherever people congregated there was talk of the Call. Gray ignored it and stayed focused on his pursuit.

The taint of the Dead Priest was stronger on the land now. It was as though the man was leaving a physical trail to follow. The air was charged with a negative energy and nature itself seemed disturbed by his passage.

The man's trail turned, heading south and west toward the Long Timber. The great forest was another wild place, but this one was in the heart of Shieldgate rather than on the frontier. It had been a haven for outlaws once, and still was in a way. It was certainly a place where the desperate tried to hide from whatever pursued them. Many folk heroes of old had some connection to the forest. And there were grimmer stories that spoke of monsters.

When he entered the Timber the mood became oppressive. The large trees loomed over the road, barring any direct daylight and covering everything in green gloom. Black birds flitted from branch to branch as though they were following him, and things were lurking in the shadows, keeping pace with his horse. The road was nearly dry, despite the rain, so thick was the tangle of branches and limbs above. Only in rare places did puddles congregate.

There were villages in the forest. Most were located many miles north on the Slate Road, but there was a handful that dotted the banks of the Scale River to the south. There was only one place ahead of him, and Gray wasn't surprised that the Dead Priest was heading in that direction.

Giver's Arch had a turbulent history. The town was built along the banks of the Crow's Banquet River, a tributary that fed the Scale, and it had once supported an abbey. Because of its remoteness the town escaped the ravages of the Doom, the great plague that killed nearly a quarter of the realm's population over 500 years ago, and was quiet during the Peasant Rebellion that followed. During the War of the Inquisition, however, it was a center of the Inquisition's power. One of High Marshal's armies had stormed the town and put all the holy men and townspeople to the sword. That was how the Crow's Banquet got its name, as the birds came to feast on the bodies that choked the waterway. Years later, the Querling family purchased the land from the High Marshal and re-established the community, though the abbey was left a ruin.

The village was now the residence of Edward Querling, the surviving heir of the Querling family. He was a strange man of peculiar science who called himself an "anti-structuralist". His theory was that humans placed conscious limits on themselves through the artificial structures they created — whether those structures were time, money, physical measurements, or even the law of the land itself. Furthermore, he believed that by freeing oneself of these structures one could be capable of anything, even flight.

He was laughed at by most and scorned by many, and earned the nickname "the Mathematician," which mocked his apparent loathing of numbers. In his youth the Mathematician had passionately promoted his ridiculous theories in the academic halls of the capital. Getting nowhere, he had retreated to his remote estate to write books instead. He was now in his fifties and had gained some followers, mostly idle and feather-headed nobles who periodically went on a pilgrimage of sorts to Giver's Arch to pay homage to the *great man*.

They also load the Mathematician's pockets with money while he loads many of the women's bellies with his bastards, Gray noted.

It was near dusk when he arrived at Giver's Arch. A flat gray sky lent its power to the approaching evening's gloom and Gray felt the Dead Priest's presence.

The forest had been cleared over a thousand years ago, first to make way for the abbey, then for the town and the fields that surrounded and supported it.

Many of the buildings on the edge of the village were abandoned; the same could be said of the fields and gardens, which were thick with weeds and overgrowth. An orchard he passed was wild and choked with thorn bushes. Pigs, goats, chickens, and sheep wandered, seemingly untended. The heart of the community, though, still stood, and the orange lamp light coming from the windows of the buildings was almost welcoming. Gray's horse's hooves squelched in the mud as he approached.

The town's square was next to the eastern bank. Beyond that was an ancient and sturdy stone bridge that some said gave the village its name. On the other side of the river was the Mathematician's manse, hidden in the trees.

The greatest glow came from the windows of the town's only remaining inn, which was located off the square. The sign above the inn's door depicted the image of an elderly lady holding a rose in her pale hand. The *Tarnished Rose. He* hitched his horse and entered the establishment.

The Mathematician's followers — his faithful — were gathered around the common room's fire, making merry. Most sat on wooden benches, laughing and clapping, while three men played a popular rill on their fiddles. A plump woman was accompanying them on a squeezebox.

Some patrons stood in clumps in the back of the room, tankards and bottles in hand, but only a few noticed Gray enter. One of them, a dandy with a yellow coat, square jaw, and a heavy hickory walking stick, detached from the company and came over to greet him. "Welcome, stranger," he said, a crooked grin splitting the bottom of his handsome face. His eyes flitted briefly to the guns on Gray's hips. "Come, have some wine. Join us."

Gray nodded as the rill ended. One of the fiddlers finished with a flourish of his bow and then gave a little hop, clicking his heels together when he was in the air, nearly bumping his head on the low ceiling in the process. This was met with wild applause and laughter.

What Gray saw surrounding him were mostly youthful faces, the privileged sons and daughters of wealthy families who had little work to do at home, but plenty of time to listen to the idle ramblings of the Mathematician. There were few wrinkled faces and grey hairs in this crowd. And he saw only two people of lesser means — a man in a patched and threadbare coat who stared into the fire in the hearth, clutching a wine bottle, and a woman whose face was more painted than the rest and was missing one of her front teeth. She was tucked under the arm of a fat-faced fool. *Both are staying warm in their own ways,* he thought.

The man who had greeted him extended a hand. "Henry Owens," he said. When Gray shook it, he noted how smooth it was. *No calluses for this one.* He examined Owens closely. He had a square jaw, thick dark hair that stuck from under the brim of his hat, a wide, flat nose, and bright intelligent eyes. There was no hint that the Dead Priest had any hold on him.

"John Gray," was all Gray gave him.

After a moment of silence, Owens asked, "What brings you to our little corner of the realm, sir? Have you come to hear the words of Lord Querling?" He eyed Gray up and down and smiled, "You hardly seem the type."

"I have little interest in what the Mathematician has to say," Gray agreed with a nod.

"Then *why* are you here?" Owens wondered, offering an open bottle of wine to Gray.

Gray sniffed at the bottle's contents suspiciously before taking a swig. It was a very sweet and it took all his effort to not spit out what little he had in his mouth. He swallowed. "I'm looking for someone."

Owens chuckled. "Aren't we all?"

Gray grunted. "I'm not looking for a woman. I'm looking for a man who I have some business with." He handed the bottle back to Owens and decided to change the subject. "So what does this Mathematician talk about anyway?"

Owens shrugged. "The same things that he's been talking about for decades now. How numbers, figures, and all fixed structures are evil. This includes, of course, marriage, money, business, etcetera, etcetera," he ticked the items off on his fingers as he listed them. "Truth be told, I don't listen to a word he says." A smile tugged at the corners of his mouth. "Like you, I have limited interest in what Querling has to say."

"Then why are *you* here?" Gray asked.

Owens raised an eyebrow. "Why, I'm here with a woman who *I* have some business with." He laughed, and Gray smiled.

The pair talked while the Mathematician's admirers carried on around them. The woman Owens came with was named Scarlet Henry. She was up at the manse with a dozen other followers of the anti-structuralist. Owens wasn't pleased about it, but was worried he'd upset his lady friend if he voiced his opinions about the Mathematician too fiercely.

"Everything the academics say about him is true. The man is both deluded and a fraud," he said quietly, so only

Gray could hear. "He talks about the evils of money, but gladly takes the donations of his admirers. I am thoroughly convinced he is wealthy beyond belief, so freely do these fools pile gifts of coin and other things upon him." He looked at the company around them with distaste.

"He is quite open about his opinions on sex," Owens continued. "He declares marriage is just a convention made by man to shackle man, but men and women should love freely and openly. And when it comes to women, they should be free and open — with him mostly. He dips his spoon into any honey pot that opens for him and most of the women here do."

Owens paused for a moment, perhaps thinking about what the Mathematician was doing with his friend, Scarlet, because he suddenly snarled, "I want to throttle the man." Realizing he had raised his voice, he dropped back down to nearly a whisper. "Still, there is something charismatic about him. I don't know what it is. I want to hate him, but I can't."

Gray decided it was time to ask about the Dead Priest. "Has there been a rider through here recently? Dressed mostly in black and carrying guns?"

"This would be your *business associate*." The smile was back on Owens' face. "Yes. He arrived two days ago."

Gray felt his heart hammering. He was close to his prey and was prepared for the showdown that would ensue. He kept his voice calm as he asked, "Where's he at?"

"He went to Querling's manse."

"Then I must make my way there, too." He turned to go, but Owens put a hand on his arm and stopped him. "My dear fellow, he's not there anymore."

"When did he leave?" Gray shook his arm free from Owens' grasp. "What did he do while he was here?" There was no friendliness in Gray's tone. It was time to get some answers.

If Owens was put off by Gray's abruptness he didn't let it show. "He stayed the night and left very early the next morning. He met with Querling and they had a long, secretive chat in Querling's inner sanctum, a place reserved for only the truly devout and prettiest women. I am neither, so I wasn't privy to their conversation. Scarlet was, though. However, if you want to know more, I suggest you talk to the Mathematician himself."

"I'll do just that." Gray tipped his hat to Owens. "Thanks for the wine and company." Owens said nothing, but the smile was there and he tipped his hat in return. Gray left the inn, untied and mounted his horse, and started toward Querling's.

It was dark, with only the feeble orange light from a few windows spilling onto the narrow street. His shadow, long and twisted, stretched in front of him as he made his way across the stone bridge, his horse's shoes ringing on the stones. On the other side of the bridge, the road slipped into the near complete blackness of the forest. Ahead and to the right he could see some lights far back through the trees. Two whitewashed pillars marked the gravel lane that led to the house. Gray turned his horse and made his way down it.

He came up to the main house, large and looming. Most of the house was several centuries old, reflecting a more elegant time, but the central part was new, built in recent memory. Lanterns flanked the front doors, the yellow light from them filling the stone porch and leaking out onto the gravel beyond. There was no light coming from any of the windows.

Gray hitched his horse to a rail and walked up the doors. The heavy bronze knockers, complete with grotesque gargoyle faces, were old, and they seemed to drink in the light rather than reflect it. He grabbed a knocker and rapped hard. He waited for only a few seconds before knocking again.

He heard the bolts being drawn and the door was opened. It was bright inside the manse, and Gray could hardly make out the shadowed face of the servant. He was insignificant looking and sleight of frame, with a neatly trimmed beard. Gray could see he was smiling.

"I am here to see the master of the house," Gray said. The man opened his mouth to say something, probably to turn him away, but Gray had already thrown open his coat showing his badge of office, as well as the guns on his hips.

The man blinked, his eyes flicking from the silver star pinned to Gray's breast pocket to the holstered guns at his sides. Gray pushed his way past the man into a large entrance hall.

The man coughed lightly. "And you are?"

"John Gray, Fifth Wheel. I am here to parley with the Math— ... Master Querling. I have questions for him."

The man smiled, but it looked more like a grimace. His complexion was sallow in the brighter light of the hall. "I will let the master know you are here. Please wait. I will return shortly." Gray nodded.

The man went down the hall and through a door on the left. As Gray waited he took in the surroundings. Despite a supposed aversion to money, the Mathematician had spared no expense in the upkeep of his home. The floorboards were new, and freshly waxed and polished, as was the rosewood paneling. Several ornate chandeliers — loaded with beeswax candles — hung from the ceiling, and there were additional candles in shiny brass sconces on the walls. There were also oil paintings, portraits, most likely of Querling's ancestors and above them a few nudes, pretty women in provocative poses.

After a few minutes the servant returned. He was still wearing a smile, which was now less of a grimace. "The master will be happy to see you," he said. "Shall I take your coat?"

"Thank you, no," Gray responded, waving away the man's outstretched hand. "Lead on."

The smile-grimace returned. "As you wish." The eyes flicked to the guns again. "This way."

Gray was led to a large parlor. It was an elegant chamber with carved oak trim, hand-painted yellow wallpaper patterned with green leaves and ivy, and a thick blue rug that nearly covered the entire floor. A fire roared in a large fireplace and there was an ornate brazier located in each corner of the room. Each brazier was fashioned to look like a dragon and had thick blue smoke leaking from the nostrils. The fireplace and braziers made the room uncomfortably warm and the air was filled with the musky scent of incense. Seated on the floor, on a large cushion with his back to the fireplace, was the Mathematician. Surrounding him were his followers, all women dressed in silk pajamas like the princess-pretenders of Far Reach. Their clothing revealed as much as any lowborn doxy's, and more. They lounged seductively on cushions of their own and their eyes were on him as he entered. A few of them gave him lusty stares. Despite himself, he felt his manhood stir. It had been a while since he had been with a woman, the last being a wench in Barres Beacon who was no great prize. A startling-looking creature with bright red hair was leaning on the Mathematician's shoulder, her hand resting idly in his lap. Gray wondered if this was Owens' Scarlet.

These women were clearly chosen for their attractiveness and would have stood out at any ball or social occasion. Gray was surprised and somewhat disappointed by the Mathematician's appearance, however. He looked ordinary, almost shabby. *The great prophet looks like a bumpkin, a rural teacher, or a city clerk,* he thought. His clothing was drab. He had no remarkable features *except* his pale gray eyes, which glared out at Gray and the world from the shadows.

The Mathematician dismissed the servant with a flick of his fingers. The man bowed and made his way out. "Who have we here?" the Mathematician asked. He spoke clearly and without hesitation.

Gray bowed slightly and touched the brim of his hat. "I am John Gray, Fifth Wheel, Knight of the Realm." Because of the shadows he could not be certain, he thought he saw one of the Mathematician's eyebrows rise. The eyes of his followers did not waver and stayed fixed on the visitor. "I have some questions for you."

The Mathematician gestured toward an empty cushion near Gray's feet. "Have a seat and we will talk. Would you like something to drink?"

Gray shook his head. "I don't want to impose on your hospitality. I intend to be brief."

"Well, you might not be thirsty, but I am." The Mathematician chuckled and some of the ladies around him chuckled as well. He lazily picked up a crystal goblet from the floor beside him and presented it to the red-haired woman at his elbow. "Scarlet, be a darling and get me some wine."

This *was* Owens' companion then.

"Of course," Scarlet said, removing her hand from his groin and taking the glass. As she stood up, the slit in her pajamas opened, revealing her bare thighs and the patch of red hair between them. Gray caught the scent of her perfume as she walked past him and went to the sideboard to fill the Mathematician's glass from a decanter there. When she passed by him again to return to the Mathematician's side, Gray could see the silhouette of her bare buttocks. Again, his manhood stirred and he shifted uncomfortably on his cushion.

"Is something bothering you?" the Mathematician asked as Scarlet smiled, almost knowingly. "You look stressed and agitated, sir. Too many hard days on the trail, I'd wager, doing the realm's *good* work. Well *good* work should be *rewarded*. After all, what is life without rewards? What is life if it is consumed by one's duty and labor?"

Gray had no words, so the Mathematician pressed forward. "Scarlet," he said, turning to her. "Be a good girl and comfort our weary traveler. Rub his shoulders and soothe his weary bones."

She got up and moved over to Gray. He drank in the promise of her form beneath her flimsy clothes before she slipped in beside him. He felt her warmth immediately. It was nearly unnatural, and her perfume filled his nostrils, making him lightheaded. He struggled to find his thoughts and he felt Scarlet's warm hands on the back of his neck.

"You, sir, are a *prisoner*," the Mathematician said. Gray tensed, but relaxed as the man continued. "You are a prisoner to duty and duty is nothing more than structure imposed by one person upon another."

"I am no prisoner to duty," Gray managed to say, conscious now of how much he was enjoying Scarlet's magic fingers.

The Mathematician laughed at that and the women joined in. Scarlet's laughter was soft and close to Gray's ear. He could feel her breath on his neck. "Oh, but you *are*. It was duty that brought you here and it was the *messenger* that told me you would come."

"Who is this *messenger?*" Gray's words were heavy in his mouth, almost slurred. He felt Scarlet's lips on his neck, her hands running down his sides toward his waist.

"Why, he is the man you seek. He is the man you pursue, although you do not *really* know why you pursue him." Gray, though, *did* know. The man was a Dead Priest. He felt Scarlet tugging at his belt, the belt that held his guns. His hands shot down and clamped on her wrists. She cried out in pain. The spell was broken.

"What sort of sorcery is this?" Gray shouted, his wits returning quickly. He pushed Scarlet away as though she were some great, clinging spider.

"Ho, ho," chuckled the Mathematician. Something in the man's manner reminded Gray of Predrag Laundry. "You *are* a tense fellow."

"You are trying to put me under some spell," Gray said, his hands on the grips of his guns. "Are you some form of sorcerer? Sorcery is a great crime. It is—"

The Mathematician waved Gray's accusation aside as he took another sip of wine. "Ridiculous." Gray could see his smile, his teeth flashing in the dull orange light of the room. "I am no more a sorcerer than you."

"Then the man you call *the messenger* has left some of his power behind and bewitched you."

"No," snapped the Mathematician. "He did *not* bewitch me. He enlightened me. He told me *you* would come. *You*," he stabbed a finger at Gray, "some *lawman*, a *slave* of structure and the realm."

"I am *no* slave," Gray replied calmly.

"You barge into *my* home, *demanding* answers to questions, scaring *my* guests," he gestured at Scarlet who indeed looked frightened. "Come here, my darling," he said soothingly, patting the floor beside him. She moved over to him and he placed a comforting arm over her shoulders.

"This so-called *messenger* is a Dead Priest," Gray snapped. "He summoned an abomination that killed many innocent people."

The room was silent and the eyes of the women were fixed on him. The Mathematician drained his glass and placed it on the floor. He placed his hands together and rested his chin on the tips of his long fingers, looking long and hard at the Fifth Wheel. Finally, he said, "You have *your* story and the messenger has his. The question I must ask myself is which story do I believe?"

He stood up. Gray was struck by his height. He was six and half feet tall and slender. His drab clothes hung loosely on his frame. He absently stroked Scarlet's hair. "You know," he said, turning toward the fire and turning his back on Gray, "the thing I hate most about human laws is how unnatural many of them are. How *against* nature most of them are."

"How so?" Gray asked, angry with himself for asking because he did not want to get into a philosophical discussion with this man.

The Mathematician bent down and started prodding the logs in the fire with a heavy iron poker. "The law says stealing is wrong. And yet in nature, it is perfectly natural to steal. The raccoon steals from the nest, the bee steals from the flower, the fish steals from the sea, and so on. And we steal as well. We steal from the land. We steal from nature all the time. We do so for the same reason that any animal does. We do so to survive.

"So when man's law says, stealing is wrong, it means stealing select things — human things — coins, cash and property — is wrong. The law says steal certain things, but not others. *This* is the structure that I abhor." He poked furiously into the embers, stirring up the flames as he did so. Gray said nothing.

"The law says a man can only have one wife. This, too, is against nature. For it is in our nature to procreate, or attempt to procreate, as frequently as possible." He stood up and turned to face Gray, his eyes blazing. "This is the structure I abhor." He stepped forward and stood by Scarlet, who looked up at the man adoringly.

"The law says, killing is wrong, and yet in nature killing occurs all the time," he leveled the poker at Gray, his hand shaking. "The wolf *kills* the deer, the fox *kills* the hen, the spider *kills* the fly, and so on. And we kill as well. In fact, we *happily kill* to set a good table and we invite friends and family around that table to laugh over and feast upon the carcass.

"So when man's law says, *killing is wrong*, it means killing certain things — humans and living property — is wrong. And, at *this* moment, *this* is the structure that I abhor."

He raised the poker over his head and screeched at the top of his lungs, "Ladies, *kill* this agent of structure so that we may laugh over and feast upon his carcass."

As a single host, the women in the room shrieked and sprang toward Gray. He had very little time to react, as he had been transfixed by the passion with which the Mathematician had delivered his words. He sidestepped the closest women and freed himself from the grasp of another. Scarlet managed to rake her fingernails across his face. He stumbled back and drew his guns. The Mathematician was wading forward through his followers, the poker above his head, with murder in his eyes. Gray squeezed off two shots, one from each gun. The first shot caught some unfortunate woman in the head as she leapt in front of the Mathematician, her skull, brains, and blood spraying those around her. The other bullet found its mark in the middle of the Mathematician's coat. The prophet stumbled and fell. The furious shrieks of the women turned to screams of fear and they shrank away to the edges of the room.

Gray heard the sounds of footsteps behind him and turned to see the servant rushing in from the hall. The man had a shotgun in his hands and the Fifth Wheel decided to give him no chance to use it. He put three quick bullets into him, and the servant fell to the floor, dead.

The shrieks had subsided to sobs and groans. Gray stepped forward and stood over the Mathematician, who was still alive, but bleeding out and writhing in pain. The iron poker lay discarded several feet away. Gray leveled a gun at the man's head. "Your bullshit talk is over and now I will have my answers. Did the Dead Priest give you a name? Did he tell you where he was going?"

The Mathematician coughed up some blood and glared at Gray. Gray put his boot on the man's wound and pressed. The Mathematician shrieked and the women joined in with shrieks of their own.

"Once again, I ask," Gray said through gritted teeth, "what was his name and where was he going?"

There was still defiance in the Mathematician, but there was a great deal of pain also. He decided to cough out an answer rather than face the Fifth Wheel's boot again. "He said his name was Paulus," he coughed, "and he had business near the Seawall border with a Marshal's Man, Sterngirth."

Gray knew of Marshal's Man Wallace Sterngirth. He was sometimes called the Giant because rumor was he was close to seven feet tall. He had a fierce reputation and renowned temper. Regardless of his reputation and temperament, he was Marshal's Man of the Four Valley Region, a region plagued with banditry. The Fifth Wheel was not welcome there, as Sterngirth had his own private army and used it to maintain the law and make war on the bandits. He was a reclusive sort and his people were reclusive as well, sticking to their own. "What would a Dead Priest want from Wallace Sterngirth?" Gray wondered aloud.

"I do not know," the Mathematician answered. He gasped in pain, and added, "He did not say."

Gray looked down at the anti-structuralist and felt no pity for him. With his eyes locked on the Mathematician, he said to the women in the room, "I am leaving now. This one here may live or he may die. I suggest that after I depart you run to town and find a doctor as quick as you can. You know what occurred here. I did what I had to do to maintain the law of the land." He swept his gaze over the women huddled against the walls. "Consider yourselves lucky that I am not taking any action against *you*; that I am overlooking your open hostility toward a Knight of the Realm."

With that, he quickly made his way out of the Mathematician's manse and collected his horse. He mounted up, now armed with a name and a destination. He knew his quarry and he knew where his quarry was headed.

Twenty-Seven

The Dead Priest — Quentus

Leaving the bone yard they had traveled south and east, leaving West Marque behind and entering the Eastern Range as they crossed the Murk. Now they were making their way through the northern tip of the Silent Woods. *And they are silent*, Quentus said to himself. *Almost as silent as this girl.* She sat in front of him on the saddle, tucked tightly between his legs. He looked down at the top of her head, which was swaying ever so slightly with the horse's step. "A nice day, isn't it, child?" Above, through the gaps in the green leaves, the sky was blue, not a cloud in sight. The blue was made more vibrant by the bright spring sun. *It'll be summer in a few days.*

The girl stayed silent. She had only whispered a few times in Salene's ear. *And that is a good start*, he decided. He gently patted her shoulder and glanced over at Salene. She was staring at him, amusement in her eyes. He sighed. Her lips curled into a smile.

"It's two against one, I see, girl," Quentus huffed. The girl gave a slight shrug and a sound that could mean agreement. Quentus' jaw dropped for a second, and then he shook with quiet laughter. "I see how it's going to be, then," he said through a smile of his own. And maybe, just maybe, the girl was wearing a smile too.

The resilience of children is amazing, he thought. *If I'd gone through half what she has endured, I'd be broken.*

You did *go through the trial of the dark rite*, a voice that was not quite his own whispered inside him, taking him back to that time on the Blasted Rock, and knocking the smile from his lips. He quickly stilled that voice before it could say anything else.

It was near mid-day and they would stop soon to rest, take a bite, and quench their thirst. Up ahead he heard the sound of a brook or stream. *We'll stop there,* he decided. He signaled to Salene and they moved ahead.

The water poured over the rocks, cool, clear, and inviting. But a closer look revealed that there was a certain thickness to it — *like mucus,* Quentus thought. Below the surface he could see thick clots of slimy green algae hanging over the sides of the rocks like fingers. The green was off-putting, the color of something that one would think would cling to the walls of a sick person's bowels. There was a smell in the air, too, of rot and decay.

Poison.

Quentus' lips curled and he crinkled his nose. He turned away in disgust. He felt the spongy wetness of the ground beneath his feet. With each step he heard a sucking sound as the earth gripped the bottom of his boots.

"The water's sour," he said, "and I don't like the look of the grass that grows here either." The grass was a bluish-green and it looked like it was covered in dust. .

"Gray grass," Salene noted. "The horses shouldn't eat it."

Quentus mounted up. "Maybe up ahead there'll be some better ground."

Salene glanced around at the woods surrounding them. "I doubt it," she muttered. "We'll probably have to eat and drink in our saddles."

She was right. If anything, the ground grew worse. Soon all the trees were dead and covered in a silver mold, and tall shelves of fungus the color of old bone hugged the base of nearly every tree. "Grave fungus," Quentus spat. He could smell it. A smell of rot and decay mixed with a terrible sweetness. It was a wretched smell, nausea-inducing and cloying all at once. The only living things that Quentus could see were large orange ants with bloated and mottled abdomens. They swarmed over the fungal mounds.

And there was *something* else.

He had sensed they were being followed since they left the stream. He chanced glances when he could, scanning the woods around them for any sign of their pursuer. He would like to have used his far-sight, but he couldn't risk it. It would upset the girl. More than that, it might upset whatever was locked up inside her. *I'd much rather face whatever is out there.*

Suddenly, he saw it. It was just a quick glimpse of a darker shadow sliding in and out of the gloom of the forest. Whatever it was, it was big and moving fast, stalking some prey. *Stalking us*, he realized.

Was it a Range wolf? He wondered. He had seen a pair when they came out of the bone yard, far off in the distance. They were partially hidden in the tall grass and moving quickly away, perhaps having already learned the danger of mounted humans. They were young and small, a year or two old, most likely pushed out of their pack to start one of their own.

No. Whatever it was that was lurking in the woods was no Range wolf. Even the solitary males that could grow to immense size weren't *that* big. It wasn't a bear, either. He felt the hairs rising on the back of his neck.

This thing was not afraid of them. It saw them as potential food. It was cautious as well, which meant a certain kind of cunning, if not intelligence. He thought hard, trying to figure what exactly the creature was, and what it was planning. *It won't strike in the day,* he decided. *It had had an opportunity to do so when we were at the stream. It will wait until night.*

His dark eyes flicked toward Tabby. She was riding with Salene now. *Hasn't she suffered enough? Must she see the horrors that haunt the Eastern Range so soon?*

He clenched his free fist, the one that wasn't holding the horse's reins. Even so, the horse whickered, sensing the unease of its rider. *The thing will die.* He was determined. *It won't harm her.*

His hand slipped down to the butt of his pistol. His thumb slid over the smooth wood of the grip and he found comfort in it. *I'll just be the distraction, though. Salene will take the shot that will bring it down.*

He moved them north toward the edge of the wood, and he pushed the pace as much as he dared. He did not want the child to notice something was amiss.

Their pace wasn't fast enough. They were near the edge of the woods, not out of them, by the time the sun started to dip low in the west. He would have preferred to have open ground surrounding them so whatever it was would expose itself when it attacked. If they had had another hour, they would have been clear. He sighed as he dismounted and started to make camp.

The site had its merits. The trees were thin and small, and they even had a few green leaves on them, long twisted things. The undergrowth was sparse and there were some patches of green grass that the horses could forage through for clover. They were also on a small hillock and had a commanding view of the ground around them. *Will it be enough?* He hoped so.

He led the horses to the north side of the camp, while Salene gathered kindling to start a fire.

The girl pulled out the small iron cooking pot, plates, and the food they had left — rice, beans, hard bread, dried peas, and some meat from a rabbit they had caught the day before. They had plenty of rice and dried beans, but little else. *We'll have to find some game when we get clear of these woods — maybe antelope or a Range ox.* While the prospect of getting some meat pleased him, heading out into the open, away from the shelter of the trees did not. There were outlaws and others from West Marque that prowled this deep into the Eastern Range. They wouldn't be clear of them for many miles yet, *and then we'll face other hazards.*

He carefully checked the horses as he rubbed them down. They were in exceptional health, thanks more to Salene's care than his. Her people lived in their saddles, and they relied heavily on their horses. When a horse was lost on the Glaze through neglect, the rider was often lost with it. A man or woman who could not tend his or her horse was not fit to be part of the tribe.

His horse's name was Not'motter, *Night Mother*, in the girl's tongue, the tongue of West Marque. He was a gelding whose mother had been black as night. Only his mane matched his mother's coloring; the rest of him was a rich reddish brown. Salene's horse had a blonde mane and was the color of sand. The mare was graceful and powerful, *like her rider,* and her name was Sanwaevoya in the desert tongue, or *Dune Rider.* The horses got along, except when Dune Rider's blood flowed. The mare could be testy then, and Night Mother sometimes thought he still had testicles and would challenge her.

Quentus looked closely for any parasites and gave their legs and hooves one more going over before he was satisfied. Seeing nothing wrong, he left them to graze.

He walked up to the top of the rise, standing away from the fire where Salene and the girl were busy. He looked around, peering hard into the trees. Nothing. *Maybe it is frightened to come out of the shadows into the failing light of day,* he thought. *But soon it'll have the cover of darkness, all the cover it needs,* the other voice whispered inside of him.

He nearly jumped out of his skin when Salene's hand settled on his shoulder. He spun around on her and could tell she knew something was wrong.

"What is it, my love?" She spoke to him in the language of her people, the language of the desert. It was a graceful language, whereas his was blunt and brutal. When they spoke in his tongue it upset the girl, so they had stopped, speaking mostly in the language of West Marque, and only in Salene's tongue when they didn't want the girl to know what they were talking about.

"Something is out there," he replied. "I think it is hunting and we are the prey."

"I know," she said flatly. "I caught a glimpse of it earlier." Quentus was not surprised that she had already noticed it. He was surprised, though, that she had not mentioned it to him earlier. I *didn't tell her either*, he reminded himself. "It's unnatural in shape," she continued, "and it's huge."

"If it's so big, how has it eluded us?" He wondered. "Why can't we see it clearly?"

Salene shrugged. "There are some animals that can blend in with their surroundings. Maybe this is one." Her voice was calm, but when he searched her eyes he saw her concern was as great as his. "I was hoping it would go away," there was nervousness in her voice now, "give up, and look for something easier. But there's so *little* life in these woods. All I saw were a few twisted birds in the branches. There is *nothing* for it to eat here, except us."

"What are you two talking about?" The girl's voice surprised them both. They turned to look at her. She looked very afraid. "What's wrong?" She stamped her foot and curled her hands into fists, thrusting them down by her side. Her eyes were starting to fill with tears.

Salene moved over quickly to comfort her. "Hush," she said gently in the language of West Marque. "All is well." She put her arms around Tabby and hugged her, then brushed away the tears that were now falling from the girl's cheeks. "We were just talking about the road ahead."

"You're lying," the girl yelled. Salene shook her head, but the girl pushed herself away. "I know it. I see it."

Quentus stepped forward. "You're right." He saw no further reason to keep the truth from her. "There is something out there." He swept his hand toward the thicker woods to the south.

"What is it?" she asked.

Quentus shook his head. "We don't know, but it's been following us and we must be on our guard. *All* of us. That includes you. Extra eyes and ears are always welcome when you are on the lookout."

He dared to walk up to her and she did not shy away. He put his hands gently on her shoulders. She flinched, but just for a second. "Can you be strong, Tabby? Can you be another set of eyes and ears? Can you swallow your fear and let us know calmly if you see or hear anything?"

She seemed to mull that over and the expression on her face was such that, had the situation not been so serious, Quentus would have laughed. She bit her bottom lip and nodded. I can," she said, and then added with a fierceness, "I will."

— «» —

They ate in silence, each of them lost in private thought. Quentus shoveled the half-boiled rice into his mouth and chewed. He avoided staring directly at the flames of the campfire and kept his eyes on the woods. He strained to hear something, anything, but these woods were not giving up any secrets. It was very silent.

After they ate, they sat with their backs to the fire, looking out. Salene had her rifle and Quentus kept his hand close to his pistol.

Hours passed. He was tired. His eyes were heavy. The air was too warm, too comforting. It was no longer early spring or even mid spring. Sometimes the evenings were cool in spring. The nip of cool air would be welcome right now. He looked up. Above, the moon was waxing. Then he went back to scanning the woods.

Maybe it won't come, he thought. *Maybe it* has *given up.*

That's wishful thinking, the other voice inside him whispered. *It's there, watching and waiting for the right moment.*

There was a sudden shriek. It was a horrible sound. The horses screamed and reared. And suddenly something came out of the darkness. *How did it get so close?* Quentus wondered, as it seemed to materialize in front of him. The smell hit him. It wasn't the fungus that stank back in the woods. It was this *thing.* He gagged.

It was a chitinous mass, the color and translucency of shed snakeskin. Below the surface, he saw dark juices flowing and moving around under its shell. Its eyes, if they could be called that, were two ugly orbs on armored stalks that rose above the spiky block that was its head. And below the eyes was the mouth, cavernous and open, with ropes of slick saliva and mucus dangling from a jagged set of half-rotted teeth — row upon row of them disappearing into the darkness of its maw. A translucent whip swung out from its mouth, as long as a river reed. And at the end of it was a barbed stinger, black and dripping puss-colored venom.

"A demon," Quentus yelled, meaning it in the truest sense of the word. It was some spirit of this poisonous land that had been warped by a malevolent hand for some dark purpose. The man or woman who the hand belonged to had probably died thousands of years ago, and its purpose with them. But this thing was still here, an evil legacy.

Tabitha and Salene screamed almost as one. Maybe he screamed as well — a terrified chorus whose wail echoed off the sick and dead trees around them.

Tabby ran and it rushed toward her, mouth open, hissing and chittering. A feeling of dismay hit Quentus like a hammer. *Too fast. No chance.* The dismay was slowing him down. His hand was dipping toward his gun, but not quickly enough.

It was almost on her now. She shrank back and into a ball, covering her head with her hands. It was about to strike, its hungry mouth open and its stinger lolling like a dog's tongue. And then something happened. Some phantom shape reared up out of Tabby, some wild spirit, a pale vortex with a hundred angry inhuman faces, a hundred jagged blades of smoke, striking at the thing. The demon recoiled as if it had hit a wall. And Quentus shot.

He fired as quickly as his fingers and hand would allow, the bullets ripping into its head. Boney plates shattered and fragmented. Puss and ichor flew. It was knocked on its side by the multiple impacts. Its legs flailed, seeking some purchase.

Salene fired while Quentus reloaded as fast as he could. The thing rolled and staggered to its feet as the bullets from Salene's rifle plowed into it, sending it reeling. She took out an eye and a piece of its maw fell away. She blew off one of its legs. Puss was pouring from its many wounds.

It turned, looking to retreat into the darkness of the woods. Quentus was done reloading and he fired into its abdomen as it fled.

It disappeared, but its moans, almost like sobs, echoed through the night, along with the sound of snapping branches and crashing trees as it lumbered away, broken. It roared once in frustration and kept retreating.

He blinked his eyes, the ghost image of the phantom that had struck out from the girl fading into the night.

"Is it dead?" Tabby asked a moment later. Quentus spun and looked at her. She looked as meek as ever, peering out between her fingers with frightened eyes. *What happened? What did I see?* It didn't matter. Relief washed over him, and he went to her, engulfing her in a big hug. And Salene was there too, weeping and hugging her with him.

He looked down at her and she was looking at him. "And it's all thanks to you, I think. I don't know what I saw, but I think you saved all of us, girl.".

Twenty-Eight

The Novice — Marcus Dawn

Marcus' long coat was buttoned up to the collar and he was wrapped in a heavy wool cloak, which he pulled tighter around him with his mitten-covered hands. The cold air made him want to sneeze. He looked across the bay, the water like slabs of rolling gray slate, and was unimpressed by what he saw — a large stone quay, backed by a line of timber buildings and nothing else. Behind the buildings was bleak, snow-covered ground and treeless hills. This was considered civilization in Axefell.

The smell of the sea was there, ever present. It sickened him and he felt his stomach roil. When he was young he had enjoyed trips to the seaside with his family. But it was always summer, the sands of the beaches warm beneath his toes, and Mother was there to laugh encouragingly at Marcus and his siblings while they played, wrestled, and swam. This journey to Axefell made him hate the sea. He suffered from seasickness for two weeks as the boat plowed its way through rough waters. He lay below deck, confined to a stuffy cabin, puking his guts out. He had no appetite, but the ship's cook, or so the man called himself, forced Marcus to choke down bowls of broth, which inevitably came back up. He lay in the puke and sometimes his own piss and muck because there was no one was there to tend to his needs. The crewmen were rough and weathered. They thought little of their sniveling ward, foisted on them by the church, and made no attempts to hide their disgust for

Marcus Dawn. "Priest killer", they called him. When Marcus felt well enough to leave the stifling confines of the cabin and explore the deck of the ship he heard one crewmember whisper to another that they should throw him overboard. And frankly Marcus didn't care. He would have welcomed a watery grave, but no one lifted a hand against him.

For several weeks there was little to see but endless ocean, and often he looked at that through a veil of wind-whipped rain; he soon realized the Thunderfall Sea came by its name honestly. He knew the ship was beating up the coast, but any signs of the coast were hidden by miserable weather. Even when they entered Troubled Passage he saw little. Occasionally, he spied a sea bird or a large fish that caught his attention, but nothing more. The crew avoided conversation with him and when he ate his evening meals with the captain and other officers of the ship they engaged him little. Misery was his chief companion, second only to the hatred he had for his father. His father's command had placed him on this ship, bound for a land that was clearly forsaken by the Giver. At night, with his guts boiling, Marcus plotted ways to return to Seawall and exact his revenge on his dear old dad. He fantasized about murdering Lord Dawn. It was good sport, but it left him empty and bitter, and feeling helpless in the morning. Most likely he would never see his father again. There was even a good possibly his father would outlive him.

A hand slapped down on his shoulder, startling him. "This is what passes for late spring in Axefell, boy," the ship's captain said with a laugh, his warm, sour breath hitting Marcus' cheek. "Expect cold weather for several weeks yet and then insufferable heat. Summer is short, but it runs hot in these parts." There was nothing in appearance to separate the captain from his crew. He wore the same drab, salt-stained clothes as the other sailors and had the same cracked, wind-burnt face. He had yellow teeth and thin graying hair. Coarse whiskers covered his chin and traveled down his neck before they disappeared into the collar of his coat. He was in his thirties, but looked fifty. The crew whispered into Marcus' ears that their captain liked to fuck boys. But Marcus suspected it was a lie meant to scare him. If anything, the captain seemed to have a large appetite for members of the female sex, as he spoke of women often.

"Hmmm, it looks like a charming place," Marcus drawled, tasting the bile at the back of his throat.

The captain looked at him, a slight smile on his face. "Still got some spirit in you, eh? Time in the cells and exile to the north hasn't taken the wind out of your sails?" The smile vanished and the man's expression turned grim. He looked at the approaching shore. "This place will tame you, or it will *kill* you." He turned back to Marcus and eyed him up and down. "In your case, I think it will kill you."

He turned away and called out to the crew. "Make ready to bring us into port! There are goods, wine, and warm beds awaiting us! And there are women, too! So make haste and look smart. I don't want to die before I get in one last fuck." He laughed loud and long.

Once the ship was secured to the quay, Marcus was ushered ashore and sent on his way. "Head to the Witch's Tit, lad," the captain said to him, gesturing toward a large and shabby–looking seaside hotel — what might be called an inn in these parts. "One of the Brothers will meet you there, I'm sure — today, tomorrow, or Giver knows when. I did my part, now off with you."

Marcus surveyed the countryside. There was nothing to stop him from wandering off in any direction he chose. The captain must have guessed his thoughts because he started to chuckle and said, "I'd give you a day, maybe two, out there on your own." He squinted at Marcus. "Take your medicine and meet with the brothers. They will take care of you." He gently pushed Marcus in the direction of the Tit.

It was warm and suffocating inside the inn's common room. Smoke from two fireplaces mingled with smoke from many clay pipes. The smell of sweat and the sea mixed with the smell of tar, tobacco smoke, cooked meat, and strong beer. There were only a few places to sit and the best chairs were taken. Marcus found a seat on a bench by the door. He held the canvas bag, which contained his worldly belongings, including a purse of gold, close to his chest. No one noticed him, not even the big–bosomed waitress. She was large and ugly, with thin blonde hair and pimple on the end of her nose, but she still commanded the attention of the room, especially the packs of lusty sailors.

He sat for an hour, maybe two, when a man came down the stairs, saw him, and approached. He was tall, with brown hair going grey, and had a long face. He wore a greatcoat, fur-lined and made of heavy wool. He had a scar on his forehead and pale grey eyes — eyes that seemed to stare into a man rather than at him. Marcus averted his gaze as the man walked toward him.

"Marcus Dawn?" he asked. Marcus looked up into the grey, searching eyes, and nodded. "I am Brother Cleo. I won't call you brother yet, because that title is not easily earned. Get your things and come with me." Marcus slung his bag over his shoulder and followed Cleo across the room to the stairs.

"We have a few days of travel ahead of us," Cleo said as they climbed the steps. "We missed the only train by a few days, so that means hard walking for us. You'll have time to bathe, if you wish, and judging by your smell I think you should." Marcus sniffed himself self-consciously as they made their way down the hall. Cleo unlocked a door and gestured for Marcus to enter a small room. He reluctantly stepped inside while Cleo stayed in the hall. He handed Marcus the key. "I'll order you a bath and some food. We'll leave shortly." He turned and left.

Two plain-looking women poured Marcus' bath in a small tin tub that looked beaten and abused. He also had two boiled eggs and some bread. Although he was cramped in the tub, it was remarkably refreshing and cleansing. He scrutinized his arms and legs as he washed himself. He was not thick-boned like his father and two older brothers. His limbs were thin and brown. His hands were long, his fingers delicate. "A piano player's hands," his mother had said once admiringly. To which his father had replied, "A milkmaid's hands, more like."

He stepped out of the tub feeling renewed. He was free of the stink of the sea and his breakfast sat well in his stomach. He put on his clothes, gathered his things, and went downstairs.

Cleo was waiting for him and ready to go. A travel bag was slung from one shoulder and he carried a walking stick in his hand. He put his hand on Marcus' shoulder and guided him out the door. "We will not tarry," he said on the street. "We have ground to cover and time to make up."

"I didn't realize we were on a schedule," Marcus remarked, feeling his old energy return.

"We are always on a schedule," Cleo said, "one appointed us by the Giver." He clipped Marcus on the shin with his walking stick, wood on bone, and Marcus cried out in pain.

"This is not Jonah's Sword, Novice," Cleo continued as he walked with long strides. He did not look at Marcus but kept his eyes fixed on the road ahead. "No one here will take lip from you. Here you listen or pay the consequences." Marcus hobbled along as quickly as he could, trying to keep pace with the much taller man.

"You have a strong spirit, Marcus Dawn, but it's a bad spirit, a spirit that needs tempering." Marcus watched as Cleo pulled a heavy pistol from his pocket. The holy man checked to see that it was loaded and returned it to its place. "You temper steel by beating it, over and over. The same will be done to you, if necessary." He turned his gray eyes on Marcus and Marcus looked away, surveying the surrounding countryside. It was empty and uninviting. He looked back at Cleo, who nodded. "Good. Now we walk."

Twenty-Nine

The Lady of Seawall — Genevieve Goodregard

In one fluid motion, Genevieve raised the bow and drew back the string, feeling its tension on her fingers, feeling the pull in her muscles, and released. The arrow — a thin wooden shaft fixed with white goose feathers — flew. The shot looked good, but struck shy of the mark.

"Close, my lady," one of the hens behind her said. Her ladies-in-waiting were gathered together under a pavilion, hiding from the summer sun, enjoying cakes and iced tea.

They were in an enclosed yard behind the house, the noises of the city around them muffled by the high stone walls. Overhead the clear summer sky was unblemished by clouds.

It was hot, humid, and Genevieve was sweating. But she didn't mind. She brushed away a few strands of hair that were stuck to her forehead. She was wearing soft leather breeches and a dark blue silk blouse which clung to her skin, showing her form. She was still thin and willowy and lacking breasts, *like I was when I was young*, she thought.

But she didn't care.

She *felt* young.

It had been nearly a year since she last drew an arrow. She was rusty, she knew. She also knew that archery was supposed to be beneath the Lady of Seawall — or any lady of high nobility, for that matter.

But I was not always the Lady of Seawall, she thought as she drew another arrow from the quiver beside her, nocked, and loosed again. *Once I was a Noble woman.* The arrow thrummed close to the center of the target, and her ladies cheered. It was a ragged cheer. They were more interested in their gossip than in their lady's queer fascination with archery.

A smile touched her lips.

Her family's last was name Noble, but the Nobles were low nobility. On the social ladder they were just above the landed folk, a rung above simple farmers and shopkeepers. That was the reason why Genevieve was allowed to engage in a common sport. *That was the reason I was allowed to become so good at it.* Her father encouraged her in it, much to her mother's dismay. How mother had ranted and complained, but her rants and complaints fell on Seymour Noble's deaf ears.

Genevieve's father was a stubborn man, and he held little regard for what the high nobility considered proper. He was also very wealthy, and proud of that, too. His family's wealth had allowed him to land a woman from one of the important Seawall families, a family of high nobility — a Goodchance, and none other than Cecilia Goodchance. The Goodchances had power and influence, but they sorely lacked money, something that Seymour Noble had in abundance. And so a match was made.

From that union came Genevieve Noble, Melody Nobel, and a litter of other babes who died in their infancy. Mother tried to give Father a son, to give Genevieve and Melody a little brother to play with, and she did. She gave birth to two boys, in fact, but neither lived beyond their cradles. They were buried in tiny graves in the Noble family plot — next to Father and Mother. A little girl was buried there as well, Nadia, who Genevieve could scarcely remember. Nadia was four when the fever took her. A final child, the last, did not even grow in her mother's womb. It was nothing but a mass of clotted blood on a bundle of rags, which was quickly buried in the back garden — and dug up by the family dogs, if the servants' gossip was true.

It was a sore point for Genevieve's mother that she could not give Seymour his sons. *He had me and Melody instead.* Mother passed much of that pain, guilt, and disappointment in herself onto her two living daughters, both of whom had enough children of their own and sons of their own. That pain was transferred onto the girls through harsh words, delivered with a sharp, cutting tongue.

Angry, Genevieve released another arrow. This one struck the wall behind the target and split apart with a crack.

"A shame, my lady," one of her ladies shouted out. Genevieve shot an angry glare at her ladies over her shoulder. The smiles disappeared from their privileged lips. They were all high born, cultured, and well versed in the subtle machinations of high society. They had all received their *woman's education.*

Genevieve snatched up another arrow and thought of the education she had received. When she was young she suffered the best tutors, and when her breasts began to grow her mother sent her off to a convent school, to learn next to girls whose family names meant something in Seawall, and sometimes the realm. There, she became and heard the gossip of the other girls, that the Nobles were Common once and had purchased the Noble name for ten silver marques. That gossip resulted in Genevieve's first, and only, physical confrontation when she singled out the source of the gossip, Sissy Goldspun. Sissy was a mean and mouthy little creature. Genevieve had left that fray with her head held high, a torn dress, and scraped elbows and knees. Sissy had stumbled away, sobbing, with a split lip and broken nose — a nose that remained crooked to this day, and caused Genevieve no guilt whatsoever whenever she saw it.

Oh, how father had laughed when he heard about that. He laughed even harder at mother's embarrassment and shame.

Genevieve released her arrow and relished the satisfying sound of it hissing into the bale, well in the center of the target. She flexed her fingers. They were already sore and she had only fired a dozen arrows. The archery butt was nothing more than a bale of hay, and the target was nothing more than a white kerchief with a red dot painted in its center. But they would do, they would more than do. She forgot how much she enjoyed sending arrows toward the target.

She waited as the servant — one of the houseboys — removed the arrow before she drew another. The boy cleared the area and she nocked again. She loosed and felt the snap of the bowstring on the bracer that protected her left forearm and wrist.

There was a groan of disappointment from her ladies as this arrow fell farther from the center of the target than the last. *Not one of them could draw back the string,* she thought, *and they would miss the side of a barn if they could manage to fire an arrow.*

Genevieve adjusted the bracer slightly. It was a worn piece of green leather, an artifact from her youth that she had kept. The first bow that her father had gotten her was long gone, a toy that was replaced by newer and grander weapons, but the bracer remained. *And it still fits.*

The bow she was holding now was a beautiful thing. The stave was made of yew, specifically crafted for her hand and dimensions. It was hers, something she had gotten for herself, in secret. She later found out that Sylvan had known everything and had made certain the bowyer had done his very best when making it. Still, when she had handed over the money and the bowyer had handed over the bow she felt a certain thrill, thinking that her husband remained ignorant.

All wives should have their secrets — even if they aren't really secrets at all.

She also had a case crafted for the bow. It was nearly as fine as the bow itself, green leather lined with velvet, with silver clasps, and her name embossed on it in gold. *Genevieve Goodregard.*

Goodregard. Her husband's name, and now hers.

She drew another arrow and fired. It struck the side of the target.

"Perhaps my lady needs some refreshment," she heard one of her ladies cry. She waved the remark away.

Sylvan was a good husband, fine and handsome, but he had not been Genevieve's choice. *Mother had made that match.* She had loosed Genevieve like an arrow into society and hit her intended mark, attaching her daughter to the eldest son of the Marshal of Seawall.

Had it been the other, *had it been* my *intended mark, my life would have been very different.*

She tried to remember his face, but couldn't. Twenty-five years was too wide a gulf for any clear memories from her youth to cross … and she had only seen him a few times.

He was Sylvan's brother, Xavier. *I desired him, but so too did all the single women in the realm and most of the married women, I imagine.* She grabbed another arrow.

Xavier Goodregard was the type of man women dreamt of when they slept, only to wake flushed and exhausted. She loosed her arrow and grinned as it struck very close to the middle of the target.

He was tall, handsome, oh, so very handsome. He was gallant, a good dancer, exceptional conversationalist, good rider, and according to rumor, well-versed in bed play. He was a fairytale prince, a shadow that his older brother, Sylvan, and his younger brother, Brand, had to live under. He eclipsed all men who had the misfortune to keep his company — and the company he kept was large, as all the men loved him. They all wanted to be around him because they wanted to be him.

He was a hero, *and he was a great fool.* He read too many romances and put too much stock in romantic heroes. And in his quest to emulate those bits of fiction, he chose a hero's death, a romantic death — which, in the end, is really just death. He commanded the rearguard in the last war, covering the retreat of what was left of Seawall's army as it limped home after its final defeat. He fought hard, he fought well, and he died. His sacrifice earned his father an easy peace, a peace that Sylvan and Genevieve now enjoyed. Why? Because Ablechance Mainhouse was like most men. He liked heroes, especially martial ones.

"You have lost your best," High Marshal Mainhouse had said to Sylvan's father when they met to negotiate the terms. Everyone expected the terms would be harsh, until Mainhouse added. "You lost your son, and that's enough."

Sylvan's father apologized for his wrongs, swore his loyalty to the Mainhouse family, recognized Ablechance as the true High Marshal of the Realm ... and all was forgiven.

But not forgotten. The pride of Seawall would not allow it.

Pride. The badge that men liked to wear on their puffed out chests; the burden that men carried so easily.

She snatched up another arrow and loosed it, feeling it all come back. The arrow struck the edge of the bright red circle. Her ladies cheered.

The pride of Seawall is different from the pride of Shieldgate. In Shieldgate pride is a cool thing that comes accompanied with a stiff upper lip. In Seawall pride burns hot and it takes a long time for it too cool. Perhaps, it never cools.

How stupid men are, she thought. Ablechance Mainhouse could have ended it all, the Goodregard family, Seawall itself, but he chose to forgive and forget because some boy gave his life in a noble retreat. She felt the sneer on her lip and uncurled it.

Men seldom kick an opponent when he is down. Women, on the other hand, scratch their opponent's eyes out the moment they are vulnerable.

And so she married Sylvan. Xavier had died in battle and the youngest Goodregard boy, Brand, died shortly after the war from his wounds. He was always the weak one. Genevieve remembered he had a nice smile.

She heard a disruption behind her and turned to see Bishop Michael entering the courtyard. He was smiling, his eyes fixed on the plump, pretty ladies of the court. He gave them a gracious bow, *too gracious for a Bishop*, Genevieve thought, and then turned to give Genevieve an even more gracious bow. She favored him with a slight smile and turned back to her archery work.

Let him wait, she thought. *He chose to keep me in the dark regarding the Dawn boy and now he can wait and wonder why I summoned him here.*

As she gathered up another arrow, she thought about Michael. That he was Genevieve's confessor was her mother's work. *She* had selected him. Yes, the Metropolitan appointed him, but his appointment had her mother's smell on it. On the surface, Michael was to be Genevieve's spiritual guide and confidant in all religious matters. Beneath it all though, he was there to report to Mother. *Just like my previous confessor.*

Before Michael, her confessor had been Bishop Thaddeus. Thaddeus was an old man, presented to her when she became the Lady of Seawall. She had giggled then at the thought that she needed a confessor. Thaddeus was dutiful, in his way, and he was friendly. He was also a drunk. He had lost his wife and children to the Yellow Fever when he was a young man and he hoped to find them again at the bottom of a bottle. All he did was drown his memories of them — *and let slip to me that he was acting as my mother's agent.* As fond of drink as he was, he was still very devout, and impressed on his new ward, the Lady of Seawall, the importance of prayer — prayers in the morning, prayers in the afternoon, and prayers in the evenings. It was good preparation for when she met the equally devout Michael.

She had first met Bishop Michael ten years ago. He had been ushered into her chambers in the palace in Starfall, Seafall's capital. He looked very young then, and she supposed she had looked very young as well. Her son, Roland, was just a small boy and her daughter Susan was little more than an infant, a toddling little thing who always found her way under Genevieve's feet. Jane was just a seed growing in her womb, and Genevieve still wore black on the Giver's day, as she continued to mourn the death of her favorite cousin.

Michael was as charming as he could be, but he struggled to act courtly. Genevieve knew that his background was more common than hers. That his mother was one of the landed folk and his father the lowest of the low nobility, some country squire — the kind who stank of the stables, entered prize pigs and cows into country fairs, disdained any form of learning, and held betting, drinking, and drunkenness in high regard.

Michael was not even Michael at all, she thought. He became Michael, as Michael was the name given to him when he joined the Church. His real name was Gideon Morgan. *Never trust a man with two first names.*

She released the arrow, hit the target but missed the mark, and gathered up another.

I knew his true purpose even back then. She recalled the triumph she felt when he ceased to be her mother's agent and became her own. *He betrayed Mother's confidence and he gained mine, and together we conspired and hatched this current scheme.*

"Bishop Michael," she called to him. She held the bow and arrow in front her. He looked up, and placed his cup down. "Come here. We must talk."

He excused himself from the company of her ladies-in-waiting and made his way over. He gave her a bow, his hands clasped in front of him as if in prayer. He was wearing a black priest's robe made of light cloth. "I did not know you were such a competent archer, my lady."

"And I did not know you were such a little sneak thief, Bishop," she returned. She gave him a smile to soften the remark.

"My lady?"

She drew and shot; the arrow struck the target, but was far from the center. She was out of arrows now, and she signaled to the houseboy to gather up more. "You did not tell me that one of Edward Dawn's sons was accused of murder."

Michael smiled, his expression betraying nothing. "I knew when you summoned me here that you were upset with me," he said.

"Well, why wasn't I informed? Why is it that I learned about it from my husband?"

The bishop shrugged and smiled again. It was a smile that she would love to see smashed in with a hammer. "It was an inconsequential matter."

Genevieve gave a bitter chuckle. "Hardly inconsequential when the accused happens to be the son of one of my husband's most important retainers."

"He is the *youngest* son of one of your husband's important retainers, and not well liked by his father." Michael said.

Genevieve had learned as much as she could of Marcus Dawn. Her own memories of the boy were dim and scattered. She recalled a thin, reedy boy with fine features and a girl's curls hiding behind his mother's skirts. He would have been six or seven at the time. That thin, reedy boy had grown into a thin, reedy youth — a mean and arrogant youth, if the stories were true. His curls were gone, but his feminine features remained. She could believe that Lord Dawn would have little love for a son like that. Lord Dawn thought all men should be strong and exude that strength, like him. *And his two older boys.* "Still."

"I didn't think it was important enough to bother you with."

"I will decide what is important. I..." She trailed off as the houseboy scurried up with a bundle of arrows. He quickly filled the quiver and then returned to his safe spot behind a low wall.

"You have preparations to make, the nobility of the realm to entertain," Michael pointed out.

"Yes, I do. And don't you think something like this could color the proceedings?"

He stared at her, a smug look plastered on his face. It was the kind of look Genevieve's mother gave before lecturing or scolding her. Michael was smart enough to avoid doing either. "I am sorry," he said. "Next time I will tell you first."

"Thank you," she said.

"Have you heard from your sister? Is she coming for the Oath Swearing?" Michael asked, trying to change the subject.

"No," Genevieve replied. It was disappointing, and it was typical of her sister. She would like to see Melody, would like to pump her for information and gossip of all that was going on in southern Seawall, but she was pregnant again, perhaps with her last child, although Genevieve wouldn't be surprised if her sister continued to have children well into her old age.

Genevieve envied her sister in many ways. She and her husband were left to manage the Noble estate and enjoy the full beauty of the south that Genevieve had grown up in. Oh, how she longed to see southern Seawall again, its hills and mountains, its deep valleys and rolling hills, its wonderful vineyards.

The Noble estate will be Roland's one day, she thought, *and my sister and then her eldest son will manage it for him if he is so inclined.* She picked up another arrow and rolled the smooth wooden shaft around in her fingers, admiring the fletcher's work.

If all plays out as I hope, Roland will have to manage much more than my father's estate. He will have to manage the Realm. "I wish I could have another son," she whispered.

"My lady?"

She looked at Michael. "I said, I wished I could have another son."

"Why?" Michael looked confused.

"So Roland could have a brother ... to help him manage things."

"He'll have you and your father for as long as the Giver wills it," Michael offered. "And his friends, the sons of the Marshal's Men of Seawall, as well."

Some friends, Genevieve thought. The older Dawn boys were brutes, like their father, but lacked any of their father's better qualities — and the youngest was possibly a murderer. The rest were ... well, they were boys.

"He'll have his sisters," she muttered.

"My lady?"

"Nothing, Michael. Nothing." She had neglected Susan's upbringing. She had left her education in the hands of tutors and the Ladies of the Church. *The Church. Why does the Church still have teeth?* She wondered.

It doesn't, she suddenly realized. *As science advances, every year it loses some of its teeth. Soon it will be just gums and words and have no bite at all.* She looked up at Michael and saw it there, plain on his face, the hidden fear of all holy men, that they were losing their power over people. And Michael, zealot that he was, was more fearful of that than the others. *He likes having power over others, over me.*

"Let us not keep secrets from one another," she said sweetly. "We need each other to achieve our goals," she said.

"And what are our goals, my lady?" A smile was there, but it wasn't the sure smile he usually wore.

She drew back the bowstring and aimed. "You want the Church to have teeth again, and I want ... I want ... I want revenge for Seawall." She relaxed her fingers and the arrow flew, it flew straight and true, and struck the center of bull's-eye. Behind her the ladies of Seawall let out a loud cheer.

Thirty

The Fifth Wheel — John Gray

Gray knew the Dead Priest's name now, Paulus. And Paulus knew he was being pursued. But how did he know? The Mathematician had called him a messenger and the messenger had said Gray was coming. Sorcery. It was the simplest answer. It was the only answer.

When Gray fled the Mathematician's manse — yes, he decided he had fled — he had hidden in the woods for several days, riding parallel to the forest road. The Dead Priest had ridden that road boldly and hard. There were few travelers on the forest road, especially at this time of the year, and the Dead Priest knew that, so he went for speed rather than subterfuge.

It was a week before Gray exited the forest and was able to take to the Seawall road in full pursuit. But slow moving carriages and crowds of people all heading west to Jonah's Sword hampered his progress. They considered themselves holy pilgrims of a sort, and it was said there would be a hundred thousand visitors or more in that city — all to take in the Call, or rather the entertainments that accompanied it.

There would be tournaments, balls, and great merriment. There would also be violence and young hearts would be broken as love was quickly won and just as quickly lost. The best of the realm would be there, displaying their talents, and so would the worst. Gray would be glad to avoid it.

As he rode, he thought about the Dead Priest. *What was the sorcerer's purpose? What business did he have with*

Wallace Sterngirth? Did he intend to kill the man? Or was it something else? If he was a messenger, as the Mathematician claimed, then what message could he possibly be bringing?

While the many travelers were nuisances, hindering his pursuit, they also helped. They had eyes and ears and kept him on his quarry's trail. It was easy to track the Dead Priest, as he was still dressed head to toe in black. The same black cloth that he wore as a uniform was now betraying him. He was also noticeably aloof and kept his own company. On the pilgrim's trail, keeping company with others was expected and the fact that he refused to made him stand out like horns on a cat.

It was the end of spring and the beginning of summer. The rains were less frequent and it was time for the first harvest followed by the summer planting. The last of the winter crop had been removed and the ground had been tilled in preparation for the new season. While food was fresh and plentiful, the publicans and innkeepers kept their prices high because the demand for their produce was high. And the travelers wanted nothing more than to stuff their faces and fill their bellies. The Call was certainly doing a good job of fattening waists as well as purses.

Gray rarely found an inn that had an available room and even when he did, the prices were too high for him. He was forced to sleep outdoors, camping next to the road. It did not matter, though. He was used to hard living while riding the frontier and the Range, and besides, there were many sharing the road with him and he seldom had to sit by a fire by himself.

For many of these so-called pilgrims it was an adventure, a break from the idle living to which they were accustomed. Many were the small nobility of the realm, the type who filled their schedules with hunting excursions, riding, cards, parties, and balls. They had replaced that with a journey to Seawall, where they would pick it all back up again. The truly wealthy and powerful traveled by train or by boat. The ones who traveled these roads couldn't afford the luxury — or, more rarely, were too miserly. It was easy for Gray to tell which was which, those who lacked great amounts of coin and those who lacked generosity. The ones with the leaner purses were the ones who were quick to share fire, food, drink, and their company. Those with fat purses tended to offer a cold shoulder. *Fat purses stay fat by lean spending*, his father had often said. He had lived up to that, as he was never known for his generosity. Gray knew the same streak ran through him. He was generous with friends *(and I have few enough of those)*, but struggled to share his fire or food with strangers.

Very few landed folk traveled the road to Jonah's Sword, just a few enterprising tinkers and merchants who fleeced the travelers as they could. No, the landed folk would do what they always did — work the soil and provide for the rest.

— «» —

By the time he had narrowed the gap between himself and Paulus, he was closing in on the seat of Wallace Sterngirth; a half-day's ride ahead was the Four Valley Region.

The valleys that made up the Four Valley Region ran north to south. They were great cuts in the land, each walled with rocky hills and jagged spires. Rivers snaked along their bottoms and eventually merged far south, joining into a single rushing force that dominated a wider valley of its own. That valley and the mighty river in it — the Thunder Flow — ended abruptly at a great falls, Heaven's Drop. The falls took the force of water 500 feet down into Great Sword Lake, which eventually became Great Sword Bay and emptied into the sea.

The Four Valley Region was another geographic barrier, fragmenting the land, a second line of defense for Shieldgate. North and west, beyond the Four Valleys, was the Green Table Plains - often just called the Table. It was rich farmland and richer pasture that skirted the Teeth, the mountains that separated Shieldgate from Seawall. Geography, more than anything else, worked against the cohesion of the realm.

Driving through the four valleys was another valley, this one running east to west. It was a narrow and savage gash. It was called the Bleeding Star Cut. A flaming red star, which fell from the heavens when men were primitives and lived in scattered nomadic tribes, was said to have done the cutting.

No matter the history, Gray knew the Cut was the only way to enter the Four Valley Region and it was the only way to cross it. The Dead Priest, sorcerer or not, would have to utilize the same access point as everyone else. He'd have to pass through the Valley Gate and go across the Anvil of the Heavens, an ancient stone bridge — a high road really, in truth as well as name — that had been maintained over the centuries and continued to serve the people of the realm. He hoped to intercept Paulus before he reached the bridge.

A storm, marked by great black banks of clouds, was gathering on the western horizon. He'd be riding right into it and if it hit when he was on the Anvil he'd be in some danger. This made the urgency to finally catch the Dead Priest even more acute. That's why he was dismayed when he turned a corner on the road only to see a knot of travelers blocking it.

At first he thought some accident had occurred on the road itself, but then realized most of the attention was on the field just off to the right. There was a group of men gathered there, staring at something on the ground. Gray felt the hairs go up on the back of his neck. Somehow he knew the Dead Priest was behind this newest disturbance.

Seeing Gray and seeing the shield of office on his coat, people on the road started waving frantically and calling out. Gray rode up, facing a knot of frightened faces. "What's going on here?" he snapped.

An older man who was well dressed stepped forward to answer the question. "There's b-b-been some m-murder in that field over there," he managed. He pointed to where the group of men were standing.

Gray nodded and directed his horse toward them. He was about twenty feet away when he smelled the blood, and his horse did, too. Gray steadied the creature, dismounted and headed over. He could see now that the men were standing around several bodies. They parted quickly to let Gray in to see the carnage. There on the ground, in the tall green grass and early summer flowers, lay a man, a woman, and a child. The child was a girl no older than eight or nine. All were naked, covered in flies, and had massive holes in their chests where their hearts had been removed. *Blood magic.*

"Wh—what h—happened to them?" a full—faced fellow wondered. Gray could tell from a glance this one had seen little death in his life. He was pale, slightly green, and there was vomit on the ruffled collar of his shirt and down the front of his well-tailored coat.

"I know the *creature* that's responsible for this," Gray said through gritted teeth, "and rest assured, if I move quickly, he will be brought to justice for his crimes."

He swiped at a fly that was buzzing around his face. "We must do right by these poor people and see them properly buried and cared for. Clothe them and take them to the nearest inn, public house, church, or sheriff's office down the road," he continued. "See that they are identified, so their next of kin can be informed."

He looked hard at the full-faced man, the one bold enough to speak to him first. "Do you think you can see that done?" The man nodded. "Good. Then get to it. You best hurry, because it looks like a storm is coming." Gray looked at the horizon where the clouds continued to gather.

He quickly returned to his horse, mounted up and put his heels to its sides, spurring it into a gallop. He'd catch up to Paulus before this day was done or die trying. He wanted to bring him to justice, so he could see him burn. More likely though, he'd have to mete out justice himself, and plant lead into the man's head and heart. He'd empty both guns into him. He owed the man a dozen bullets, at least. One for each life that he had taken on Gray's watch. One for each life that Gray somehow felt responsible for.

As he raced past the crowd that was gathered on the road the wind blew up in his face and he felt the raindrops on his cheeks. This storm was going to be a powerful one for sure and maybe it'd match the righteous anger that was rising in his breast.

— «» —

Although Gray was angry, he kept his senses. Experience had taught him that. When he was young he had blown several horses in his eagerness to catch some dirt rider or lowlife. As a result, a few of those outlaws managed to slip away. Not this time. He carefully paced his horse.

The rain was falling steady now, and the hills and rocky peaks of the Four Valleys were in front of him. The Seawall road, covered in gravel and flint, was a grey ribbon running through the green fields leading up to the Valley Gate. He could see the whitewashed exteriors of the small village that serviced Valley Gate and sat on the border of Lord Sterngirth's land. Several bolts of yellow and purple lightning flashed over the hills and moments later came the roll of thunder. Gray's horse lowered its ears.

By the time he reached the village, the rain was falling in sheets. The wind was up and lightning forked this way and that in the sky. Thunder rumbled and the air around him was charged and heavy. All travelers had stopped for the night at the Last Drop inn, a large building that dominated the village. Horses lined the hitching posts in front of the building where a groom and stable boys were collecting them to lead them to the nearby stable. Through the windows Gray could see the inn's many patrons, enjoying food, drink, and each other's company. Gray felt a stab of nostalgia seeing those smiling faces, bathed in the orange glow of candle and lamplight. It made him think back to when he was a young child and spent time with his mother's family. They were a happy bunch and those early days were some of his favorites. He exchanged that innocent joy of childhood early in life for duty.

He brushed aside the thought as he rode up to the Valley Gate. It was an imposing structure with a large gatehouse, outbuildings, stables, and a set of iron gates. Those gates were rusty and had not been closed in a generation. The same light that emanated from the windows of the Last Drop emanated from the gatehouses. He also saw that the smiles on the faces of the guards sitting in those gatehouses were the same as those on the faces of the inn's patrons. These were soft men in a comfortable position — pensioners, favorites, and the youngest sons of petty noble families. The one closest to the window saw Gray approaching. He was in his thirties, with a jowly red face and ridiculous sideburns. The man grimaced as he realized he'd have to brave a bit of rain and do his duty. By the time Gray rode up the fellow had stepped outside. He had thrown a greatcoat over his back and a rifle hung loosely over his shoulder. He held up a hand. "Can't let you pass, I'm afraid," he said loudly, over the rain slashing the cobbles. "Too dangerous on account of the rain." He looked apologetically at Gray and then up at the sky. "You'll have to head back to the inn."

Gray showed the guard his badge and snarled, "I am on the High Marshal's business. Who was the last person to pass?" The man blinked at Gray, saying nothing, so Gray shouted and said again, *"Who was the last person to pass?"*

"I— I d—don't know, sir," the guard stammered. Gray's shouting drew the attention of the other guards, and they threw open the door, guns in hand, and gathered in the doorway. Gray let them see he was a Fifth Wheel. "Does any damn fool one of you know who the last person to pass through this gate was?"

One of them, whose hair was sprinkled with gray and appeared more worn than the others, spoke. "He was a lone rider, like you," the man said, raising his forefinger to make the point. "He was dressed in black and riding hard. Passed through here just a while ago, before the rain really hit and we decided it was time to turn people away 'til it passed."

"How far do you think he got?" Gray asked. "Is he still on the Anvil or is he in the valleys?"

"He'd still be on the Anvil, I'd reckon," the guard replied. "And if not, he won't 'find a way into the valleys until he's got almost to Pecking, which is a good hour's ride away. There's a trail round 'bout there where you can slip off to Far Market." It seemed like the man was about to speak more about the local geography, but Gray cut him off with a tip of his hat before spurring forward through the gate and onto the Anvil of the Heavens.

The Anvil was a marvel, a stretch of high road and ancient stone bridges that pushed through the more jagged land of the Four Valley region. Nasty weather was even nastier on the Anvil, and as soon as Gray passed through the Gate he knew why the guards were turning away travelers. The wind whipped at his clothes and the rain tore across his face and cut into his eyes. His horse's ears were flat and its eyes rolled wildly. Still, he had to urge it forward and the horse obeyed.

The clouds above were boiling now, and lightning flashed and forked into the nearby hills, followed by crashes of thunder. He rode hard, and as he approached a span of bridge he drew on the reins and slowed, then brought his mount to a stop. In the middle of the span was a man who appeared to be kneeling, as though in prayer. At each side of the man burned a small red flame, perhaps from a candle or torch. And there was only one thing that would allow fire to burn in such rain. Sorcery.

Gray now faced Paulus, the Dead Priest, the sorcerer. He thought of the deadly dance he and Predrag Landry had so many years ago. It took place in the middle of Feather's Cap, in the middle of a dead town where no one was left alive except for the killer, Landry. It was like any other gunfight. If there was any sorcery at play, Gray did not notice it. Would this dance be the same or would it be different? Landry was the only sorcerer who Gray had confronted and Landry did not deal in demons like this Paulus did. But Gray saw no demon here, only Paulus.

"*Sorcerer*," Gray called out. "I have come to bring you to justice. I would prefer to take you before a court of the realm so you are given your proper due, but if I must I will see that you pay the price in lead." The wind seemed to whip his words away, so he yelled louder. "I know that you have killed people and I know that you are a servant of the Enemy."

Even from a distance, Gray could see that the one called Paulus was smiling. He was speaking, not loudly, but still Gray could hear his words as though the Dead Priest were talking into his ear. "Yes, I have killed people and I *am* a servant of the one *you* call the Enemy, although he is no enemy of mine. Still you will *not* bring me to justice, *not* today." His accent was thick, but his words clear.

Gray reached for his guns and something closed around his wrists. He looked down and saw tendrils of earth wrapped around his arms, holding them fast. His horse screamed and reared. As it did, the tendrils hauled him down to the ground. His horse turned and ran. Paulus' laughter echoed around him. He thrashed around to throw off the grasping mortar and stone, to haul himself to his feet. He still could not pull his guns free.

Paulus was chanting. The words that came from the Dead Priest's mouth were foreign to Gray's ears. They were harsh and cutting words that seemed to vibrate in the air around him. The ground between Gray and Paulus stirred and heaved, and with a shriek it took on the form of a demon. Its voice was the voice of a man, woman, and child, blended together in a horrible chorus. It was not as large as the demon he had faced in Dead Tree, but Gray recoiled nonetheless.

His hands were now free, and he ripped his pistols from their holsters to shoot down the sorcerer. The demon, though, protected its master and stood between Gray and Paulus. "*Not* today," Paulus yelled over the rain and a crash of thunder. "Not today. Rest assured we will have our parley, but only when you're ready to listen and understand." Gray tried to get off a shot, but the demon got in the way, the bullet plowing into its middle.

It shrieked in anger, not pain. Maybe it felt no pain.

Paulus was chanting again, fiercely and loudly, the words cutting into Gray and hammering his brain. The demon raised its fists and slammed them down on the bridge. It did so again, and again, in rhythm with its master's words. Gray began to fire wildly into the creature, as he now understood its purpose. It was going to bring down the bridge span.

While it failed to collapse the whole span, it did manage to bring down the part where Gray was standing. The flagstones and timber beneath him gave way and he fell. The demon fell, too, disintegrating as it went. Paulus' laughter followed them. "We'll have our parley soon enough, Fifth Wheel," he whispered into the air and into Gray's ear.

How is that possible? Gray thought, as he tumbled to his doom. *Will we talk in hell?* Below him was the dark of the approaching night and a rushing river. Maybe if he hit the river, he'd survive. He was hopeful. But the river seemed to be coming up very fast, and he wasn't in any position to make the best entrance. He was going to hit the water, hard. His breath was forced out of him as he smacked into the surface and was quickly smothered by the cold, roaring torrent.

The Book of West Marque Saga

The Call (Volume One)
tinyurl.com/edge6017

All In (Volume Two)
tinyurl.com/edge6023

If you enjoyed this read

Please leave a review on Amazon, Facebook, Good Reads or Instagram.

It takes less than five minutes and it really does make a difference.

If you're not sure how to leave a review on Amazon:

1. *Go to amazon.com.*

2. *Type in The Call by Richard Parkinson and when you see it, click on it.*

3. *Scroll down to Customer Reviews. Nearby you'll see a box labeled Write a Review. Click it.*

4. *Now, if you've never written a review before on Amazon, they might ask you to create a name for yourself.*

5. *Reviews can be as simple as, "Loved the book! Can't wait for the Next!" (Please don't give the story away.)*

And that's it!

Brian Hades, publisher

Author Bio

Richard Parkinson was born in Montreal and raised in southwestern Ontario. He wandered around the wilderness from job to job, taking the occasional university course. He played solider as a historical re-enactor, hit the stage as a wannabe rock star, tried his hand as a puppeteer running his own Punch & Judy show, and worked hard on his quest to become a "renaissance man". The results were equal to Don Quixote's quest to revive chivalry and many of Richard's friends took on the role of the sensible Sancho Panza. On the side, he dabbled in homebrew RPG design with the enthusiasm of a medieval alchemist. Unfortunately, he often enjoyed the same results as the medieval alchemist, sometimes explosive and always realizing that base metals could not be turned to gold. He then fell into journalism.

Richard lives in Essex, Ontario with his wife, two dogs, and four children.

Need something new to read?

If you liked The Call, you should also consider these other EDGE-Lite titles…

From Moon to Joshua

by Matthew Moffitt

The Real Devil is The One Waiting Inside of You...

Drayaden Sinclaire lives by three rules: he kills when he needs to, never before; he always pays his debts, and he never draws his sword. But when a town mysteriously vanishes into the hot wind of the Desert Land, Drayaden's world is turned upside down.

The search as to whom or what caused the destruction forces Drayaden to confront the very thing he fears most: himself. No one is safe and no one is ready.

About Matthew Moffitt

Matthew Moffitt lives with his wife in South Dakota, where they go to graduate school and take care of their cat, Sherlock. Growing up, Matt read everything he could get his hands on — science fiction, fantasy, murder-mystery, comic books, and even his mother's endless piles of romance novels. One day he got the bright idea to write, which he stuck to, feeling he could make a difference to those around him. He currently writes science fiction and fantasy, drawing from his experiences as a budding clinical psychologist.

Grimenna

by N. K. Blazevic

When Courage Finds Hope...

Evil is roosting in the lord's keep, corrupting the land and feeding off its growing despair. When Paiva Ibbie, a young sheepherder's daughter, joins her aunt to work in the kitchens, she brings with her a flicker of hope from a village in the north that remains untouched by darkness. Her good spirit is a threat to the evil's work and it will stop at nothing to ensure that Paiva's hope is turned into the darkest of despair.

About Natasha K. Blazevic

Natasha K. Blazevic lives in St André D'Argenteuil, Quebec. She studied art in college but, after a year, fled to the countryside of the Quebec Laurentians where she apprenticed as a stone mason and began to cultivate her love of art and animals in earnest. She is a beekeeper and considers herself a student of life with a keen interest in the natural world. She hopes her book Grimenna can not only entertain and enchant readers, but can help to promote a green renaissance.

Bad Rock Beat Down
(Book Two in The Milky Way Repo Series)

by Michael Prelee

A Sci-Fi Crime in a Dirty, Corrupt Universe.

The starship repossession agents of Milky Way Repo are sent to the desolate settlement of Bad Rock to retrieve a vessel. Once there, they become entangled with a notorious thug running a smuggling operation for the Syndicate. Struggling to do the right thing while trying to complete their job, things go seriously awry with deadly consequences.

"The Milky Way Repo universe is populated by hard working men and women who are trying to make their way in a tough world. They are scrappy business owners who find themselves beset by criminals in the course of doing their jobs. How they deal with this adversity makes for entertaining stories." — Michael Prelee, author

About Michael Prelee

Michael Prelee is a graduate of Youngstown State University. He resides in Northeast Ohio with his family where he enjoys writing.

Beltrunner

by Sean O'Brien

From The Best Traditions of Hard Science-Fiction.

Collier South has been belt mining his entire life. He's watched the small independents around him get swallowed up by the bigger corporations, forced out of their livelihoods by corporate creep. But he isn't about to settle or sellout. Broke and desperate, Collier has one last chance to land a strike. What he discovers instead has the power to change not only his life but the fate of the entire system. That is if he can keep his discovery out of corporate hands and survive the ensuing manhunt

About Sean O'Brien

Sean O'Brien is an educator and writer from Southern California. He was named Educator of the Year by the California League of High Schools and has been a head varsity football coach, television broadcaster, and Gilbert and Sullivan singer (though not a good one). He's the author of A Muse of Fire, Wondrous Strange, and Vale of Stars.

The Red Wraith

by Nick Wisseman

Magic Awakens in Early America...

On the eve of the Harvest Ceremony, Naysin, a child of the Lepane nation, manifests powers of a dual deity forever torn in two by light and darkness. Cast into exile by his clan for being a spawn of human and spirit, Naysin is lost in a world of change as pale men from the sea arrive to plunder the riches of the Earth. Guided only by the devious facets of his spirit father, Naysin has no choice but to master his powers to survive the destruction of his people. For Naysin, it is a path of darkness and death that will take him from one end of the land to the other and down into the depths of infamy.

About Nick Wisseman

Nick Wisseman lives in Bear Lake, Michigan with his wife, daughter, fifty cats, twenty horses, and ten dogs. (Okay, there are actually ten times less pets than that, but most days it feels like more.) He's not quite sure why he loves writing twisted fiction, but there's no stopping the weirdness once he's in front of a computer.

For more EDGE titles and information about upcoming speculative fiction please visit us at:

www.edgewebsite.com

Don't forget to sign-up for our Special Offers

CPSIA information can be obtained
at www.ICGtesting.com
Printed in the USA
BVHW031741010419
544261BV00001B/39/P